# You People

# You People

NIKITA LALWANI

VIKING
*an imprint of*
PENGUIN BOOKS

VIKING

UK | USA | Canada | Ireland | Australia
India | New Zealand | South Africa

Viking is part of the Penguin Random House group of companies
whose addresses can be found at global.penguinrandomhouse.com

First published 2020
001

Copyright © Nikita Lalwani, 2020
The moral right of the author has been asserted

Extract on p. vii from *Poems of Akhmatova*,
selected, translated and introduced by Stanley Kunitz
with Max Hayward (1997, 1973) © Anna Akhmatova

Set in 11/13 pt Bembo Book MT Std
Typeset by Jouve (UK), Milton Keynes
Printed and bound in Great Britain by Clays Ltd, Elcograf S.p.A.

A CIP catalogue record for this book is available from the British Library

ISBN: 978-0-241-40953-4

www.greenpenguin.co.uk

Penguin Random House is committed to a
sustainable future for our business, our readers
and our planet. This book is made from Forest
Stewardship Council® certified paper.

*For Vik, and that love, hidden in dream.*
*For Anoushka Tiger, Shay Raag and Ishika Lotus:*
*all the stars of joy.*

*'As if through a straw, you drink my soul.*
*I know — it's bitter and intoxicating.'*

Anna Akhmatova (1911)

# PART ONE

# NIA

There he is, in memory, standing behind the bar of the restaurant, pouring that vile drink he used to love, a sickly Martini from the long bottle with those big empty letters on the label. Kind eyes, imperious too, the leather trench coat all the way to the floor, its seedy sheen reflected somehow on his face. There is the face itself: angular, the brown depth of his colouring, black kinks of hair rippling to his shoulders like a soft perm, the bizarre gold hoop in the right ear. The hi-lo voice is there, insinuating itself through twists and turns like mercury in a barometer when he speaks – taking the temperature of things, divining the climate. All of this distracting the eye from his looks, which are striking, exceptional even, you would probably have to call him beautiful.

She is right there, in the same memory, about to reply, but a bit more blurred around the edges. It is likely that she was dressed up, she wanted a job of course: so it would have been the black jersey dress, tight on the bust, hemline a bit too short, and inappropriate shoes – the chunky maroon creepers with massive silver buckles. Aiming for 'voluptuous', but without quite the correct regalia of accessories. One of the three outfits she was circulating in those days, and the only one that could aim to satisfy the criteria of 'smart' in the advert. Sometimes she would wear a crimson Kashmiri shawl with it, lifted from her mum's cupboard, drape it over her shoulders, a bit of red lipstick to match, as though she was going to a formal winter event, like a prom in the fifties or something.

She can't remember if she had the shawl on but she remembers the feeling well – that she looked confusing, that he was eyeing her with a curiosity that he didn't bother to conceal. Mostly, she can watch the two of them in this memory without rushing ahead, slip inside the vein that funnels the language between them, and

3

marvel that it is happening, pretend she does not know what will come next.

'I do apologize,' he says, offering her a cigarette. 'Would you like some tea? Coffee? A glass of wine? Just . . . do let me know, lah! Some water?'

She is shaking her head. The attention is intimidating.

'Nah, I'm good,' she says. 'Don't worry.'

And that is when she first experiences his smile. She is just nineteen, lying her way through the world but telling him the truth for some reason, and he's thirty-three, thirty-four max, giving it the big patron act in the restaurant, lighting up a cigarette and funnelling the smoke through the side of his mouth as he raises his eyebrows and regards her at leisure. Tac! The palatal click of satisfaction as he taps the ash into a square vessel of smoked brown glass. His fingernails are fastidiously clean and she is curling her own away from sight in response.

He's good. Surely he is good? He is the altruist we need on each street corner. The one who's got your back, can help you stand up after the fall. He's wise: King Solomon capable of enough empathy and hubris to decide who deserves the baby. He is a walking set of choices and consequences: love thy neighbour, the greater good, take your pick. This image of him – of them – filters and echoes through her memory, there are a thousand iterations or more. She can never be certain of its imprint or impact.

She tells herself the story as it unfolds from this moment. She does it to understand him, and so to believe in his cure.

# SHAN

Shan is walking in Archway, cheered by the discordant heat as he moves alongside the massive dual carriageway outside his estate of residence. He stops at the traffic lights, lets the buses sear their crimson optimism onto his retina. Colour, his mother would say, brings joy, wonder, power.

He can see the kid who comes with his mama every day on the way to school. He fascinates him, this kid, he has long brown curls that bounce to his shoulders, pale flushed skin, he rides a beat-up blue scooter, four years is he, or five? Lifting his leg up behind him as he goes down the road, like a dancer, the same pride, the same demonstration of ease, someone skating on ice, not a narrow pavement next to a huge river of traffic. *Look, I can do this*, his body says silently, as he sails past Shan at the crossing, almost at exactly the same time every day. Today there is blossom in his hair, in Shan's hair too – the road is planted with mammoth trees that bestow leaves and the tiniest of white-sheened petals on them all, from on high. This is London, thinks Shan, this contrary indication of motor-loud madness and real, actual breathing life. Humans, trucks, petals.

The kid is staring at an older man in an electric wheelchair who sometimes joins them at this 8.34 a.m. confluence at the lights. The man: pink-cheeked, grey-haired, tidy short sideburns, is raised momentarily from the cautious expression that he tends to employ when he is motoring along, raised to smile at the boy, and up at his mother.

'Why is that man in a chair that moves along like that?' says the boy, curling back against his mother's body, suddenly shy at the man's smile. His voice is high, sonorous, the sentence dances like the melody on a bansuri, an up-turn of curiosity at the end.

Like tha-a-at? He is sweet, thinks Shan: some kind of pale honey skin he has, long lashes, a dream-sweet.

'Because maybe his legs don't work right now,' says the mother, crouching down so she can hush up her voice.

'Why his legs doesn't work?' sings the boy's voice, dancing over the articulated lorries, the tangled chain of cars and bikes. And again, the descant high, louder, when he gets no response:

'But WHY his legs doesn't work? Why, Mama, why?'

She hides a smile and instead of answering tucks some dark blonde strands back into her ponytail, fingers at her collar, one hand is enough for the job, the other is on her kid, getting ready to guide him with his scooter. The lights change and they walk across quickly. Shan can hear the boy still shouting on the other side.

'WHY DOESN'T HIS LEGS DOESN'T WORK?'

Give him an answer, thinks Shan, also smiling as he watches the boy reattach himself to his scooter and flamboyantly sail off, right past the charity shop and always-empty optician's to the round-about, where he halts, obediently, for his mother to catch up. Surely you can make one up. Stop his anxiety, really? There are so many reasons why someone's legs wouldn't work. You could choose the most benevolent, make something of it, use it to teach the kid something.

His own son is a couple of years older. What is he doing right now? The question assails Shan without warning, pollutes him with despair, a toxin that is suddenly in his lungs as he crosses the same fat zebra path and walks to the tube station. It's his own fault. He relaxed too much, didn't guard against it. The mind betrays when you loosen control.

His mother comes to him again, wringing out wet clothes during an afternoon in Jaffna, giving him the eye of concern. If you wash a cloth, over and over, it becomes bleached out, she's saying in this memory, relishing the chance to impart life lessons when presented with such useful methods of illustration. Such is the test that life throws at your honour. Your honour is the colour of the self, it should be steadfast. To be dishonoured, to be found out, to be revealed to be false – it is to be leached of all your colour as a person, to watch it dissolve into the water and slip away through the gutter down the alley.

His mind surges with a mix of sayings from his mother. *Love your neighbour, but don't take down the dividing wall. In a treeless country the castor plant is a big tree. Dig your well before you are thirsty. During the daylight a person will not fall into a pit that he fell into during the night. The poor search for food and the rich search for hunger.*

*When well united and together, one plus one equals eleven,* thinks Shan. But he and Devaki are apart.

'Mama!' shouts the boy as Shan walks past them. The kid is staring back at the display of frames in the optician's window.

'Can I have a eye test, Mama?' he shouts, little voice in an agile somersault over the traffic. And then, again, high flute of a sound. 'CAN I HAVE A EYE TEST! A EYE TEST!'

Shan closes his eyes against the force of memory, takes the free newspaper at the underground ticket barriers and returns to the bus stop. He is still early enough to eat something in the kitchen before his shift at the restaurant begins. The sky is viscous and turquoise: the hot, demented turquoise of a day filled with promises.

# NIA

In those days they were all a bit in love with Tuli, everyone who worked for him in the restaurant. They couldn't help it, somehow it came with the territory: a solid admiration leavened with a kind of vulnerable unrequited romance. Nia considered this oddity often: she really did mean all of them – male or female, front of house or in the kitchen, take your pick – the waiting staff (Ava from Spain), the gaggle of South Asian cooks (Shan, Rajan, Guna, Vasanthan), even Ashan, the clipped French Tamil guy who shared the lease with him, purveyor of crucial expertise from working at 'the Pizza Express'. This is how they appeared to her, even though, or maybe because, Tuli was so infuriating and endearing in equal measure. It wasn't just because they were beholden to him. You could argue that he had rescued everyone who was there from something or someone, but this was more to do with his manner, his way of being.

When Nia started working there she was proud of the fact that he didn't affect her, but soon enough this indifference to his charms was undermined by the fact that she envied him – she wanted to *be* him rather than the object of his affection. He was so expansive, a bit arrogant with it sure, but that heart . . . To possess such a heart, to look outward like that, rather than inward to the hidden pockets of the self as she did. An audacious heart. It seemed to thud against his lanky frame with its own strength and vibration, exulting in a freedom from the scrutiny of others.

Oh, it was an emotional time of ups and downs and she would often veer from her happy chatty persona at work to such a loneliness when the sun went down, as though the whole of the day's cheer had been an elaborate gossamer web and now the web was ripped, there was nowhere to hide. She would spend her days off without speaking to anyone and there was a kind of bruise in her speech when she tried to talk upon return to the restaurant. But it was always there, solid and accommodating, happy for her to slide back in once she had pinned her apron and hair.

She stared at everything and everyone in the beginning, ignoring the veneer of detachment that protected other commuters in the mornings. It was the summer of 2003 when Nia joined the restaurant, and that particular part of south-west London was just beginning to gear up for gentrification. You could see the bankers – male and female alike – dipping their toes in, walking past the burger joints and chicken shops with appraising gazes, bodies taut with the effort of remaining open-minded. Tentatively making it down to the imposing residential squares they had heard about, and staring up at the red-brick and stucco mansion blocks and sliding timber sash windows. They would go up to the hushed communal gardens that lay at the centre of these squares, and lean on the railings, not worried by the locked gates that always caught her out. Instead they seemed to be practising for a lifestyle that appeared to be entirely up to them. She saw them on her way to and from the restaurant and marvelled at this idea radiating out from them, that the responsibility of shaping a life was all down to the choices you might make. They seemed full to bursting with choices.

She had loved the place instantly, in fact she loved the whole process – walking from the tube and turning down the small road, past the greasy spoon, the betting place, the Australian pub on the corner, till she was right there, standing at the panelled glass doors and looking up at 'PIZZERIA VESUVIO', each word hammered in gold and angled to form two sharp mountain slopes. They were warm days at the start of that summer, and these huge baroque capitals would be flashing with reflected sunlight against a vermilion background, whilst underneath you had all the offerings in a humble white font: 'Caffè, Restaurant, Pizza, Pasta. Vesuvio: Your home from home!'

Inside, the space was laid out pretty traditionally: twenty small square tables on the ground floor with the till, counter and wine racks at the back, near the kitchen. Diaphanous white tablecloths, small accordions of folded paper printed with photos of diners and the splashy headline: 'Welcome to the magic of Vesuvio!' One candle per table, along with single stems in water – a pink rose or carnation usually. A spiral staircase at the front led up to a function room, with the bar at one end and leather sofas at the other – this was the area where Tuli entertained guests, unless it was hired out for a private party, but also where the staff mostly had their meals between shifts.

Some of the Sri Lankan cooks lived above this first floor in a flat that Nia had heard about, and she'd witness them disappearing at the end of the night through another door near the bar. She'd watch them go through a dark portal into relative privacy, one or two guys at a time, catch a glimpse of an impossibly steep flight of stairs, register the knitted warmth of their murmurs after the door was locked from the inside and they were no longer visible. There was something fascinating about the definitive way in which they sealed themselves off. They were different from her, in that they had a clear end to the day, some place that they wanted to go when work was done, even if it was just upstairs.

In contrast, she always lingered when her hours were through, unsure as to what she should do next. There was a perk for staff: on your day off you could come to the restaurant with a friend and both eat a meal for free – you knew not to choose the steak of course, and to stick to pizza or pasta, at most a glass or two of house wine, but it was still pretty generous. Nia was aware that she didn't have anyone to bring with her on these days, but Ava would swing by with a different friend from a different country each week for lunch it seemed, before heading out to comb the sights and sounds of London. The cooks preferred to avail themselves of the promised meal at night – hanging out and chattering on crates in the kitchen as usual, directing those on duty to cook their favourites. Sometimes Tuli would send in a bottle of whisky for those who were off duty and everyone would be happy.

Nia was pretty sure that Tuli was a Catholic even though he wasn't often at church; he was all bound up with Patrick, the priest from Laurier Square. They had a thing going on Fridays at closing where they gathered leftover sandwiches from the supermarkets and bundled them with a batch of pizzas from the restaurant, leaving by midnight to distribute the goods on the streets. One time she even found herself going to Tuli in a state of chaos, asking him to help convert her to Christianity. He sent her on her way, shaking his head in mock sorrow and ruffling her hair at the nonsense of it.

'Are you mad?' he said, laughing with an edge to it, the way you do when confronted with an insult of some sort. 'Nia, what do you take me for? Bounty hunter, marking out my place in heaven type of thing? Scalps hanging from a satchel as I'm walking into the sunset? Really? What about your Hindu blood, can't you mainline some more of that into your veins at least? When you come from so much, why would you look elsewhere?'

It made her smile. There was something undeniably funny about this, even though he did mean what he was saying. Something to do with 'Hindu' sounding so exotic, the way he pronounced it with his questioning twang. And that it was directed at someone who looked like Nia. 'An affront' was how her mother had described her relationship to her skin. She wasn't far wrong – it was no secret that Nia wished for more of her father's colouring. People around the restaurant mostly mistook her for Italian with her permanent bisque tan and dark hair. In fact, she was quite sure that was one of the reasons Tuli hired her.

'Where are you from?' he'd asked at that very first meeting, minutes after she'd swung through the door to ask for a job.

'I grew up in Newport,' she said. 'Welsh mother, Indian father. Mostly Welsh mother without Indian father.'

'Ah,' he said, as though he understood everything necessary from that clutch of sentences. 'Got it. Come.' Pulling out a chair in front of the bar. 'Please, do sit down.'

Often Tuli would come back from the nightly rounds with a single oddball of choice – an unshaven man in thready denim with a smell to match and a bag of loud opinions, or more of a smarter guy in a white shirt – someone clocking off from a shift stacking shelves at Tesco, say, or even the red-eyed halal butcher from two doors down. One regular, a white guy in a battered brown suit and brogues, a hovering impatience in his face, was a pimp apparently. Tuli had revealed this to Nia after the man had left, mainly because she asked him the question directly.

By this time she had figured out that although Tuli operated on a need-to-know basis, he didn't lie; this seemed to be part of his personal code, a pact he had made with himself. She had the idea that she could find things out, providing he was in the mood to respond rather than evade. It was all about coming up with the right question, the correct code to unlock the safe. And she was very curious about all of it.

He'd sit them down, these finds of his, at the front of Vesuvio where they'd smoke and talk while Nia was spraying the counters or polishing the bevelled glass at the front of the bar with newspaper, and she'd bring them a free pizza of some kind usually, but also leftovers to nibble with him – bruschetta with tomatoes and garlic, or sticky giant olives rolled in a blood chilli sauce. She was attractive to a certain kind of man, and she'd often get a nod of approval, maybe a grunt of acknowledgement for the bust and hips in front of them, their eyes lingering at her waist, cinched in with an apron. She, in turn, wasn't sure if they expected her to giggle like a naughty milkmaid in response, but she took it in her stride, it was no big deal. Sometimes these stragglers would play chess – by candlelight, no less, with Tuli always making a point to put Bach on the stereo – and there would be something almost regal, timeless, about the two faces in concentration when set against that music, seemingly blissful in shadow as they moved those wooden pieces to oblivion.

Every now and then he would disappear to the back to check the freezer contents in the kitchen for the next day, eye up the pizza oven or get that pale serpentine bottle labelled 'Martini' from upstairs, a huge carton of Marlboro Lights to go with it. Sometimes, it was just some cash from the plastic bag that was always hanging behind the counter. While he was gone, his guests would stare at the theatrical masks on the walls, try to make sense of the framed gondolas sliding through pastel sunsets, the strangely erotic quadrants of lace that he had pinned up too, in the name of building 'character' into the place.

One of Nia's long-term jobs was to conceive of a cosmetic makeover for Vesuvio, sort the decor out. Although it grieved Tuli to admit it, he knew it didn't quite work and she knew he wanted to give her a project that might prove satisfying. The *dee-cor* she would call it, only knowing this word from books she had read. It was an unexpected tic, to have these aberrations in fluency, even though she'd grown up with books around her, a tic that fascinated him. And he was usually ruthless in response.

'Sorry, but just checking, Nia – when I interviewed you, I had a sense that English was your first language, lah?' he said once, ramping his accent up the ladder of South East Asia with this emphasizing word he liked – 'lah!' – whenever she stubbed her toe on one of these boulders.

'Yes, but I didn't grow up with ponces.'

'You grew up with whom exactly? The salt of the Welsh and Bengali earth?' A pitying look for her predicament.

'The former.'

'And you got yourself to Oxford by your bootstraps.'

'Yes, good, you've got the picture.'

'Because it's not easy being a nurse's daughter. Too busy keeping it real in the green grass of Wales?'

'I'd have thought you wouldn't be obsessed with pronunciation like British people. Did they bother with that sort of thing when you were growing up in Singapore?'

'Oooh. Oooh!' And then with naked joy, 'Trying to analyse me, is it? Aren't we fancy when we get on our high horse!'

And he got out this teddy bear he kept behind the bar – big beige nylon-furred thing the length of his forearm – and made it dance on the worktop while he hummed a melody for it.

Always, in these exchanges, Nia would throw something at him at this point: a scrunched-up crimson napkin, her ballpoint pen with the nib extended like a dart, or the whole notepad she used for taking orders, while his shoulders shook with silent laughter, hand over his heart as though, dear Lord, there was no way to contain it.

# SHAN

'He has become obsessed with Jesus Christ,' says Ava, presenting her phone to Shan. 'He love him. I say, look Theo, you are just five years, when you are older I will answer your questions then. He say no, answer me now, why did Jesus Christ have such bad friends that they kill him? What am I to say then?'

Shan smiles and shrugs sympathetically. Ava looks after this child for just two afternoons a week, when she is not working at the restaurant, but she has clearly become very attached to him. There is something endearing about her when she describes his tics, something in the indulgent tone of her voice.

'His parents, they really don't like God,' she continues, 'they don't like all this Jesus talk, really the father is main one, he wants everything to be exactly how he says. But I can't control him, Theo, he love Jesus Christ, whenever he see a picture of Jesus or a book about it or the cross, anything, he go to it, and he just stand there, staring at it, with this big eyes, I tell you, is crazy! I say don't ask me all this now, wait until you are older and then we can talk about it, OK?'

Shan takes the phone from Ava and looks at the picture, begins composing an appropriate response to this pious child. He likes it when she bashes the parents, it is oddly relaxing, a kind of balm of mundane patter that smooths itself right over him. Instead of an image of devotion he sees a small brown-haired boy holding a fluorescent toy gun, making a fierce face at the camera. Shan frowns instinctively, takes a sip of his coffee, distracts himself by looking up at the watercolour scenes adorning the walls, the tearful clown puppets and ridged, lacy fans. He relishes these morning moments at the restaurant, with the other cooks yet to swarm in, soaking the air with their assertions and accusations.

'But Shan, why you making a face like that!' she says, taking the spray from the shelf and squirting small circles of foam over the bar counter between them. 'You look at it – is made of plastic! Is just a toy! He get it because he complete his reading, after two weeks of reading one book, is a reward for him. Come on!'

Ava takes her cloth and wipes down the wooden surface with an enviable vigour. He is still waking up, really.

'Sunny!' She sings with a coaxing tone to her voice, as if to lure him back into good humour. It is the song from the sixties, the one by Stevie Wonder. She sings it as though it is written all for him, a private joke of some sort, this pet name. 'Sunny!' She makes a face at him, tips her head to one side and makes herself cross-eyed to suggest she is losing her mind.

Shan laughs. He is fascinated with the defiant bulge of muscles in her small arms, he can see them as she leans over to complete the job, her whole physicality is streaked with the force of these tight lines of feminine power. She is a woman who defies categorization in terms of age: long grey hair in waves down her shoulders, pinned back at the front with grips, youthful angular face with lightly tanned skin, a few lines barely framing the eyes and mouth, her black apron tied meticulously around narrow hips. Conscientious, small and strong. A woman who tells him that she saves up the scraps of money that she doesn't send back to her family in Valencia (her sister needs it mostly, for her kids, has a delinquent drunken husband she needs to kick out of her home) for her own, very odd idea of luxury: a monthly visit to a climbing wall in some big mall complex in west London.

He says her name to himself. Ava Amada. She has a brusque, no-nonsense manner about her that suggests an incontrovertible history: some kind of extracted wisdom that makes it pointless to argue. There is something relaxing about her particular brand of conviction, he thinks, as he mops up some olive oil with the remainder of his bruschetta, sucks on the pieces of tomato, attempts to assess the experience with the blunt narcissism of a customer. They've been trying out the recipe at the restaurant with less garlic, have added tiny weathered particles of capsicum, which Shan knows to be a mistake, knows it definitively now that he can feel them on his tongue. But he is new, he knows the deal, keep your thoughts to yourself.

She returns to the bar and begins polishing glasses.

'Do you need help?' she asks, moving her towel over a glass so that the squeak repeats itself again and again, in a satisfying rhythm. Her eyes have mischief in them. Green now, grey before, a gentle change with the light. At her neck there is a crystal, a tiny rose-coloured dagger of stone, hanging from a black leather necklet.

'I mean, is that why you are here early today?' says Ava. 'Did you come to see Tuli for help?'

'No,' says Shan, disguising his annoyance with a cough. 'I'm OK.'

She laughs and a quick glint of silver is visible in her mouth, like bullion.

'What did he do, to help you, in fact?' asks Shan, turning the question back on her. 'We never discussed that.'

His tone is sharper than he intended, but Ava does not find the question to be an insult.

'What didn't he do?' she says, crouching down with a piece of cloth to polish the tiling display on the floor, large glossy hexagons in terracotta and jade, flanked by a mosaic border. 'You can say I have a big debt for how he has helped me but he does not mind that I cannot repay him. But I will be a friend to him always.'

How old is Ava? he thinks, as he watches her eyes refract the light back to him: olivine fragments of a meteorite, set forward like that in her tanned skin. Thirty-five? His own age. Forty? Forty-five? Even fifty, it is possible, with that long soft waterfall of grey hair, rippling with curl. It is impossible to say but he watches her pert behind, snug and righteous in stonewashed jeans, tied up like a present and topped off with the black bow of the apron strings, as it leaves the room and disappears through the door to the kitchen.

Ten minutes later, he is in the kitchen alone, slicing chicken, stacking the neutral oblongs of flesh on a crumpled cellophane skin, when he hears raised voices in the main space. He frowns. There is something of an aggravated quality to the discussion, and one of the voices belongs to Ava.

'Calm down, Elene!' she is saying, as he comes through the door to stand near them at the countertop and till. 'Just calm it now, Elene!'

Elene is hysterical, her face is wet with tears behind her spectacles and she keeps pulling at the fringe of her chunky dark hair. She is the Georgian waitress who works in the Polish café three doors away, and often comes over for a coffee or bite to eat with Ava. She usually has an air of girlish good humour about her, chuckles away and whispers surreptitiously during their meets as though she has escaped from school lessons rather than an adult job, for a coveted break. Today, however, she is panicked and it has the unnerving effect of making her seem older, less naive than usual.

'But she's there right now,' she says, urging Ava to listen by grabbing her arms, gulping her breath as she speaks. 'Woman police, she's there now, right now, telling Krystian to sign a paper and he won't sign it, he keeps saying, "The man in kitchen is just washing his hands. He is my friend." Keeps on saying this. "He is my friend. Washing his hands." And the lady police is speaking in her walkie-talkie all the time. What is going to happen, Ava? If he signs it he will have to pay thousands and thousands fine, people are saying? And what about Tendai? There's a big van outside, he's sitting in there with the hoops and silver chain on his hands? On the back seat? Lots of people from the street standing and watching, Ava, you don't know – there's another police at the driving seat too, a man, asking the crowd questions out his window of the car, pointing at the Chinese shop, I mean he is even pointing here to Vesuvio—'

'OK,' says Ava, taking Elene's elbow and walking her to the door. 'Thank you. Is good you came here. Now go back, Elene.'

Elene nods and starts crying again. Ava firmly manoeuvres her out the front, turns the girl's body so that she faces left and puts both hands on her back with a gentle nod and murmur of consolation, masking the fact that she is literally pushing her down the street. She shuts the door, pulls down the blinds and comes back to Shan.

'Go,' Ava says to him, gesturing towards the back door of the kitchen. She comes up close to him. In the sudden darkness of the room, her voice is a terrifying, scouring rasp of a whisper. 'Go now, Shan.'

Outside, there are people shouting: thick voices pummelling against horns. A door is slammed, and then they hear a car alarm singing up and down, see-sawing madly through his head.

Ava keeps her voice deep but raises the volume, as if to shake him into action.

'Just GO! This is the direction, Shan. Is all set up by Tuli. Anybody comes, then is you, Rajan and Guna – you three must to leave from the back before they get past us to the kitchen. Me and Nia – we keep them talking. The other cooks, legal ones, stay – they got their documents upstairs.' She points again, thrusting her hand to urge him out.

And then, the shouting seems louder. He thinks he can hear expletives. FUCK YOU. FUCK OFF. But he can't be sure if it is in his head, he can't separate the noise out into words. Can Ava hear it?

There is something in him that rejects the fact that he has to leave. The problem is, if he accepts that this is for real, then it is to shake hands with a pestilent understanding. The acceptance will actually be crippling for him, because it will be an acceptance of the total instability of his life. And that way lies a terror that he must not encounter. So, what then? It can all crack open and swallow him like this at any moment? Really? Is that what it is to live, now?

'Shan, bloody stop . . . standing,' says Ava, her eyes glistening now with a ferocity that is turning hostile. He is endangering them all with his inaction. 'What, you worried about Tuli or something?'

He shakes his head and begins unpinning his hat.

'Shan, I am telling you for last time,' says Ava, fixing on him with what he has to accept is real, obstinate rage. 'You go. NOW. THROUGH THE BACK. What you want, a practice for this bloody thing like is fire alarm drill or something? You can see I am here. I am doing the restaurant care, what you waiting for, just go!'

He turns and walks through the kitchen, keeps going, out through the rear doorway, past the pipes, the belching fumes and vapours, hoists himself over the small brick wall that borders the yard. After the murky quiet of the restaurant, the sun is agitating his eyes. His heart is like a defective gun that is shooting off all over the place.

Where to go now? He stands on the corner of the back road and removes the offending garments, folds the hat and apron till the thick white squares of cloth are almost small enough to fit between his palms and outstretched fingers.

He looks out at the high-rise buildings in the distance, thinks of the anonymous inhabitants, the families who are living out their lives in these grids in the sky.

Here he is, saving himself again, rather than those he loves. Now that he is out of there, he feels a sudden desire to scream. A single note, over and over. Where do people go to scream in privacy? His legs are shaking as he walks, he is tripping over his feet as he tries now to run, so that he falls over in the alley itself. He hits the pavement on his side as an image of a dead body comes to him, the same body as always, wrapped in white, dark blood blotching the fabric with the remnants of life. *Ratatatatat* go the bullets in his chest, faithless and worthless. *Ratatatatat*.

# NIA

She was at the crossing with a song in her head, grateful for the warm lick of sun in the sky, waiting for the traffic to pass. The pavements too were starting to fill with people, it was almost time for the monthly street market.

The road to the restaurant was blocked off at one end. She couldn't see through to Vesuvio, the view was obstructed by a large white van and a small crowd. They were gathered outside the Polish greasy spoon, stretching back towards the Aussie pub. She could recognize some of them – the guys from the Chinese place, the attendants from the launderette. A man and a woman in blue Tesco polo shirts were conferring across the narrow part of the road, near the betting shop.

They were staring at something or someone. She followed the eye line and saw him: a man in black uniform, only then registering the small luminous yellow rectangles stitched on the front, the walkie-talkie in his hand, the words 'UK BORDER AGENCY' on his back. A red-haired woman walked out and stood behind him, bronze highlights crowning her short figure, clothed in the same outfit, speaking into her radio and attaching it to her chest.

Oh, shit, Nia thought. Elene. Is she legal? She must be. Surely.

The crowd were pushing in a little now and she couldn't see the Tesco duo any more. There were about ten people in Nia's way, give or take a few, mostly men of varying sizes, rumbling with a low, apprehensive energy. They emanated heat, there was a smell that was a jumble of all their different years.

'Where you GOING?' one of them shouted, emphasizing the final word, as though kicking off a football chant or a protest march. 'Where you GOING?'

'LEAVE HIM!' said another.

She waited, tentatively pushing herself up onto her toes, on the outskirts. She wanted to call out, let Elene know she was there, but her voice would have no chance against the noise, the volume was increasing with every minute. God knows who they were taking away. 'Him' suggested it was one of the cooks. Or even the proprietor himself – was it possible?

Her phone was going against her hand in the front pocket of her jacket. She had long ago switched off the ringtone, so that it was only capable of a faint vibration, because there was really only one person who called her these days. She pulled it out with jittery fingers, worried that someone was ringng from Vesuvio. She hadn't even considered the possibility that this chaos might have reached her own place of work.

But it was her sister. She pressed the button required to reject the call.

The last time she had answered a call from Mira, there was honestly no rhyme or reason to it, in fact it was a kind of idleness that meant Nia pressed 'accept'. And then, before clocking what she'd done, she had to speak to her.

'Banana brains!' Nia said, into the receiver, before she could get her guard up. She was upstairs at the restaurant, sorting out the mini fridge behind the bar.

'It's not funny, Nia,' came the reply, plaintive in spite of itself.

'Tomato head!' Nia said, as if all the old nicknames could form a carpet between them, a magic corridor of embroidered fabric from here to Newport, shrink time and space, put them in the same protected continuum.

'Nia, stop it.'

'Peach face! How's it going?'

'Nia, it's two weeks I've been trying you for—'

'What is it?' The words cut through quickly, suddenly sharp. 'What does she want, then?'

'She's bad, Nia – you don't know how she's been, it's worse than usual—'

She could hear a scuffle of voices in the background, the strident tones of their mother. She couldn't decipher her words but the energy was intense.

'How much does she want?' Nia said.

'Nia, for fuck's sake, what do you want to always be bringing it down to that, it's not just cash—'

'How much?'

Mira didn't reply. Instead Nia could hear her mother's voice making its way loudly through the noise until it was right up close to the phone.

'Who you talking to? Who you talking to? You talking to that stuck-up bitch in London? Tell that fucking ungrateful slut something from me—'

It went muffled then, Mira had covered the phone with her hand. When she came back, she sounded worried.

'Nia?' So tentative and vulnerable that it made Nia screw up her eyes.

'How much?' she said.

'Nia, don't be like that.'

'How much, Mira?'

'I've been doing the skips again—'

'What the fuck, Mira.'

'Nia, she just wants to see you—'

She hung up. It was her sweet baby sister Mira, yes, but she dropped it on the bar counter, the phone, after ending the call. It was suddenly burning, or so it felt, and she put herself downstairs, into another room, got away from its radioactive waves. *She just wants to see you. Just.*

Still, after an hour, she went back, held the pernicious thing in her hand and rang the bank. She put fifty quid in Mira's account. It was a significant part of her week's wages. By 'doing the skips', Mira meant she was doing what they had done whenever things got to their worst and their mother was out of action – gone to the skips of the local supermarkets after dark and rifled through the packages for unused food. The safest parts were from the bakery – bread rolls,

Danish pastries, bagels, all baked that morning and thrown that night. They didn't ever take the fish or meat, even if they were in three layers of clingfilm, not just because you might get sick, but because by that point, if you were rifling through rubbish, you weren't about to start cooking when you got back.

She was fifteen now. Nia thought of her small face – you could always read it as easily as those Love Heart sweets with the messages printed on them – imagined those peachy cheeks full of almond croissant and retched suddenly, holding her hand tightly over her stomach.

After half an hour, she found a way to leave her shift early. It was unlike her, to cry sickness at work like this, but she couldn't shake the nausea. The air was sticky and dingy when she emerged from Vesuvio, there was very little light on the street and Nia was muffled by the absence, as though it was oxygen that was missing, rather than illumination. Something was wrong with the street lamp. She stepped around a heap of glass on the kerb. Twinkling and sharp, the diamanté mass of crystals on the paving, lying next to a car with a crater smashed into its window. She walked quickly to the underground station, speeding up on seeing Sue, the regular sleeper on that patch. She was visible from a distance, arranging her dull navy sleeping bag and provisions near the tube entrance. Nia tried to get past without fishing through her bag for the coins she'd normally pass to her on the way home.

'Oh, dear,' Sue said, when their eyes invariably locked. She had a stripy woollen hat on and her ears were poking out from her long brown hair. She frowned and pushed her glasses up the bridge of her nose, her pale digits in fingerless gloves. 'Is it a difficult day today, love? No good?' She had been sleeping on that bit of the street since before Nia had arrived and she had a routine for this particular hour before midnight – she'd often be arranging or replacing the big piece of cardboard underneath her bedding, at other times she'd be sitting cross-legged and smoking, acknowledging passers-by, occasional chat with some of them. If it was very late, she might have a can or two sitting near her rucksack.

Nia nodded, tears welling, feeling regret once she was in through the ticket barriers.

'Sue, I'm sorry . . .' she muttered, although it was to herself.

She had a scarf and another pair of gloves for Sue in her bag as it happened, had picked them up in a charity shop for a pittance. She usually gave her something like that once a week, she'd accept more than she'd reject, Sue, and they were relatively friendly. Probably, she made Nia think of her mum in some way, she didn't overthink it, but she looked forward to seeing her. She knew her preferences by now, to get Sue a fruit salad rather than a doughnut if she was feeling flush when she went into Tesco, for example.

But that day she had spoken to her little sister; it was all laced up so tightly, Nia's heart, and she didn't want to look at her. She felt so lonely, and she knew Sue had it worse, but Nia didn't have any space in her chest for it – all in all the whole thing was what her mother would have called a shit sandwich.

# SHAN

*Thalai muzhuguthal.* Literal translation: to pour water over someone's head. Actual meaning: to cut off a relationship. Shan is soothing his confusion as he walks, soothing it through the repetition of this phrase, polishing it over like a piece of brass. He is thinking of Devaki and the many unsuccessful attempts he has made to get hold of her. He wants, of course, to believe that her silence is down to anger, rather than because she is dead. But if she was pouring water on their marriage, surely she wouldn't do it this way?

Ava is always talking about finger strength when it comes to climbing – training your capacity to hold on to crucial crags of rock as you ascend. That is how it feels when he rifles through his past with Devaki – he is trying his best to grasp on to clues that will help him believe that she is alive.

It is true that as a couple, he and Devaki had specialized in awful arguments. He would leave the soiled furnace of their words when it was too overwhelming – and walk out of the house for hours – coming back to find that she was a wreck, shaking with the spent violence of a thousand tears. He was careful with her then, not always hiding his shameful pleasure at this: that she cared so much about the two of them, had cried so much. That she loved him the way he did her, with a rueful obsession, each of them destined to make the other bend in their direction.

She was the academic, the one with a permanent lab position. He was the one who couldn't get a steady job at the university. And of course, there was Karu: the impulsive dreaming up of their child's future was what united them most poetically, but also what divided them. She ran the house. She was so competent, so unequivocally beautiful, so kind when she felt it was right . . . just so exactly Devaki. Her only public flaw as she saw it, was her weight – she

26

wrestled with her appetite, which fluctuated cruelly and held her hostage in its sudden, emotional, manifestations. Privately, there was her wildness: part of her allure, but injurious too. It inflamed every spat with acute urgency, as though they were about to go out to a firing squad if they didn't get to the truth.

There was that saying – do you want to be happy in marriage or do you want to be right? He had come across it in one of those books sold on the footpath in Jaffna, amidst a raft of paperbacks that all seemed to be versions of *How to Win Friends and Influence People*.

Now, he wants nothing more than for them to be stuck in the worst fight of their lives, a shocking, seismic disagreement of international proportions. How wonderful it would be, if this loss of dialogue between them was just because she was full of silent fury. Radiantly alive, and full of fury. He would be happy with that.

He is inside and outside the world at once. Sometimes when he bathes in the morning, he is so spent by this simple act that he sits on the plastic flooring in the towel after he has dried himself, unable to get up and dress. He keeps his eyes open, craving the fevered salty melt that would surely come with tears. But there is nothing there. He just shivers instead. If he closes his eyes, he sees blood, and then comes the image of his son. If he is not careful, he will hear his son speak.


Crush and fade, slip and follow. He is making a concerted effort to walk away from the restaurant in a calm way, and to avoid thinking about the immigration van that he can see out of the corner of his eye as he leaves Vesuvio behind him. Very soon he is surrounded by people, due to a temporary market on one of the short roads between the restaurant and bus stop. Cheese, potted jams, breads and pickles – each stand is oddly specific with regard to contents, and customers are hovering over these goods as though they are precious stones.

There is a man behind Shan who shares his frustration at getting through the crowd, he is a Japanese man of similar build who is more resolute than him when it comes to keeping up speed. He moves along the street with an open book in one hand, directing the lead of his dog in the other, stubbornly continuing to read as he pushes his way through the mass. Stops his reading only to cross the road, and then resumes the curious, fervent task of consuming his book whilst walking. The golden-haired dog at his side accommodates its owner without complaint, bends in its body to stay on the pavement. Shan watches them disappear around the corner, admiring the man's resolve. There is a lot to be said for such persistence.

Barely ten minutes go by before he receives Ava's text.

*Come back. They are gone. Elene say they drive away.*

And there you are. It is oddly deflating to read it. There is even still time to make it back before his shift begins. He must go back, but he can't feel relieved. What is there to stop them returning?

He is back on their street within minutes of receiving the text, and the van is indeed gone, leaving an open space of some relief when he looks down the clear road. But when he walks under the striped plastic hood at the front of Vesuvio, in through the front door, the shaking begins again. It's still too early for the other cooks or Tuli, and so he tries his best to begin as normal, opens out his hat and apron so that they are ready to wear. Ava sees him, clocks the disturbance in him. He has been staring at the items for too long, leaning himself against a chair at one point.

'Is a shock,' she says quietly, moving in to help him to sit down. 'You need to stop for a minute, Shan. Just wait.'

He shakes her off and is up again, walking back out through the kitchen into the yard, the same route exactly, over the same back wall, blindly, frowning hard, walking, just walking till he reaches a thick green hedge of some sort to his left side. People can see you, but they don't see what you are. He still wants more than anything to shout, the need is fermenting dangerously inside him. It is a basic right, surely, to be able to shout without fear of condemnation? He stops and puts his face in the wet needles, immerses in the sensation of a hundred tiny sharp points against his skin, and only then does he feel the demons begin to leave his body.

Later, he is working hard when he hears Tuli breeze into the main space of the restaurant with his usual greetings. Ava's voice joins the noise, she is relaying everything with pattering speed. For a moment Shan thinks about going to join in with the explanations. The boss would probably receive him the way he does everyone: with a show of warmth and understanding, even though news of a raid on the street will be unwelcome and bring its own tensions. But he can't trust himself to talk. There is no benefit to seeking out an audience with Tuli right now, he thinks. Ava will do the needful. Let Ava do it.

# NIA

Under Tuli's watch, the restaurant had an unofficial open-door policy for waifs and strays and Nia knew she was no different in that respect. She had just been thrown out of university, after a year at an illustrious institution, and in not so many words, she had ejected herself out of the family home too.

She had embellished the truth of her parents, in the conversations with Tuli after their first meeting. Her father was a doctor, apparently, yes, but her mother wasn't a nurse. She didn't see this latter untruth as actively lying to him. It was just that she didn't want to get into it, it was a placeholder of sorts. For a start, it was difficult to summarize her mother's multifarious ways of earning money into a kind of career.

Arriving in Newport at eighteen, the young Sharon Collins had begun temping as a secretary at various firms, at times she'd also been one of those people with clipboards on the street for market research, sometimes working at call centres, for a while she was apparently a bank clerk at Nationwide – all this before Nia was born, which was when she was twenty-two years old. Most jobs lasted for a few months at least, but never really over a year. She grew up in Dinas Powys, a small town in the Vale of Glamorgan that was fortified at weekends by visitors to its castle and Iron Age ruins. A civil servant father who was slowly ascending the ranks at the Inland Revenue, and a mother whose job was 'to maintain her looks and the house they lived in'. That's how Sharon told it to her daughters. Parents who she wanted nothing to do with, but whom she was now forced to tap for cash at intervals, a humiliation that was increasing in frequency as the years went on.

How, then, was Nia to describe her own mother? Well, if you were going to talk about the sweet side first, that solid, satisfying element which ran down her spine like the hard chocolate centre of a Feast ice-cream bar, it would be romance. The hippy rosehip variety. She was turning her life into this big sculpture of romance as far as Nia could see – looking back – with a succession of relationships (some long, some short, but she and Mira didn't know much about their fathers except for their respective ethnicities: Bengali for Nia, Tibetan for Mira), and their mother had a sylph-like quality that went well with this project. Long cocoa hair to her hips, pearly smooth skin, wandering around naked and peaceful of a morning, just because it was, of course, absurd to cover up your body. Generous curves, attractive ones, not from this time we live in, more like the kind you might see in the National Gallery on the second floor. When she had gone through puberty, Nia could remember looking at her mother's breasts: the large swing of them, the big areolas of the nipples. She could imagine Sharon dancing through fields of daisies to some bongo tune until she died.

Before the descent, of course.

So, yes, Sharon Collins was the kind of mother who played 'She's a Rainbow' by the Rolling Stones when she was feeling light on a Sunday afternoon, baking muffins or painting a bed-frame in the council flat she'd been allocated as a single parent, shouting the rhymes out triumphantly, feeling them to be her own mantra of possibility. The same magical traits came into play when her mother started losing it. She ran a full house, always had lots of friends visiting, she was brimming with compliments and she meant them, she had figured out personal dynamics – how to flatter and be sincere at the same time. In truth, Nia admired her for it. A kitchen crowded with people eating veggie chilli and rolling fags to world music while Nia and Mira played with their kids. But how harsh it was, when the bubbles turned to loneliness. It happened fast, but it must have been building slowly behind the scenes.

There is no big moment of transition that Nia can peg it on, when she looks back. Only that the booze became part of Mum's diet somehow, and meals seemed less important. On week nights she would often be drinking alone and passing out on the couch, so Nia would sort out dinner. The days were suddenly centred around getting hold of the bottles; this task took on a new urgency, and replaced all other priorities. Then came the manipulation, the same flattery, the deceit. A long, endless list of first times ensued: the first time Nia could remember her mother stealing something from a shop, the first time she looked at her daughters with the sooty eyes of unknowing when they came home from school and roused her from bed. The first time Nia realized their mum was ill enough to be dependent on them, a patient softened from bravado to vulnerability.

Nia was allocated the dangerous roles, being four years older than Mira. She was the one sent to buy alcohol, when Mum was too weak to pretend it would ever change. The first time she gave Nia directions, the first time she gave her the pin to her card, the first time Nia covered up for social services. The first time Mum wet herself and Nia picked her up off the bathroom floor. The first time the gas and electricity got cut off, or one of the girls was mocked for smelling bad at school, the first time they got refused entry on a bus because Sharon herself stank of booze.

She never asked Nia to call her grandparents though, that seemed to be the boundary wall. Ringing them was something she delayed and delayed till there was no other option. Then, she'd sober up especially, straighten her clothes, like she was going to church or something, and perform the rare, polite, call and response. A piece of performance art, delivered in frictionless, measured tones on the phone. Sometimes, she'd do this call from a phone box and Nia would watch her from outside, through the scarlet-lined grid of glass, bemused that her mother could communicate like this when needed, betrayed by the simplicity of her ability to be sober for this kind of occasion, but not for her two children.

Where was this self-control when she let herself beat them? Ramming Nia against the living-room wall because she wouldn't go and get her what she needed, or slapping Mira's face repeatedly till the red swelled up in a lurid fan of shame on her right cheek. It was hard for her, bringing them up on her own, Nia could concede that. Sometimes it was too hard.

'You filthy fucking beast,' she'd spit out, if she trailed in to find Nia reading in the kitchen late at night, eating toast and ignoring her wails from the bedroom. 'You filthy fucking bitch.' In the beginning, the abuse sounded false in her mouth, as though she was trying on a piece of clothing that was an awkward fit, a hand-me-down of extremity for those moments when needs must. But gradually, she made the invective her own.

Mira was resourceful. When they got hungry, she'd perform bizarre acts of faith – find money hidden round the flat because of her persistence (coins under the sofa, in the cracks of the mattress, behind the fridge), or turn frozen peas into a whole meal with butter and pepper. She'd get sympathy food from her friends' families, walking to and from their homes when there was no petrol money or if the sleep-ins had extended to marathons. Mummy's got the flu. Mummy's a bit depressed at the minute. It's hard doing it all yourself. Thank you so much. That's so nice of you. Shepherd's pie! She'll be so pleased, I'm sure it'll help her get over this bug. Mummy, Mummy, Mummy.

Nia was working at the McDonald's drive-in on weekends and through the holidays at that time, it helped a lot. She always saved some of it, though, hiding as much of the money away as she could, maybe fifteen, twenty per cent of her earnings, and when Mira started at a local pizzeria, Nia assumed her sister would do the same. But she never did, just prostrated herself at the feet of their mother with that sunflower smile she had, and gave it all to her like a donation to some crooked guru in an ashram. People were still visiting the flat at the weekend, but now instead of the partying parents and their kids, Mum had a different crowd for companions. They hailed from all kinds of ages and backgrounds – people she seemed to have collected from a particular club in town that ran nights full of lasers and beanbags and considered itself to be alternative. 'Experimentalist' was the word on the flyer. Sometimes Nia would look back and try and imagine the visage of her father, Mira's father too, back into the living room during this period of her life, both of them sketched in like artist's impressions of wanted people. There were clearly drugs around now as well, and they'd see these people collapsed on the couch and the floor on a Friday night when they came home, Mum floppy with pleasure, barely acknowledging them.

To say it was embarrassing would be to miss the point entirely. Looking back, it's a picture of herself and Mira sleepwalking through school, their jobs too, always stepping around or over the wilful disarray of their lives, each clamping a fist securely over the heart, and focusing on nailing the basics whenever possible – food, warmth, bathing – no room for superfluous emotion.

There were regulars who only turned up at the weekend, but stayed overnight. A woman in her forties who walked around in her underwear by day, carrying her scarred body in a kind of apologetic way, like a lean shopping bag of goods past their best-before date. A tall gentle lad in his early twenties who always wore a glo-beads bracelet, on whom Nia attempted to have a distant crush for a while. He stole lead from the roofs of empty houses and sold it to the 'pikeys', the travellers camped on the outskirts of Newport. A taxi driver, who ran drugs to the rich parts of town on the side – Beechwood and Christchurch. Benign, they were, in some sense, and always figuring out the agreed moral compass – really very judgemental of those who committed violent crime, for example. A guy they knew got vilified, he had walked into the newsagent in the parallel street with a knife when he was clucking, suffering a withdrawal from heroin that became too much to bear.

'Can you believe it?' the underwear woman said. 'It's awful, I didn't know he had it in him!'

Their mother was quick to agree. 'Crazy, just crazy. Poor Ranjit, he must have been bloody terrified. He'll be feeling so unsafe in his own shop now, he's open till midnight, fucking hard for him.'

Ranjit was unlikely to be looking at them with such benevolent empathy in return. Their mum had nicked bottles off his shelves more than once. Nia knew it because she recognized the yellow stickers, the clear boxy font of the numbers printed on them. She only did it when she had people coming over, but if Nia ever went in there with Mira, he'd give them an aggrieved frown of a look that basically said 'My eyes are right on you', and she didn't blame him for it. Big family packs of Doritos, small jars of pitted olives would appear with the booze on those days, and they'd feast on them urgently, always worried that the days ahead were going to be scant.

Nia began to remove herself from their company. Instead of dropping out of school, she went in through the gates for every minute she could, as though it was a free spa, literally siphoned every last breath of freedom made available by the timetable and then on to the library. It meant she was out of the house until six-thirty most weekdays at least. More if she went on to her night shifts. She felt bad that their mum was more and more likely to be drinking at home alone, but Mira was with her and in this way, shamelessly, Nia planned her escape. She found out about the special access scheme for people from schools like theirs, and spent months carrying the forms around, figuring out how to square the circle and fit into it. Even then, it was a shock for all of them when she left for university. Politics, philosophy and economics. Three courses rolled into one.

But Nia hadn't counted on the fact that she loved them, and that this fact would generate a desire to return almost straight away. Love, or you could call it co-dependence, according to how you saw it. She'd always thought them to be much the same thing, really. Those long college halls, teeming with such sleek, gruesomely confident people, all her own age. They were more than a little terrifying. She went back to Newport so much in that first term, missed so much that she was under formal observation from a month into her time at university. *Baby I can't live without you* came the texts. *Little Mira can't do it all on her own. She's crushed without you. We would do anything just to see your face Nia. Please, baby.* She had access to proper money now, she had student loans and she was needed.

'Sent down' they called it, when you got asked to leave that particular university, and though Nia railed against the hierarchy implied by this top-heavy phrase, she was broken enough by failing her first-year exams that on some level she believed it. No one wants to look in a mirror that is cracked with their own failure, but it felt like she had fractured a dream that belonged to all of them. Especially for Sharon Collins, their dear, paranoid mother, lonely so much of the time as they were getting older, for whom shame was always a hidden possibility, a sly ditch that required navigation on a daily basis. She was proud Nia had done it, made it out of Newport, even though she spent all her time trying to suck her back.

But Nia was so angry when she got thrown out of college, it was all packed in her, tight and burning like tobacco in a pipe. She blamed them, and after the years of dreaming and planning, the loss was too much to comprehend; it was horrific, the idea that she'd thrown it away. She couldn't forgive her mother either. The last visit home was on a Saturday night. Mira was sleeping over at some girl's house and the flat was full of Mum's 'friends'. She was just lying there, inert on the sofa when Nia walked in, you could have been forgiven for thinking she was dead. A huge parade of empty glass bottles populated the long table at the side of the room, their transparent forms as defiant as nudists on a beach. And no one there seemed to give a shit about her state. They were all just co-existing happily with her long silent slab of a body.

She wasn't dead – that body with its countless familiar coves and promontories, where the two of them had nestled and slept when younger – it did finally rouse itself after some time. But Nia saw it as one of those gestalt moments that people write about. Where all your understanding coheres into a meaningful whole, and you can see it flaring on the horizon, how it all fits together. All of their mother's desires and impulses were circling those bottles, she wanted them so much more than Mira or Nia, or anything else.

She ruminated over it all constantly once she'd left, waking at night in fits of sweat and loneliness, pressuring herself to understand it, as though wisdom was like a mathematical proof, eluding her only because she was messing up one of the steps. When it became too much, she would reanimate her mother's image back to someone who was a real, empathetic human. A mother who had no fear of spiders, would pick them up by their legs and release them to freedom out the door. A vegetarian mother who still craved a good hearty lasagne in the winter – she had made it with soft aubergine oozing around the solid crunch of celery. Mum could knit a stylish cowl when she had the wool – who knew where she got the pattern. She still wanted to go to night school and study something. Above Sharon Collins there always hovered the spectre of those parents they never saw – shadowy figures about whom Mira and Nia often speculated. Did Mum's father beat her? Or was it the other thing, even? They didn't know what led to her demons and they didn't want to ask.

And so, Nia fled to London because someone at college knew someone who had a spare couch. 'Till you get yourself sorted,' they said. It was such an optimistic idea, that one could just go out and get oneself sorted, and when the black came upon her, on those days that were stencilled with despair, she would recite it to herself with different emphases. Lightly, say, effortless. Just till you get yourself sorted, mate. Or kindly, like you'd imagine of a lady serving bara brith in a café, fat slabs of raisin-studded comfort on paper-cut doilies. Just till you get yourself sorted, love. And in Nia's mind it stayed, there was no one to really discuss these things with in those days. The fledgling university friendships she had formed were quickly wilting under the grey cumulus of youthful embarrassment at her circumstances. They were of course all still there, those people, continuing on the undergraduate track, tunnelling their way through parallel futures in what she imagined by now to be a huge Borgesian library, a universe twanging with string theory and discourse, full of infinite options. The failure felt so epic in its dimensions. Already she was looking back at life and saying to herself, *I was young then*, as though that idea of youth was over. She had the sense that she'd do this always, whatever her age in the future, struggling with this curtailed experience, pushing forward on the treadmill of the moment even as it carried her back, over and over.

She used most of her earnings for rent once she had lodgings (a spare room in a basement flat in Brixton that she had found in the paper, a junior doctor for a flatmate who was mostly absent), and ate at the restaurant. There wasn't much left but she used what she had to buy cheap clothes, taken with the idea that she could fashion herself and her future place in the world if she got the outer layer right. A handful of tiny fabric roses, turquoise, each smaller than the nail on a pinkie, to stitch onto a plunging neckline. Large vinyl flower buttons as well, candyfloss pink with a vanilla calyx, to customize a second-hand coat from the market and propel it into the realm of the sublime. A military coat, that one, made from new cloth but faded to vintage, carefully 'distressed', and yes, she would think of this word too, as she walked to and from the restaurant in that coat, feet instinctively avoiding the undertow of the street: kebab polystyrene, glass splinters, the glossy slips of pub flyers. Consider its meaning as though it could yield wisdom – fancy that maybe you could manage your life's distress in this way, spread it over your face to maximize aesthetic potential.

Even as a child she was always taken with the story of Cinderella, in spite of it being sexist and all, just for the idea of transformation. It was surely the most appealing inhabitant of the fairy-tale canon: the idea that a dress could change you like that, a pair of shoes, materialize you in the moonlight so that you were finally visible. That it could be so easy.

She had her mother's curves and hair, but a new voice by now, shorn of the Welsh wool. That was one of the first things she did at Oxford, along with getting rid of her home-bleached locks. She remembered wearing those new vowels like furs, feeling that showy and ridiculous. It wasn't just the accent, it was the timbre of her voice. She'd worked on lowering it from the baby-girl pitch to which it sometimes leaned.

Mira was still stuck there with Mum, and the guilt of this was constant. But they weren't really speaking and there was no way

Nia was going back. Instead, being around Tuli in that restaurant, right there watching the granular decisions he held like sand in his palm, so fearlessly every day, she hoped that she would learn how to spread light instead of darkness.

When she walked to the bus stop alone each night she could hear a soundtrack in her head – she was a character in a film, she would nod her head to it, revel in the cinematic suture with normality, let it lance the space between her ears. In a long narrow alley once, floodlit with dirty yellow from a lamp post, she could remember running, leaping, swinging herself round it and almost howling at the moon, rejoicing in the space, willing herself into being, willing her life to begin again.

# SHAN

He can tell it is a different kind of crowd tonight, mainly by the way in which Ava breezes in and out of the kitchen with a lightness in her step. She is enjoying her role in the group, it is casual, there is none of the harried atmosphere that accompanies the weekends, for example, when the local wealthy take up the tables downstairs.

'Slow down. Slow down!' he says when she turns to leave with a platter of prawns in garlic and chilli that he has just cooked on a lazy lick of flame, slowly, over many minutes. He puts a bowl of wooden cocktail sticks onto her tray and they look to him, these sticks, as though they are all lying in each other's arms, soldiers sleeping in a mass, unaware of how close they are.

'Are you mad? I am not a slow person, matey,' she says, laughing. 'You got the wrong person, it is not in my style to be slow.'

'Taste one?' He spears a prawn and boldly holds it near her mouth. There are only two other cooks in there at this point and he is emboldened by the fact that their backs are turned. They are rolling out pizza dough amidst a stream of nutty vowels and consonants, using the absence of the group eyes for a moment of quiet intimacy.

She laughs at him, presents a face of perfect perplexity and almost skips out of the room.

He wonders what Ava sees when she looks at him. His pride has always been his hair – the big thick improbable swirl of it, faithful to the egotistical requirements of his head. His father's hair, his grandfather's too – worn regally, whatever the era – matched for audacity only by the full slant of his nose. He touches his cheeks. The side lines of beard are there, he still shaves them in but there is always too much fullness in the moustache area. Still, it is good to have hair, that much is true. Even now, it doesn't fall out or turn white, it seems astonishing to him, how it has endured. But he has lost his signature quiff, its grandiloquent height and presence. Those luxury tinctures he used to apply: the styling creams and potions, they are from another life.

Outside, the room reverberates with secret meaning: people shout, guffaw, murmur and wallow in a gluttonous state of abandonment. It all sounds like pleasure to him.

The cooks are all sitting, hovering on the tips of their stools, some are seated on the vegetable crates, and the words have clustered into a heated cloud above them.

'Why shouldn't they have their defence? They can't just let their children, their wives be killed?' Shan says. He employs a measured tone, deliberately, as though he is asking about the weather. He can hear himself saying 'they', 'their' as though he is not part of the stream, as though he can separate himself from the thousands of Tamils who have been killed by the Sri Lankan government. This makes him appear odd, he knows that, suspicious even, but he can't help it. He can't say 'we', 'us', everything that would help smooth things over, he just can't do it. At the word 'we', he imagines his house in Jaffna imploding: the ceilings collapsing, flames quickened in time-lapse, the suspended violence of the debris.

Every person he has met in the kitchen is, on some level, like him. They all work here and live in the apartment at the top of the building, five of them on mattresses in two rooms, saving and squirrelling away their earnings in a grand act of collective hibernation. The restaurant is one of several known addresses in London for Tamils coming over from Sri Lanka. Shan is the newest recruit and he is grateful to live separately, even though it is far away, at least an hour and a half on the buses. It is not just that he is the only one who has a university degree, more that he hopes very much that he will not be working in the restaurant business for long.

These guys, however, they all seem very oriented towards a shared dream: acquiring their own restaurant. Coming in like this to their odd constructed family, he has no way of avoiding the necessary background introductions. He is being surreptitiously checked on everything, starting with his allegiances, he can see them glancing at his face when they discuss *Eelam*, the dream state for which the LTTE have been fighting all these years, he can feel their tiny prodding statements as they check whether he is a believer or a blasphemer. Although they speak English when with Tuli, or the waitresses, the kitchen is generally a place for discussions like these, a bartering of ideas that can only take place in the mother tongue.

'In war we suffer, in peace we suffer,' one says, eyeing Shan up speculatively. 'But one day Eelam will come.'

Shan does not respond, even though he knows that the guy is looking for a nod of assent from him.

'Why does the government feel they can kill Tamil people?' says another. 'Because only Sinhala people are *real* people in Sri Lanka. Tamil people are a different thing for them.'

'No one is talking of history in these newspapers here,' comes in a third. 'They say the LTTE is terrorist, that the Tigers have been fighting the government for thirty years but no one is talking about how it began. How the government is turning Sri Lanka to blood. They want Sinhala people to live and Tamils to die.'

'We have lost so much, what does it matter,' says another finally, looking Shan directly in the eye. 'Main thing is we must not forget those who are still living in our country. We must do what we can to help. We can all do our duty and send money home to help build Eelam.'

Shan lets the exchange pass over him, the way it does when they discuss their various applications. Once they brought in all the letters they had received from the UK Home Office at different points, for comparison of key phrases:

'. . . *the Secretary of State does not consider Tamils to be a persecuted group* . . .'

'. . . *members of the civilian population, whatever their religion or ethnic group, have nothing to fear from routine actions and enquiries made by the authorities in Sri Lanka* . . .'

Then, the mortuary lists – every last auntie's cousin's wife's brother who has been killed by these so-called 'routine actions'. These lists are long and gut-churning, bulbous with details. Shan does not enjoy this mixture of morbidity and pedantry, even though the others all seem to find it cathartic.

Even worse are the excerpts from court proceedings. Guna, easily the most social and excitable of them, has taken to collecting these from his wider circle, and reading out the most salacious chunks. His preference is for transcripts of speeches by actual judges, and he reads the lines in English, with a decent attempt at a haughty Anglo whine:

> *'The appellant* claims *to suffer from the effects of torture but I find that this is all part of the smokescreen. He has persisted in maintaining a* false story *and his conduct in seeking anonymity in the course of proceedings before the Tribunal is but another aspect of the smokescreen which he has thrown up.'*

Shan usually keeps a low profile when Guna's showmanship gets going. But today, due to his relative newness and the novelty that he brings, the topic for analysis is inevitably turning to Shan himself.

'I am from a hotel family,' Shan tells the cooks, all five of them attentive, but with varying levels of warmth and dubiousness on their faces. 'We have three hotels in one street and there are four of us cousins – brothers. Our sister left two years ago, married to a business family in Colombo, air-conditioning units, myself I studied Geology in Jaffna and took over one hotel after graduating—'

The hotel family is a fiction that comes easily now, after multiple tellings over the months, blended as it is with the useful, non-threatening facts of his actual degree and college.

'What, man?' says Guna. 'Nothing, nothing doing, so you have a degree, and we don't – you think here they are, what, actually caring about this shit? What – you are about to go to the job centre and ask for some kind of lecturing post in a fancy university then? Ha! Welcome, sir, please, do have your six pounds an hour, you can also be happy to pick up every coin when they leave their tables and then bring it back to count with us for tips like a *naye* on the street or what?'

Shan rolls his eyes.

'I don't mind working hard,' he says. 'I am out of danger myself. There is a lot to be glad for in this country . . .'

'Out of danger, are you mad?' says Guna. 'You think you have a special magic passport hidden up your backside or something? Just please look in the mirror, dear prince – for these people your face has TIGER written all over it, like a holy text.'

Guna bares his teeth, produces an efficient, clipped growl.

'Agggh! Wild tiger! Like this: aaagh! So crazy! You even read that newspaper they hand out at the train station – how can you bring that shit in here, man, seriously – front page is always which fucking *kusukundi* bombed which bastard *vesai moan* and then they stare at you like this when you go past them on the moving stairs and you even shake your bag like this just to scare them?'

He swells with the excitement of his words, absorbs the murmurs and laughs of the group, wobbles on his stool and delivers his next line with an egregious sense of drama.

'Shan, man, tell me one thing, did you at least do some of your trip on the aeroplane? They let you through without stopping and stripping you down to your underwear in the airport? Oh, you thought it was sexy time for Shan baby? Yes! Come on. Confess to me. DO it, man.'

They laugh in unison, open the door out to the yard. Two of them stand in the doorway and light up their cigarettes. It is entertaining to have a new boy to toss around, in front of whom they can appear worldly.

I get it, thinks Shan as he rolls up his sleeves and pins his cap back on to his head. He thinks of his journey to this country. Tearing up his passport, the moment when he did it, handing over the money, the gold, everything that he could have owned to be relinquished in that one gesture, getting on that first boat. The volatile glory of hope, how it came and went insidiously over the ensuing months of travel, this sickly desire like the white phosphorus clouds of chemical warfare – depleting you and then disappearing without a trace.

Weeks of waiting in small abandoned rooms in different cities, your speech clotted thick with suspicion and fear, hard shell closing in on you like a crab if anyone looks you in the eye. Features and colouring of humans changing as often as the transport methods. Trucks, steamers, one aeroplane. Your self, you hope, can elongate or contract as necessary, swap or drain itself of colour, whatever it takes to disappear into each environment: you join a list of creatures that have made camouflage their daily practice – the Bat Faced Toad, Common Baron Caterpillar, Dead Leaf Mantis, the Wolf Spider. No questions, keep your conversation at a minimum. If you get caught, hold your hands up and ask for asylum, whatever the country, just accept that you didn't make it to the UK, and make your life there, instead, it's better than nothing. Make your life in Moscow, Moldovia, Belarus, Lesbos, even Kuala Lumpur if you have to. Don't sit around crying, just take it – you got this far, at least – that is how you speak when you rehearse the story you'll tell yourself. You can all live here: Devaki, Karu baby, all three of you. You can and you will.

Remember your new name at all times, you can network to some extent but don't be stupid and make actual friends, never remove the manacle of discipline that is necessary for this long-distance undertaking. If you slip up, it's over. Think of it as a hunger fast, a devotional marathon, a computer game in which you have only one life, anything to keep you on track. Have this 'life story' ready, or you'll end up telling the real story, the one that will get you or your loved ones killed if they start trying to check it out and those vermin at home get wind of it, the ones who come looking. Remember: having no passport is the key, everything takes longer, you've got a certain amount of time to make a new plan while you clog up the system. Take heart from this if you get caught, it's going to take them time to eject you, and time means hope, more hope, yes?

And then, after two months and thirteen days, how he had arrived in London and not been crushed in its fist and returned like Malar, Sati, Somi, and so many others, returned to be beaten, scratched, ripped or 'disappeared' – annihilated by their own government. Instead, the joining of the dots – whispered advice from hidden voices in this London network that was supposed to help him – getting sent to a room for a handful of nights in each of those addresses with such strange names: 179 Blackhorse Road, 431 Bywater Street, 3 Martyr Lane – addresses built around a hollow space of transience – a route that had required constantly threading himself through the eye of a needle, such was the deliberation and focus necessary.

Finally, the impossible discovery of Tuli, and this restaurant. A *safe house*. He had heard this phrase whispered throughout the journey but only upon meeting Tuli had it taken on any meaning – four walls that seemed to exist with the aim of protection rather than incarceration. 'Safe' is a word that has haunted him throughout his journey. Even now, every night, when he locks the door of the place where he sleeps, returning in the thick brain clot of the fearful hours – sometimes 2 a.m., sometimes 4 a.m. – to open and lock it again, it is this very word 'safe' that is in his head. A numb, drugged, sugar-haze of a word that he needs to guard against. Once they put you on a list, they can find you anywhere. They can find your wife, your child, even sooner.

But still, he takes heart from his own indestructibility. How did it happen that he, Sivaram Shan, a trainee geologist of such little consequence, had managed to get through? It felt so arbitrary but he preferred to think that there was also something in the way that he had conducted himself. His manner, his deportment, even, could it be the way he had told it? Something in his soul that was muscular, able to stand up in the ring, tighten itself and fight, in spite of the varying lucid nightmares that had convinced him it would be otherwise, that he would be deported on one of those special flights, like a fish escaping from Nilwala river, scooped out upon arrival in fresh water and released back, instead, to suffocate in the giant oil spill of origin, to drown with his entire family in the black margins of human error.

London town. The dream tusk, the end point, the hoped-for destination.

His days selling mobile phone cards here, after the detention centre – the silence, how it took such time to really speak again, his whole self reduced to a contravention of the law, thoughts drawn out in long, endless threat like those painted yellow lines on the road.

What do these guys think – that he'll get upset at their jibes? He has grown up just like them, with the sound of grenades at dinner, thrown at houses in order to silence any voices after curfew. He has huddled with his family under the kitchen table, placed his child in the safest space at the centre, between chair legs and adult legs, a finger to his lips, waiting for the army to move away and patrol other streets.

Their jibes slip off him as cleanly as water on glass. His primary emotion when he is in the kitchen is still that of untempered gratitude towards Tuli, for everything. He almost likes this kind of humour, it spells safety to him. Where's the harm in this? They are harmless enough. It is during nights like these, when jokes abound with such ease, he actually believes that maybe things are going to be OK.

# NIA

It was one of those really tiring nights at the restaurant – everyone demanding their special Saturday night so loudly – a big cacophony of bullish needs that would rise up through the centre of the downstairs space like a tower of sound, impenetrable, all of it merging into one syllable: me, me, me! Now, now, now! Everyone at it – the long, raucous, thirtieth-birthday table shouting openly for more, the wealthy lady tourists with creamy lipsticked mouths and prestige knitwear. You had your local pensioners, reading glasses magnifying their watchful eyes when looking up from the menus, or the pert suited men on dates, following your every move with a timer – making an art form of patient but pointed eye contact when waiting for another bottle.

By the end of these nights Nia knew that she'd be in a sweat and heading for bedraggled if she wasn't careful, but she didn't want to ruin her tip – all the kitchen staff were relying on it too – they pooled all the cash extras in the bag behind the counter. It was like a magic porridge pot, that bag. Whenever it was starting to bulge nicely, that was the time she'd see Tuli come and add to it, casually thrusting in piles of mixed notes as he walked past.

That night, Tuli had disappeared for a few hours, and Guna was running the kitchen with just one other cook. The room's relatively empty state offered a respite from the tornado of demands at the front of house and at one point, Nia entered, throwing her notepad down dramatically, sitting herself flat bump on one of the crates, a sound escaping her throat like a collapsing balloon, almost like flatulence. 'Aghhhhhhhhhh!' It made Guna laugh. He crinkled up his squirrelly brown eyes, dispelling the heavy restlessness that often lay behind them. His smooth face, clean-shaven as always, was merry under the lights, a few tiny greys trickling through the dark sideburns.

'Take this to the big table,' he said, producing a couple of large plates of garlic bread and nodding assuredly towards his phone on the worktop. 'Boss has sent the text, to give them something without the cost between the courses.'

'Do you have his phone number?' Nia said, her voice tilted with surprise. She gave the phone a casual glance. 'I only have his landline.'

Guna looked up at her with unease. His hand was suddenly over the phone. He did it instinctively, covering the screen in one clean movement. She could see a thin band of scarlet threads, tied and knotted around his wrist, there was a slight tremor of uncertainty as he kept his hand there.

'God, Guna, don't worry,' she said. 'I'm not going to jump on it!'

He gave her a half-smile then, goofy, urging her with his eyes to understand the awkwardness of his position.

'I was just saying . . .' She wanted to reassure him. 'He is quite private, isn't he? With all his different rules for different people. The boss. I can't work him out.'

She could see that Guna could get the gist of what she was saying, but that she was going too fast. He had decent English when speaking, and she still had to get used to the fact that it didn't work as well the other way round.

'He is . . . good person, yes?' He nodded as he said it, in order to elicit her agreement.

'Yes,' she said instantly. 'Yes, of course.'

He waited for a moment, and she could see the plan forming in his eyes. He was going to share something with her, it was decided.

'He is helping you?' he said, finally. And then, without waiting for an answer, 'He was doing it for me too. I was in the problem of gambling. You know. Cards playing and all.'

'What did he do?' She said it quietly, she knew how unusual it was for Guna to talk to her at all, let alone for him to offer up something like this.

'Just, I don't know. There was a man from casino who was saying he will come to hurt me. You know. Big man. Break the arms, the legs, for the money.'

Instead of the affirmation of a shared understanding that she was planning, she found herself giving him an astounded look. How could he say this so casually?

He shrugged. 'For the money I am supposed to pay that I have lost in the card games. Too much money only.'

Her mouth opened a little, with involuntary shock. His shrug was so regretful, there was an acceptance in it – the particularities of debt leading to broken limbs – this was, what . . . normal in his world?

'So Mr Tuli, he find out about it. I think, probably Vasanthan, Rajan, one of them tell him.' He looked up at her then, with a quickening glow in his eyes. 'But Tuli, he say, look, just you leave it with me, Guna, I make it go away.'

His hand left the phone then, as though the revelation itself had brought a new confidence to the proceedings, and he went back to the sliced baguettes on the plates, pulling apart the slices to reveal the saturated yellow centres.

'I say OK, boss, but really, how? How it just go away? He say don't worry about that all, it will go only. But you pay me *something*. Even small amount is OK, you decide it and pay what you can. Payment should be every month, we write it down, that's all.'

'Uh-huh,' she said, gathering her legs together and shifting her weight on the box, hoping not to break the spell. She couldn't quite believe that he was talking to her like this and she didn't want it to stop. The other cook was in the corner of the room, handling the oven.

'And so I start and I am still paying. I don't know what he did but I never seen that casino guy again, he disappeared, you know? Just like that, he never come back.'

The door of the kitchen was jolted open suddenly, bringing with it the hydraulic rush of voices from the dining area. Ava popped her head in briefly with a command on her face that made

Nia jump up from the crates and quickly nod back her compliance. Guna handed over the plates, and before she could think of how to honour the fact that he had confided in her, the strange privilege of it, she was threading her fingers between them, lifting the stack successfully and backing out of the door.

'Guna, thank you—' she said, faltering.

But he was already in another corner of the kitchen, crushing, chopping, slicing the fat new bulbs of garlic and not looking in her direction. His phone had disappeared from vision too, all in a glimmer of a moment, and he was now talking to the other cook in a gentle murmur that passed symbiotically between them. She had the feeling that he was regretting the conversation already, that he was trying to quietly erase it, relegating her back to the ranks of those white girls at the front of house who were best kept at arm's length.

She wanted to understand Tuli's motivation, what drove him to get so stuck into people's lives – it was one of the many things that intrigued her about him. She stored up her questions until the end of the day, usually, knowing that he operated on a need-to-know basis. She enjoyed planning the correct question, one that could provoke an answer, something that was most likely to happen if they were alone and he was released from the need to play the big boss in front of everyone.

'Do you see us all as charity cases?' Nia asked, that night, when she was stacking the chairs on the tables and sweeping the floor. 'Are we all part of a love-thy-neighbour reward scheme?'

She had Billie Holiday on the stereo, he let her choose the tracks when the shutters were down, and though his tastes were very conventional, he let her play some jazz, the old crooners mainly. There was an unofficial ban on anyone current. Ava was upstairs playing chess with Shan now they had clocked off and it was all very pleasant and atmospheric downstairs with him counting through bills and scribbling in a massive ledger-style book as he smoked. Candles lit on the table, steam on the windows and street light coming through from outside. She took the dustpan to the front door and opened it for air. The rain slipped off the striped awning in a repeating drip, heavy and regular, like a heartbeat. She could see the scarlet bleed of the sign at the Chinese grocer's, feel the wet solitude of the street as a kind of romance.

'Seriously,' Nia said again. 'Why bother? What's your reason?'

Tuli looked up suddenly and glanced out of the window.

'I'll get back to you,' he said. 'Hold the thought.'

He went through the door and crossed the road, she could see him outside, offering a light to some guy who was standing near the crates at the front of the Chinese grocery. She was held by the image – the mystery of them through the constant ellipsis of drops on the window. Tuli's face was animated, it looked as though he was teasing the guy, now putting his arm around the man and squeezing his shoulder lightly, before taking another drag on his cigarette.

Guna came through from the kitchen. He was leaving for the night, getting ready to go up to the flat. He witnessed Nia standing with the broom in her hand, the way in which she was staring at the two men, and his expression turned to exasperation.

'Look,' he said. She could see that he was battling with a reluctance at having to speak to her again. 'Nia, this is not for you.'

'What?' She could hear herself – too distant and dismissive in spite of her good intentions – she was straining towards the window as though there was a chance of hearing the conversation.

'Is drugs,' he said, jolting his face forward as though this information was self-explanatory. 'Drugs dealer.'

'And?'

'Is *drugs dealers*!' he said again, reinforcing the words with overly clear enunciation.

'I understand, Guna.' She made a point of examining the man in question, demonstrating that she was looking at him anew, as though with the helpful filter of Guna's information. She found herself clocking the usual signs: the immaculate trainers – large white Nikes – the ostentatious watch. 'What kind of stuff does he deal?' She infused her voice with a nonchalance; it was difficult to know how else to communicate to him that she was acquainted with this kind of thing.

'LOOK,' said Guna loudly enough that she had to look over at him. He glared at her, while his body was turning away, in the direction of the exit at the stairs. 'Is bad guy. His people, he is very bad.' He shook his head. She sensed a more intense, seething frustration in him – why did he have to go through all of this with some idiot of a girl who wouldn't just take a hint?

'I get it, Guna,' said Nia. 'OK. Calm down, man. I understand. He's a dealer. You don't like drugs . . .'

He said something that she couldn't understand. A pressurized exclamation flailed in his throat, something angry. She assumed it was in Tamil. Then he gave her a long, sombre stare.

'Is dangerous,' he said, finally. 'You don't look at him, Nia, listen. Not good he know your face. His people, one is big man for job. That man, I meet him. He come find me and say to me if you want, then don't pay to your casino guy, you pay me something instead. If you give me this much money, I can hurt the casino guy for you. If you give me this much money double, then I kill him. Which one you like?'

He gestured back at the man, who was stubbing out the cigarette with his large white wedding cake of a trainer. She had an image of him defiling the underside, the wet squelch of the burnt tobacco against the rubber sole. And then, without meaning to, she was looking directly at his face, in a kind of compulsion, doing just exactly that which she was being warned against. The dealer raised his head and held it in her direction, his eyes hidden behind tinted glasses.

A horrible nausea went through her. She turned away.

'This man his boss. You don't look at him! Move your face away, I tell you.'

She found herself looking down at the floor. Her mind was darting all over the information, she couldn't seize any of it as real, couldn't hold on to it. Her eyes were tracing the dots and lines in the mosaic tiles, hoping for clarity.

'Guna!' she said suddenly, seeing him disappear up the stairs out of the corner of her eye. 'Guna!'

He was already on the next floor. She went to the bottom of the stairs and called up at him.

'Guna! Does Tuli know?'

He was dematerializing, vanishing through the door that led up to their mysterious home, returning to that enviable dwelling place, feathered with the mutterings of his makeshift family. As he went, she imagined she could see him shrug in response. It was a movement that created a gap in her perception of it all, one that was just wide enough to introduce the salvation of doubt.

'Guna, please!' she said, plaintive and hopeful. 'Does he know?'

Angelic suddenly, he turned round and returned back to the door, seemingly to help her – the whites of his eyes and teeth now visible in the darkness, her vision adjusting as the shades of grey separated themselves out.

'He doesn't know?' She was embarrassed at the repetition but unable to find another way.

Still, he wouldn't reply.

'Does he *know*?' She said it again, insistent, hooking into him, letting the question caricature itself.

Guna nodded. It was unmistakable. His eyes met with her own in a brief, concrete moment – making sure she had understood, before he turned to leave, this time locking the door behind him, so that she was staring up the stairs into a vast and hollow nothingness, faintly imprinted with the memory of his figure.

# SHAN

In the beginning, when he would come to see Tuli, he was full of fear that a single misstep might mean he would slip, fumbling and idiotic, through a one-way portal to hell. He just couldn't understand how the man worked, and the lack of firm answers made him very uneasy, as though he was playing chess with someone who might nonchalantly change the rules, the board, the pieces – all of it, at any minute.

The idea had been for Tuli to buy Shan's debt back then. Samar had told him about it when Shan was selling mobile phone cards in the Internet café, commission only, piecemeal money. There's this guy in a restaurant not far from here, he said. He lends money, go talk to him and say I sent you. In response to the only relevant question – 'What's his rate?' – Samar had been evasive. 'It's complicated,' he said, intimating that it was best to talk to Tuli directly. 'He has different rates. Just go and see first. Lot of guys go there when they first get here from Sri Lanka.' And so, Shan had begun visiting Tuli at the restaurant, and taking part in these conversations, odd at the start, in which he had told him his life story. Sometimes they would eat, sometimes just drink. It became apparent over time that in order to borrow from this man, he was going to have to sit with him again and again, to what end? To reveal something of himself.

Initially they talked about his debt. They spoke with a formality. It rumbled through the conversation, causing Shan to halt, stumble at times, during the initial description of his life, his situation.

'Are you legal?'

'Not yet.'

'Moneylenders?'

He rationalized it as best he could. It had begun with the need to set up for the first job. The clothes, the Oyster card, a quilt, light bulbs, towel, that kind of thing. The basics. All of the queuing at the job centre, and the disappointment when he realized how hard it was going to be to get hold of enough money for starting life here. Food, of course. Soap, bleach, the list is long. Then they come round with their big men and it begins – threats to break the windows in the flat that is one small room, the fear that the landlord will find out through the other tenants. So you go to the second lender to pay off the first. Fifty per cent interest by this point so you borrow a hundred pounds and when you get paid, that is when you pay back towards your one hundred and fifty. And then you borrow more.

Slowly, haltingly, he unwound the explanation for Tuli, like silk filaments from a cocoon, presenting the strands as clearly as he could under the muted lights on that top floor of the restaurant. How he was taking all the shifts he could at the Internet café, the launderette, stacking shelves at the cash-and-carry grocer place, everything and anything to halt the flow of this tidal wave coming towards him.

Eventually, Tuli had responded with a pronouncement that was both fantastical and unnerving, a honeyed swatch of words that made him sound like a *filmi* villain, saying something that seemed surely to be a trap for Shan's battered, fatigued brain.

*How much do you want to borrow? How much do you want to pay back? How long do you want? What interest rate would you like? You set the terms and I will tell you if I can do it.*

What interest rate would you like?

Now, since working in the restaurant and seeing the people who come and go to the room upstairs for private conversations with Tuli – the homeless guys from the roads parallel, the guy with shaved head and earring who does the bins and unsuccessfully attempts to flirt with the white Brit waitress Nia (the pretty young girl who keeps herself to herself and only talks to Tuli), the Pakistani butcher from two doors away who sometimes sends huge cartons of cigarettes round for Tuli to sell, the smart black guy in his fifties with the trilby and chest-length dreadlocked hair, even Ava of course; since seeing all this, Shan has come to imagine that Tuli is operating a kind of life surgery up there, where people come and show him their sores and he decides what he believes to be a fitting course of treatment.

*What interest rate would you like?*

As if he is in a fancy barber's, waiting to be styled? Which hair-cut would sir like? But how can it be, when Shan knows that the other five cooks have a heavy loan from Tuli, at the rate of fifty per cent in just six months? Literally, 'Here is ten thousand, you give me back fifteen by Christmas.' This is what he said to them, apparently. They are saving to acquire their own chain pizza place, some branch in West Kensington, joint ownership, and they are getting close, they talk about it all the time, doing the maths constantly as they roll and cut in the kitchen. They have no other conceivable source of a mortgage, they can hardly go to a bank and so, of course, they are very happy with the arrangement. Not least because they also know that the kebab guys from West Kensington went to Tuli and got a loan at the crazy rate of liter-ally one hundred per cent. Twenty thousand deposit he gave them, twenty thousand to set up things with the business plan, and they are paying him back eighty thousand.

If Shan thinks about it too much he starts to feel dizzy. He can't find a line of logic through it. Why is he on a zero per cent deal with the guy? And that too, indefinitely. Zero, twenty, forty, a hundred per cent – how in hell does the man decide what to offer? How does he judge what someone is worth? And what is it about Shan that means he gets special treatment? It makes him feel very strange, shady, as though he has prostituted some-thing, sold a story of tawdry tears, even though the story he has told Tuli is true. And here he is, paying him back the tiny amount of fifty pounds a month, capital only (his own choice too, the figure, of course). At this rate they both know he will be paying him back for something like a decade, but the man doesn't seem to mind.

'Don't worry, lah!' Tuli says, when Shan tries to bring it up. 'I am sure one day in the future, when everything is going well for you, that you will remember me. Just leave it till then!'

And then there are all the extras the guy has given him – table lamps, a rug, a set of dinner plates and bowls, an electric kettle, two photo frames, the basket of dry food items, and finally, two hundred pounds for new clothes (not accounted for, or added to his loan) – handed to Shan one night out of the plastic bag full of cash that hangs carelessly behind the bar, twenty brown notes counted out and thrust into his hands with a whack on the back and a mere 'Take it easy! OK! Goodbye!'

Since then, things have been speeding up drastically. First, Shan was invited to observe the staff, and trial his own attempt at their prized *Vesuvio special* pizza recipe, handed down from the other partner, Ashan, the one who talks about serving time at the Pizza Express. Then, just one week ago, there was the job itself – gleaming tortuously with promise – a pearl in the vast gloom of oceanic sediment that was his life, a whole, regular wage packet.

And so, here he is, not as worried as he should be about how this is all going to come tumbling down. Because the man has kind eyes, he seems so sincere. To live in fear, asphyxiated suspicion, after everything, would be ridiculous, he can't do it. So, OK, fuck it all then, let it crush him, this mountain of rubble and debt, if this man turns out to be an elaborate sham, if this is how Shan is to finally disintegrate. Let it be so.

Later, he watches Ava spray the surfaces in the kitchen and wipe them down, smiles at the determination of her small knuckles pressed on the cloth.

'What!' she says. 'You forgot to blink today or something?'

'What are you doing tomorrow?' he says. He is taking anchovies from the tin and chopping them up, slicing them into tiny lines of silver-brown and laying them out on a wooden block to dry. 'Want to get some coffee together?' It isn't the first time he has asked her, although she has not yet agreed to meet him during her time off. He looks her directly in the eye, allows himself to feel the pulse of the contact even though it travels to his groin.

'I've got Theo,' she says. 'All day it is, I will go out with him. Then picking up his sister Therese from school and the rest of it – cooking the dinner, cleaning it up and putting them to bed for stories with Mama or Papa, which one it is who gets home first, before I come here. The poor child, the boy, he has the nits in his hair. I am going to be combing every one of those little insects from his hair before bed, is big job. You want to try it some time. Is not a joke!'

'Don't you want your own kid?' he says, in a voice that betrays his care for her.

The look she gives makes him cower slightly.

'You're so good at it . . .' He stutters, scratches his forehead in discomfort.

Ava's eyes grow in their sockets, and she slams down the bottle of cleaning fluid to signify her displeasure.

'Look, mister, just keep your questions to yourself,' she says, pursing her lips.

He thinks of his mother, how she might have described Ava, effectively, in a clean line or two. The similes of his mother, although frequent, had usually been relatively straightforward, they did the job effectively. For example: *Trapped like a frog in the mouth of a snake.* Sometimes they were edged with sarcasm. *As generous as a rain cloud.* Occasionally, however, they were transcendent. *It's as if a cow had got you by the neck with a rope and was walking round on its back legs towing you along,* she said once, of an outcome that was not just back to front, but violently absurd. At times they had been over-enthusiastic, of course, needed too much from the recipient. His hair needed a wash, it was as matted as the unopened flower of the plantain. But mostly the comparisons were impressive. They demonstrated a reach for something more.

Guiltily, he thinks, how would he explain Ava? We are friends, Ma. You know, friendship? As you would say, time pass? To pass the time. There is no way to explain it to the living, of course, to Devaki, let alone Karu baby.

The living. He turns back to the worktop. God knows if these people of his are even alive. And the bleed in his brain begins again, the toxic drip of repetitive thought. They would be in touch if they were safe. They wouldn't be silent on purpose. But they are angry with him. Still, they wouldn't do this, however angry they were. Devaki wouldn't do it to him. Which means they are not safe. Which means. Which means. Which means.

# NIA

When she looks back at that time, it is with a sense of wonder at how easy it was for her to discard unwanted information. She imagined the same of every member of staff at Vesuvio. On they all went, living their lives, turning away from whatever was uncomfortable, and towards the light, opening wide like sun-flowers. In the days that followed, Guna seemed to have no trouble behaving as though the conversations regarding Tuli had never happened. But Nia could feel a new splinter beneath the surface of her thoughts, when it came to the boss. She made excuses for him in her mind, even as she tussled with a new wariness as to his deal-ings. Part of it was the force of his physical presence, the way he swept into the restaurant: so sympathetic and certain of things. It was impossible to imagine him capable of anything disreputable, and so she wilfully put it to the back of her mind.

They had a joke at school, some of the girls in Nia's English class, that Byron the poet was fit – meaning hot, his public look was just the right mix of macho and effeminate, arrogant and absurd to make him fly. The curls, the jawbone, those braggadocio eyes. Tuli had a bit of that look about him and Nia knew he was popular with certain men in the area – he'd often be found having breakfast at the gay café around the corner and enjoying the friendly flirtation. To some extent, he seemed to court it – the attention itself – but you could also just put it down to him being open and interested.

She knew he enjoyed scavenging and on some level she liked him for it, dressing himself in the way he did, without being susceptible to the sort of expenditure that could have gone with his status. He definitely had his own kind of vanity; he looked groomed enough, for example, and had the deportment of someone who considered himself to be significant, but the reason his clothes were all black was a simple one – he got them from charity shops and keeping the colour constant was the easiest way to make everything fit together visually. It didn't stop there, he'd often take his homeless guests to get kitted out at the local Oxfam before bringing them to Vesuvio for the pizza, fags, Bach and chess experience.

But he had a rule that he accepted gifts, Tuli, and that was because a lot of people did spend their hard-earned money on treats for him, presumably out of gratitude. He didn't reject these items; if anything, he communicated the sense that they were deeply valued treasures, receiving them in an almost majestic way, with a small bow of the head that gave the moment, the present its due. So if someone gave him a jumper or a jacket as a gift then he would usually wear it the very next day, without analysis, incorporate it into the wardrobe of what Nia called his 'fascist staples'. A typical outfit might involve four differing shades of black: blazer, shirt, chinos and shoes. He didn't wear a tie or anything like that, but he generally looked smart in the evenings when he was hosting at the restaurant, even with his ponytail, formal and timeless, a citizen of the world.

The night in question, she was confused by how she ended up going with him on his rounds. She couldn't work it out: had he taken pity on her, or did he want to get to know her in some way?

She was gathering wilted carnations from the tables, making a small pile of the slimy stems with their sagging blooms.

'Would you like to take a drive?' Tuli said, pulling back his arms like a magician to reveal that he was holding her coat in his hands, in a peculiar gesture of formality. He must have brought it from the back room in advance, as though there was no question that she would go with him. 'Come,' he said, 'let's go.' He seemed to love orders, savoured these words of instruction, even when they were oppositional like that. For a flicker of a moment, she stared at him, took it in as a still-life image: her empty trench coat hanging there in his hands, his playful expression as he waited for her to fill the space.

And then, somehow, she was with him in his car and looking out of the window as they moved through the darkening world. Outside, the moon loped along, mostly hidden by branches, revealing itself briefly now and then with a great flash of optimism. There was a kind of release when she could see it burst into the sky. He was singing along to the radio. Magic FM.

He was huddled over the wheel as though he was playing an old retro arcade game in a service station, forced into the squashed space of the chair with an outsized steering wheel. At the traffic lights, hand on the gear stick, he gave her an odd look, raising his eyebrows, and she felt a little thrill, small sails billowing out in her chest.

'Happy?' he said. 'Here we go!'

Nia stifled the desire to laugh. There was something absurd about it all – the cheesy song, the way she was sitting so close to him, trying not to bump into his arm while he was driving. She didn't know much about cars, but it was not a flamboyant vehicle. The seats were well worn, the exterior faded, a little scratched. A flat, long car which felt like it was probably twenty, thirty years old.

She found herself thinking through a very definite question: is he a happy person? So many of his exclamations seemed to be clearly happy, studded with diamond-class punctuation. Happy! As though it were possible. Possible!

The sky had a mauve tinge, it looked like something makeshift to pass for the approach of night: a fiction, sky from the *Arabian Nights*. They drove past the cemetery and into one of the local residential squares, lined with tubular, white-fronted buildings. She could see a row of green recycling bins on one side of the communal gardens, their bloated shapes resting against the precise lines of the arrow-tipped railing. Chair legs sticking out of a bin: deep purplish wood, the colour of a bruise on darker skin. A black plastic stack on the ground, something electronic. He parked the car right next to the bins. There was a large ceramic dish balanced on one of them, in the shape of a cat. A resident's joke, to put it there so precariously. She leaned out of the window and squinted at it. There was a crack in its curved tail.

'The things you people throw away!' he said, getting out of the car, opening the door for Nia with his impish, unapologetic eyes scanning her all the while.

He looked at her good and long, eyebrows raised again, releasing smoke through the side of his mouth.

She began to formulate an appropriately withering reply (*come on, they may be white but these are more your people than mine, you're the one who is the big guy restaurateur in this bloody bourgeois area, the skips I know in Newport are not like this*, and so on), but standing there, looking at his tall frame rocking imperceptibly against that sky, the way he was lighting up and looking at her, she thought better of it.

He talked her through the routine. This was a good time generally to pick up discarded items in good condition; after a few hours you would have the problem of dew. You wanted to be looking for furniture rather than utensils or electrics: tables, chairs, drawers, that kind of thing. His main focus was a mirror that came right up to his chest, huge gilded beast of a thing, rare to get one so big without a single crack, he said. He positioned her arms so that they could lift it together, and soon they were shuddering along the pathway with it to his car, so that she was reflecting his crucifixion pose. Deftly, he tied it to the roof with string, in the manner of someone who has performed the act a thousand times.

She watched his fingers, as they moved quickly, lightly in the cold: adorned with two huge gold signet rings that she hadn't seen before. This was not unusual for him. Certain weeks he would turn up with an odd bit of heavy gold jewellery – a solid interlocking band at his neck like a security chain, say, or a wrist cuff in the same cat's-eye metal. That very particular 22-carat yellow. Then, in the subsequent week it would be gone and she would never see it again. She imagined that he was carrying it for people, the way you would with cash – the pieces were minimal in design and clearly not for long-term ornamentation. But it made her smile when she saw these pieces on him, they were so uncharacteristic somehow.

'Thanks for your help. I couldn't have done it without you.' He was doing this odd thing with her hair as he said it, messing it up so that it was all in her face, doing it slightly roughly, making sure that it would not be mistaken for actual tenderness.

'Where are you going now?' she said, stripping down her annoyance and taking his hand off her head, giving it back to him firmly.

'Things to do,' he said. 'Things to do. Things to do. Don't worry, I'll drop you home.'

'Who's going to get the mirror?'

'Don't know. It could go to any one of a number of people.'

'Like whom?'

'What, you want names?'

'Yeah, Tuli, names would be good!'

He raised his eyebrows, sucked on his cigarette and finally nodded.

'OK. Sure. Have you met Arman and Hasti? Young couple, were in the restaurant about a week ago, upstairs, late on Wednesday or Thursday, I forget which. Afghan couple, both late twenties? You've met them, actually, on Thursday they were in.'

Nia shook her head, frustrated. She could hear his retort without him even saying it – all Asians look the same to you, eh, Nia?

'You were handling the big table downstairs for most of the night. He's walking with a limp right now, Arman, he has fucked his leg, doesn't ring any bells?'

'Yes, yes,' she said, pleased at the fact of the memory returning with this description. 'Got it!'

He laughed then, at her enthusiasm, it seemed to soften rather than annoy him.

'He's been waiting two years for an operation. He was in the army, came over with Hasti about two years ago, she left her husband for him. Well, he's been working as a concierge but the problem is that now they cannot get benefit or go bankrupt or do anything like that because of the immigration process and they have debts . . . Arman has been in pain and really needs the operation but if he does the operation he will be out of work for six months.'

'Bloody hell,' she said. As was usual in these kinds of conversations with Tuli, her response felt inadequate, but she wanted to show she was right there listening, that he should continue.

'We're seeing it a lot now, a whole bunch of people living on the edge, everything is motoring along just about OK but one bad thing and they are really screwed. This couple are legal, they go to a proper hospital, all above board, lah, but even they have had bad things one after the other, so they are always struggling. Anyway, they live in the estate on Liliwater Road, opposite Vesuvio.'

'But don't you need a lot of space for a mirror like that?' Nia said. 'A high ceiling?'

'Quite the little worrier, aren't we? Yes, and I'm hoping they are going to be rehoused this week, in fact. We've been working on it for a while, along with applications for jobs. Come on! We need to go.'

His voice, now that he was done with the chat: mischievous, nimble as a cat going over a brick wall, with its sliding high notes. In the memory she would lie naked on the pavement under that thin pale crisp of a half-moon if she could, with the voice doing its genial dance all over her, mainly to see if it would have any effect, a kind of scientific experiment. As it was, she just nodded and obediently got back in the car.

They drove for about fifteen minutes without speaking much. When they reached Nia's road, he slowed the car till it was purring along lazily.

'Take it,' he said, gesturing at a big black bag, a bin liner that was bulging with sharp shapes. 'It's for you.'

And then, leaving no uncertainty that it was time for her to leave, he was revving the engine and shouting in a jaunty fashion, to encourage Nia to open the door and exit.

'Goodbye! Please! Do take care! OK?'

That up-down voice: on anyone else it would be slightly unhinged, she thought, smiling privately.

The bin liner was full of books. Maybe thirty books, fiction from different eras – he had lined it with two bags within bags to strengthen it. He drove off while she was still taking them out, one by one.

She coveted books in a very material way – to possess them, rather than to borrow and return from a library. If she owned the copies themselves, indefinitely, there was more chance that the contents could somehow seep into her bloodstream over time. She left books scattered near her bed in a kind of superstition, as though this osmosis could take place while she was asleep, or in the half-light upon waking.

That final year in Newport, with the money she kept back from her job, she had quickly worked out that she could buy a book a week for under a fiver if they were from the classics catalogue on the front table at Bettws library. It was a pleasurable way to improve on the heavy tomes she'd been borrowing from that geometric blue-and-white building, with its oft-vandalized exterior. She loved the place with an oscillating emotion, it was a second home by then, but she hated the ugly plastic book jackets, the ungainly size of the books. She'd buy all sorts, without worrying over the contents – from Plato's *Republic* and *Man's Search for Meaning* to books with fanciful titles like *The Unbearable Lightness of Being*. If she was on the late shift at the McDonald's drive-through, there were often large stretches of time, roseate and hopeful, when she could read uninter-rupted at the till, one hand on the book in question, those giant unifying tube lights above giving her all she needed.

But whatever she read back then, it was never with a complete ease of discovery. She couldn't escape the feeling that it was important – documentary research into the rules of existence, preparation for living a life alone, for the time when she would leave home, leave Newport for good. There had always been this relationship with fiction, she imagined it could offer her blueprints for living, loving, dying – that it could save her, let her know how things should be. But how did Tuli know all this?

# SHAN

*A Hole is to Dig* says the children's poster in the window of Archway library as Shan comes through the gully and walks past the pawnshops with their maniacal promises of cash, the bellowing calls to action. *A Hole is to Dig* it says, bequeathing calm on its surroundings, this tableau of childhood innocence in the window of a squashed building enclosed by high-rise blocks. Toes are to dance on. A watch is to hear it tick.

At the roundabout, under the drained grey of the sky, across from the ladders of windows patterning the estate, he stops at the crossing and looks at the pavement. There is a deep red stain in it, maroon and dysmorphic, a stain that has halted its movement but looks dynamic still, like it can keep going, keep stretching out its shape. It's not blood, he tells himself, it is wine. Let it be wine in one of the blue plastic bags carried by the loud young suits on their way home from the tube. A bump, a slip, and the bottle crashes to the ground, dispelling its thick purplish contents as they exclaim to each other, 'Shit!' or 'Fuck!' or 'Crap!' Any one of their single-syllable delights could work in this scenario, so easy to imagine. It could be wine. But there is no broken glass to be seen, and Shan knows the look of blood on concrete.

This is the same sky that he shares with Devaki and Karu. He looks up and lets his stale guilt wash into his chest, unseen by onlookers, and therefore just about manageable.

There's a song from the sixties that torments him when he allows himself to think of the immensity of his loss. *Oh my boatman, my beloved is on the other side of the river I am unwillingly on this side.*

He walks through the corridor of the estate; the urine is no longer for him a thing to note with shock, the kids hanging and smoking at the stairs are people to nod at, smile, acknowledge.

When he gets in, there are more demands on the floor. Red-lined threats, shouting black capitals. He doesn't have the money for his rent. The chunk he took from Tuli went so quickly after paying off the debts and he is ashamed to ask him for his first month's pay so soon after the loan. Where has the money gone? It is not as though he has been living extravagantly. What has he bought this week? Rice, cheese, socks, tea, umbrella, the Oyster card, biscuits . . . what though? He has spent too much yet again. No matter if he manages to add up each of these pounds and make a figure that comes close, he can't make the money come back.

Lying in bed, no lampshade, looking at the bulb in the ceiling till the shape comes as burnt orange when he shuts his eyes, what is this life? he thinks, what kind of man am I? He soothes himself out of despondency with trickery, imagining Ava's smile, replaying the comedy of her bewilderment at the moment that he suggested she have her own child, the awkwardness between the two of them, clutches at the way she forgave his audacity, laughs softly to himself in the dark, screws his eyes up and thus, goes to sleep.

The next day Shan rips up the bailiff demands in a kind of half-baked rage, weakened by hunger, watches the red-edged pieces of white scatter in the bin like rice paper, sweet paper, nauseating confetti of strawberries and cream, quietens his stomach which growls for food earlier and earlier each day it seems, and walks past the Greek barber's shop on Junction Road, on his way to buy vegetables from the Persian grocer. He stops, takes a couple of steps backwards. It is the boy again, he is draped in a huge tent of a green gown, raised high on one of the swing chairs, little face popping out of the material. Maybe he is three, four years old? Shan is compelled, in this new, horrible feeling of increased loneliness, to stop outside. He pretends to peruse the price list so he can look at the kid. He thinks of a song he listened to in college, by John Lennon. 'Beautiful Boy'. Again, the contraction in his heart, as he holds away the thought of his own son. Why is he standing there?

He wants to feel the awful hole in his own life, try and touch the jagged crater, puncture his own drugged state. He wants to bleed and he can't. It is perverse. The boy's mother is sitting on a chair behind her son and looking at her phone.

The door is open and Shan can hear every word.

'Will he sit still?' asks the barber. 'Or do you want to hold him in your lap?'

The mother turns the phone over and looks up. Her face softens into indulgence as she registers her child.

'Yes, he's fine,' she says. 'You'll stay still, won't you, baby?'

The boy nods, uncertain but ambitious, looks at his reflection in the mirror.

'He's a good boy, a very good boy, one of the best we've had,' says the hairdresser, smiling as he emphasizes the full-bodied vowels. He takes his scissors to the little boy's curls, throws the final pronouncement down like winning cards. 'And he knows it!'

The boy raises his eyebrows, and his expression expands in spite of himself. He is trying to control the feeling of pride that overtakes him. He catches Shan's gaze in the mirror and Shan turns away shamefacedly, a tiny burn, like a cigarette pressed against his thoughts, as he walks on, hurriedly, looking at the ground.

Soon, he is in the kitchen, nostrils full of steam and onions, rolling out the pizza dough again and again, as though he knows no other movement, and the sheer monotony of this task, and all of the thousand mundane kitchen tasks he must routinely undertake as part of this job, are suddenly forming a giant rivulet of fury inside him. By the time he has his break, he hunts down Ava and virtually forces her into a game. He needs it for his sanity and the gratitude he feels when she agrees, albeit with an indication that she will be leaving the board to shine the stair-rail between moves, is boundless.

'Come on, then,' she says, tying her apron and smoothing it down with a look of challenge, as though she is a matador in front of heckling crowds. 'Let us see if you can win today, eh? What you got?'

It is difficult to play chess with Ava without reading her

personality into the choices she makes. How would you describe the process of trying? thinks Shan. Is it a kind of anthropology? It feels like a discipline of some sort, a life skill.

For example, she knows that he will do anything to prevent the loss of his queen, and she plays him hard on this point, the fact that he will only exchange it for the opposing queen when there is no choice. But he cannot hide this trait, it seems a great luxury to him to play a game that has a queen in it – a piece that can move in any direction without constraint. If he loses his queen, he finds it hard to play on, he tries to cover his disheartened state, he knows it is a conventional way to play, but this is his nature, what to do?

Ava, on the other hand, plays to win, and risks everything at every point. Nothing ventured, nothing gained might be the manifesto tattooed in mathematical precision on her heart; at least, you'd think this if you were to watch her playing, she seems happiest when the board is whittled down to as few pieces left as possible, inexplicably wandering around the vast expanse with pleasure, relishing the same apocalyptic landscape that for Shan signifies terror, and terror alone.

Add to this the fact that chess might be the only time when she releases any biographical information: it usually is so significant that it distracts him terribly.

'You know, when I was eight years old, I nearly died, I nearly drowned,' she had said to him during one game. 'This thing they did every summer in my home town, in the carnival. All the older kids, they were fifteen years old, sixteen, they make a tower like this in the sea, standing on top of each other, higher and higher. I was in the bottom and when the tower collapsed I got trapped, they couldn't find me, I couldn't float back to the top, like I was supposed to do, I was drowning. It take them many, many minutes to come and get me and then they were pushing and pumping me to make me back to life. Have you held your breath for more than one minute, mister? This is why my father, he still will not go to the beach. He hate it. Because I was not . . . not conscious, you know? I was just lying there.'

Her hair, held with girlish combs at her temples and falling to her shoulders, seems like spun silver these days rather than grey, it shines with the luminosity of precious metal rather than seeming to be a sign of age. Maybe it looks like this because he now knows that she has had this hair since childhood – age nine, she says, like her whole family – the two brothers, her sister, her parents – all of them wandering around Valencia crowned with various shades from platinum through to brilliant white. This story, too, was revealed during chess.

'We had a hair salon in the family,' she said. 'And I grow up in it, so my mother, she is always dying my hair black so I can be like other teenagers back then. But funny, too, can you think, that we are a whole family all supposed to work in that salon, my brothers, sister and me and we all going around with this kind of hair!'

What to say to this sort of tale? Shan's reaction: to absorb it, stare and be damned. Meanwhile she had whipped his queen and chuckled quietly to herself, crinkling up with mirth whilst admonishing him for his lack of concentration.

Today they are just settling in to it, and Shan is welcoming the impossible elixir of the break, the momentary uncoiling of his worries, when Tuli walks into the room. But Tuli is acting oddly, he does not smile or greet them, instead his eyes are lost in thought and his forehead is twitching with the hint of a frown.

Shan immediately stands to attention, feels himself literally heave up on to his feet in response; it is so rare to see the man walk in without some kind of cheery, benevolent light on his face.

'Boss, everything is OK?' he says, affecting a casual demeanour but faltering. 'You are . . .?'

'Shan, can you do one thing for me?' he replies, speaking quickly.

Figure-of-eight assent from Shan as he twists his head automatically. He has been waiting for this moment of course, some chance to be of aid, although he is perturbed by the naked distress on Tuli's face. He had assumed that he would be called upon for some service at some point, considering his debt to the man.

'Just come with me next door.'

'OK, boss.'

By next door, he knows that Tuli means the butcher's place, three doors down, and within seconds, Shan is following him outside, without an explanation, but trusting, as always, the man's moves.

'Don't go in,' Tuli says, and they stand in front of their own restaurant door.

Tuli lights up. He smokes silently, and Shan knows that it is his job to just wait with him. There is the big click sound of his tongue as he holds the smoke in, it is lengthy, there is no eye contact, and Shan, in tandem, holds his nerve as he looks at the pavement, then up at the vegetable racks outside the front of the Chinese grocer's opposite.

'OK,' says Tuli, after a few minutes, stubbing the cigarette out with his boot. 'There is a man in the place, right now, white guy, dreadlocks, about thirty, looks homeless, shifty, smells a bit. Wears all blue denim?'

Shan nods. He knows exactly the person he means. It's the local junkie. Ted is his name. Or John. Or Al. Or something like that. He hovers outside the restaurant for a free pizza at closing sometimes, looks right through Shan with opaque eyes if he is the one entrusted with serving him. It begins to rain and the fine droplets make them step back so that they are under the peppermint-striped awning, watching occasional pedestrians interrupt the quiet of the small street, through the drizzle.

'When he comes out, I want you to follow him,' says Tuli. 'Just see where he goes, and keep an eye on him, stay back so he doesn't see you. Is that OK with you?'

Shan nods his assent.

'OK, boss,' he says.

Tuli frowns briefly, makes an expression of pain.

'Don't go in the butcher's, OK? And keep your distance. Don't get involved in what he tries to do. Just watch it, and come back and tell me. OK?'

He pats Shan on the back before disappearing under the awning, and it is as if the man's whole body contains a wound-up sigh that he refuses to release, a coiled spring like the kind you find in a kid's jack-in-the-box, but one that is stuck, a tension so palpable that Shan can almost feel it in his own chest.

It doesn't take long to fulfil the assignment. The man he is following is completely in his own world, weaving on the pavement at a speed that makes it easy for Shan to hang back inconspicuously. When they reach the end of their lane, he crosses the main road, quiet and keen; it's a little dangerous without using the pedestrian crossing, and Shan is momentarily blindsided by traffic between them.

He crosses and sees the dark blue jacket slip into Tesco. There is a definitive quality to the movement, and Shan runs to catch up, slowing outside the double doors before entering.

The man takes about five minutes to steal his first item. During this time, Shan loiters in various ways – close to the guy, far away, in different aisles from him – at no time does he feel noticed. The man is methodical. He steals only salmon – the plastic-packed fillets mainly, but some smoked salmon too – and he gets the goods into his fabric carrying bag very quickly, buys a pack of filters at the till to avoid suspicion and then leaves with an impressive manner, thinks Shan, it is really quite speedy and proper.

He is so busy trying to keep up with the man that he doesn't put two and two together and is quite surprised to see that they are racing right back to the halal place, where Shan hangs back and watches him through the glass door, opening the bag and handing the vacuum-packed fish over to the butcher himself. He can't see the butcher's face, but the whole exchange looks comfortable, regular, not seeming like the first time that it has happened. The junkie takes something from the butcher's palm – Shan assumes it is cash, and he leaves without counting it.

Shan takes two steps forward when the junkie walks past, moves diagonally so that the man walks right into him, he can feel himself cause the collision. Ha! he thinks at the moment of impact, which is heavy, satisfying and painful. Ha! Here I am! Yes! He feels the icy breeze on his face, enjoys the glorious twinging in his chest and left arm.

'Fuck,' says the guy, staggering for a moment. He looks up at Shan, a few of his dreads falling over the freckled skin. 'Fucking . . . what's your fucking problem?'

Shan says nothing. Just stands and stares at the guy, relishing the moment of recognition. It is the first time that the junkie has seen him, rather than looking above and beyond his shoulders. The crinkled eyes, chalky blue, are definitely returning his gaze. Shan knows he is not particularly well built, he is smaller than the man in both height and body, but he has not a droplet of fear as he stands there, pushed up against the rancid smell that is coming out of the jean-jacket in front of him.

'Yes?' Shan says, finally. He does not know if he wants them to fight, does not care, even. For once, he is right there in the present moment, steadfast and impervious. He can be anyone and everyone in this moment: he can be dignified peace incarnate, or he can take his fist and batter it against this guy's head. But he is not going to set fire to himself, that much he knows. There will be no self-immolation for him.

The man wobbles, leans back arduously as though something invisible is pressing on his chest.

'Ugh,' he says, as he slowly begins his exit. And then again, 'Ugh! Ugh!' A rasping sound as he walks, culminating in a fiesta of spitting near the entrance of the English café before he looks back at Shan and throws his hand up, two fingers arranged in a V sign.

He keeps plenty of details regarding the salmon theft at the forefront of his mind. They are all ready for the boss, should he want them, but the resultant conversation with Tuli, which happens just as the lunchtime rush has begun, is perfunctory and quick.

'OK, thank you,' says Tuli, after Shan gives him the two-line headline. He puts his hand on Shan's shoulder and gives it a brief shake, as though he is checking it for solidity. 'Thank you, now you get back to work. OK, see you later, man.'

It's a strange feeling, to go straight into the kitchen and be absorbed into the production line of lunchtime serving. The room is full of commands and responses, the other cooks are working quickly and he is soon in his hat and apron, chopping tomatoes and mozzarella while the questions in his head race to match the prickly excitement running through his body. He has no idea how his contribution will be used, but he believes, somehow, that some good will come of it. He remembers one of his most significant conversations with Tuli, back when he first started visiting the restaurant and talking to the guy about his own application for asylum status.

'It's like this,' Tuli had said, using his fist to make the gestures necessary to accompany his words. 'You know that game "rock paper scissors", right? If I am playing this game with you, then we count one, two, with our fists and on three you make a shape with your hands from that list, yes?'

He had nodded assent – the game was familiar to him.

'Technically, the rules seem simple,' continued Tuli. 'Scissors are better than paper – they cut the paper. Paper is better than rock – it covers the rock. But hang on one second. Just because scissors are better than paper, and paper is better than rock, it does not follow that scissors are better than rock. Do you follow me? In fact, as we know, if you produce a rock and I produce scissors, the rock is the one that wins – it is supposed to crush the scissors. So, this is not a status thing where you can objectively decide which item is best. Instead, it very much depends on the situation, what it is that you are up against.'

Yes, and yes: Shan had nodded again, not wanting to offend, but unsure as to what reaction the man was expecting. It was an uncontroversial explanation of a straightforward game that he was hearing.

'It's like that. Let's say that being legal is better than being illegal. So far so good, lah? Telling the truth is better than lying. Again, who is going to disagree? But if you want to apply to become legal, then by doing the application and alerting people to yourself, you are running a very large risk of being deported from the country. So, the question would be – is it better to tell all of the truth, one hundred per cent, and get deported, or is it better to tell mostly the truth, with a few untruths, and become legal?'

At which point, Tuli had raised his shoulders and given him a smile of real enjoyment, as though he was acknowledging that his words were obvious, liberatingly so, and that there was a pleasure to be had in succumbing to their inevitability. 'It's about keeping your eye on the end goal at this point.'

The conversation had not been revelatory in terms of convincing Shan to lie in his application. He had refrained from saying to Tuli, just you try going through what I have been through in the last year, and then see if you are concerned with the ethics of 'untruths' in order to live! No, the exchange had been meaningful in a different way, one that was rousing, that shook him out of his wretchedness at that time, so soon after losing phone contact with Devaki and Karu.

It was the fact that the guy was so practical and directed and correct, rather than full of well-meaning hot air. He could see the vital desire in Tuli's eyes, to win the game – in this case, to crack the code for asylum – but generally the boss had about him an ambition that was urgent, something exciting to witness, to be around.

He knows what he is doing, Shan had thought back then, and he thinks it again now, arranging thick oval slices of white cheese so that they are ready to melt on the pizza bases, the buzz of kitchen chatter winding around him, blood pulsing hard at his temples as he thinks of the possibilities, all the good ones for once, rather than bad.

# NIA

The next morning, she woke early, lying in the sheets, flushed in the close humidity of her room. She found herself pressing through the events of the previous night in sequence, trying to understand them. It wasn't as though anything outwardly significant had happened at the skip, but she felt different somehow. Through the bars on her window – it was a basement flat, on a main road – she could see myriad legs moving, rising and falling. The lacquered red of intermittent buses eclipsed and revealed the scene.

She had the new novels, stacked in delicious piles next to her bed, but some part of her wondered if anyone within a square mile of the restaurant could have been the beneficiary of that particular handout. Still, she was buzzed. Making her way to the restaurant, she was suffused with a heightened sense of the crowds around her, their needs and secrets. Just, what they could all be carrying. The commuters on the bus and then the tube, the unnamed people in slipstreams through the streets, those gristly clots of hopes and dreams. She was with them, sharing the imperative, as she was waiting at the traffic lights, or cutting through the back streets – a whole globe of Londoners united in the profound mundanity of the commute.

At the restaurant, though, it was pretty much business as usual. She did her shift and Tuli was occupied for most of it with Patrick. It was a quiet one, and the boss seemed particularly at pains to show that he wasn't giving her any special treatment – a perfunctory smile across the room while he smoked, shuffled some papers, spoke in a low voice with his companion.

And there was Patrick, so quintessentially himself – in a flurry of beatific, buttery, sanguine light – beaming in his thick grey jumper, calling to Nia to sit down and have a drink with them as soon as she walked into the place.

'Nia, please! Come dear, take a break, the place is empty. What'll you have, a glass of wine on me? Red or white, lovely?'

He was a big softie, Patrick, sentimental, ageless somewhere over sixty, partial to reciting poetry after a few glasses of wine or whisky. Sometimes, Nia would be on her way in for the early shift and she'd pass the Polish greasy spoon. Elene would shout out at her – you missed the homeless guy last night, Nia, the hopeless homeless one who comes and shouts stuff at the door, big old guy with red cheeks and white hair. And Nia would be laughing as she replied – right, Elene, yeah, Santa Claus is on the street now, is he? Hopeless homeless, that's a good one! It wasn't far off an approximation. Patrick, trilling lines from his favourite poets, could come across as a delinquent beardless St Nick for sure – Mearns and W. B. Yeats – he'd always be particularly singing them out when he'd had a few.

Social in his priestliness, Patrick, always wanting to sit and talk things through, always treating you like part of his congregation. Where are you living, Nia, are you doing just fine, now, or are you feeling lonely at all, dear? London can be harsh, though, can't it? You've got that slightly quiet look about you today, dear, what's bothering you, eh? Come see us at the church if you want some company, we've got a beautiful exhibition on at the minute by a young artist from Bromley. I tell you what, why don't you come and help out with the food parcels on Monday if you're knocking about? You'd be a tonic there in the hall, sure you would. That kind of thing. He did all of it with this grace, is the only way she knew how to describe it; he managed to be soothing rather than irritating, like he was giving you a blessed hug, aware of his charmed status and endowing you with it at the same time as being genuinely concerned about you. She knew she could rely on Patrick, he was not a fraud, there was nothing furtive about him.

Nia stacked the glasses on the counter. Most of the staff had disappeared, it being a Sunday, but Ava was still pottering around with her upstairs, cleaning the bar.

'Can I borrow you for a minute?' Tuli said, half an hour before midnight, all sheepskin warmth on the stairs, looking at her with a confidential glow in his eyes. She nodded and followed him downstairs.

Patrick was still there, and he was in full active listening mode, imperceptibly shaking his head and raising his eyebrows at intervals to show that he was bearing witness. They were talking to a man with a meaty red face and black hair, slight hint of a moustache above lips that revealed big pink gums as he spoke.

'She will change anything she likes,' the man was saying, without moving his attention from Tuli. 'She will do whatever it takes, it is not a line for her that she will step over, she makes it how she wants.'

Nia gradually ascertained that her job was to sit with them, and listen to the guy talking about his wife. She understood it within seconds due to the meaningful looks she was getting from Tuli. It was flattering, this new element of trust, and so she did what seemed to be required. She learned all about the man's situation. How he wanted a divorce because his wife had been unfaithful to him, and she was heading after his cash. How he only hit her that once, he regretted it, and now she had conflated it to a whole series of beatings that would threaten to destroy his entire existence. He was talking in a thick Eastern European accent, she had to strain to understand some words, but it was pretty clear what he was saying. He wouldn't be able to see his two-year-old. His cheeks were a little pink with the effort and she could tell he was upset as he tumbled it all out.

'He will cry if he doesn't see me,' he said, glowering with accusation as he looked from Patrick to Tuli and then back again. His forehead was furrowed into deep ridges, thick lines of flushed pink skin. 'Then what? He will cry and cry. He sees me every day, why will he understand, my boy? He is only two.'

At the end, when the man had gone, Tuli asked Nia a few questions, most of them heading towards an appraisal of the man's statements: do you think he is telling the truth?

'How do you normally do it?' she said. 'How do you normally judge this sort of thing with someone new?'

'Honestly?'

Patrick was still there but it was clear that he was not going to intervene. He hummed quietly to himself.

'Yes, honestly,' Nia said. 'Just tell me.'

Tuli shrugged, turned both of his hands upside down so his palms were facing upwards in a gesture of submission.

'It's just a gut feeling. That's all I have. Nothing else. In the end, I have to go on my gut.'

'A gut feeling.' Nia shook her head. 'It doesn't make sense. Like . . . what? Even Solomon had some trick questions up his sleeve, in the Old Testament. Isn't that a bit of a dangerous method? The gut instinct approach?'

'Nia, I don't have time right now to debate my "methods". I'm just asking your opinion here. Literally, as a young woman, I'm asking you . . . on a basic level, can you tell? I'm just trying to get a different perspective.'

'Tell what? Whether his wife has been unfaithful or whether he's only hit her once?'

He looked uncomfortable, nodded as he tapped out the ash.

'The second one,' he said.

'How do you know him?'

'You know the café in the tube? The other exit of the tube, that side, mostly takeaway with two metal tables and chairs? He runs it.'

'OK.'

'He seems to be a decent guy, by all accounts. Hungarian. Works like a maniac.'

There was something vulnerable in Tuli's face, then, moment-arily, a fissure, like he was genuinely doubting himself. Nia had never seen it before, and even then, it was over before she could reassure him. It was deadly. Like a caress or a kiss is how it felt, something so human about it, like the faintest embrace, as though he was his age for once, and not towering above it. Then, the clean slopes of his face were closing back in, containing him again, the thick, defined lips pulling at the cigarette and blowing the smoke out in a perfect line.

'Are you going to give him money?' she said. She wanted so much to help him but she couldn't just come out with a decision like that.

'Maybe some advocacy. Help him put his case across in court. What do you think?'

She looked over to Patrick for his reaction. He gave her a peaceful, anticipatory smile. It was clear that he, too, was waiting for her response.

'Come on,' Tuli said. 'This is your chance. Sock it to me. Do your worst. Do your best.'

'Tuli, I don't know what you want me to say. All I can say is . . . there is no way you have to prove that he is telling the truth. You can't know what happens behind closed doors.'

'But then you would never intervene in anything,' he said, not in an arguing way, just with this odd, eerie hush in his voice. 'Let me ask you something. What about the basic idea of just *being* there. Just taking part, responding to need, not walking on by. To be present rather than absent, to forgo being a bystander?' He shrugged. 'We are all flawed, all capable of making a mistake – the question is what happens after the mistake. In this case, he didn't do it again, lah?'

'I get it,' Nia said. 'But I'm not saying you shouldn't intervene. It's just . . . how do you know? How can any of us know without speaking to her, for example? You can be present for the wrong person, you can back the wrong horse. Of course you can. Why did you choose him, rather than her? What's your plan here? To find a way so that he doesn't pay maintenance for the kid? How is that OK?'

She was getting a bit het up by now and her voice was louder than before. It gave a momentum to things. They talked it out like this for a good ten more minutes, going through the permutations. Does it matter if he's hit her twice, and he's lying? Nia proffered.

82

Say he's hit her three times, four times, but he says he won't do it again? Does the number of times matter? Come to that, does she matter to you, her point of view?

'So, his wife is English,' Tuli said, 'and they met when she was a student. He puts her through university, she gets her degree, and now by all accounts she's got a pretty fancy job at the Science Museum. OK, so then she is unfaithful, she is the one who wants to move on, and she's got herself someone who is loaded, he's in the City, banker type of thing. Meanwhile, she says I'm going to bring up this one time that you hit me, and I want you to give up the kid to me wholesale, just you see him once a fortnight – the minimum, lah? His main thing is that he wants to keep the kid as a joint, equal parent, and the other problem is she also wants half of his home, in spite of the whole infidelity being her thing—'

'Hang on a second,' Nia said. 'What do you mean, *his* home?'

'It's his home!' He released the sentence with a yelping voice. 'Come on! *His* home, Nia, he bought it with *his* money, on top of that he put her through university, the fees, everything—'

'Their home,' she said.

'He paid for all of it!'

'Their kids.'

'She is the one breaking up the home!'

'Their home. Their kids.'

'OK, look. You know how in some couples, the guy is the nurturing one, doing it all?'

'Your point is?'

'That's how it is with them. He is the one doing the majority of the childcare, always has done, and she is saying, but I'm the mother. He is saying that the kids will end up being raised by a full-time nanny, she's never been that into the parenting thing, what's the point? Plus she is going to money, the woman is going to live with a man who has ten times the amount as him, what is to discuss in this, she is clearly trying to squeeze him for whatever she can—'

'How do you know that he'll look after the kids? He's at the underground station, running a business. He's probably there late – what do you know about how his shifts work?'

'With anyone else I would not advocate this, but in his case, he is such a caring character, you should see him with the kid.'

'But he's his father, why does he get extra Brownie points for bloody looking after his kid? He should care for his child regardless!'

It went on like this for a while until eventually, she could see them all sagging, the three of them. Patrick was still quiet, watching without intervention, as though it was Wimbledon, and Tuli finally suggested they call it a day, said he'd drive her home.

She went to the toilet, and returned to see Tuli and Patrick outside, under the awning, two tall muted shapes in low light. The street lamp threw their shadows so that they shrank and lengthened on the pavement as they moved, a pair of squeezed-out reflections in funfair mirrors. At the moment when Patrick turned to leave, pulling up the collars of his coat in preparation for walking home, Tuli produced a piece of paper from his blazer, a quarter-folded piece of A4. He pressed down on the clicking pen that also appeared in his hand at that moment, lowered his voice with an expert's decorum, and handed both to Patrick to sign. The two men managed the exchange very quickly, you wouldn't know it was surreptitious unless you were looking, she thought – Patrick folding the paper further, using his palm to steady his signature, handing it over within seconds, with a nod. She watched Tuli's hand, the long fingers closing over the white rectangle, watched it for a clue to the man, assessed the way he slipped it back into his pocket and held the door open for her as she emerged from the restaurant.

Was it linked to the man who had been talking about his wife? Was Patrick endorsing something? Why did they feel the need to make this arrangement out of her sight? The truth is, it could have been linked to any one of a number of people who came in and out of the place, and she could only guess at what was written on that page. But it kept hammering at her – this business with the

Hungarian man – how could Tuli know he was telling the truth? And even if he was, could either of them pass judgement without talking to the man's wife?

The questions were stubborn, they kept repeating themselves, refusing to leave her mind when she got into bed that night. There was an occasional flutter of expectancy, as though the answer was about to make itself known at any minute. She was sweating and turning, thinking about the bruises: Mira's in particular, but also her own. Their mother didn't have the strength to hurt them physically any more, now she just rattled about the house, a husk of a thing, spitting out vitriol rather than being taken with the urge to use her fists. But those times when she'd crossed that line . . . there were no words for the desolation they had felt, all three of them. Even Mum had suffered lacerations upon seeing the bruises the next day, but her shame was never a balm, it just came and went like everything else. Maybe this man had hit his wife just the once. Probably his presence was crucial to his child's life. Neither point gave her peace. Only as the light began to filter through the curtains did she finally fall asleep.

# SHAN

Two of the cooks are shouting at each other. Shan ignores it for a while. He is slitting a pile of prawns, taking them one by one and removing the long dark line in each digestive tract. Each thread of black waste needs lifting out with care if he is to do it with one swoop of the knife, the countless beady eyes of the prawns are bothering him today, there is a sense that he will botch this, that he is a surgeon who is not fully up to scratch.

The argument gets louder, almost as if the men involved are crying out for intervention. They are speaking in Tamil.

'Look, you just listen to me!' says Guna. 'You just tell me what is in your hand?'

The other man looks at his right hand, annoyed to be stopped mid-flow.

'What are you TALKING ABOUT?' he says, bellowing with frustration.

'You just tell me what you are holding?' says Guna, brandishing the question like a weapon. 'NO!' he says, when the other guy starts to dismiss him. 'Just tell me what it is! Say it!'

Shan looks up. The man with Guna is Rajan, a formative member of the group living in the flat at the top of the restaurant. He is not as convivial or sentimental as Guna, and sometimes seems to baulk at the emotional demands placed on him by his room-mate. A beat passes, and Rajan responds, frowning heavily, unable to hide his exasperation.

'It is a cup of TEA, you can see that much, what are you going BLIND now or what?' he says.

'Oho!' says Guna, relishing the role of challenger, accompanying the utterance with a slow self-congratulatory nod. 'Yes, it is that exactly. Eh? Isn't it? A cup of tea, yes?'

His partner in the discussion shakes his head in despair, he is talking to a lunatic.

'Guna, what are you saying? I have to go and finish the fridge, just get on with it.'

'Now you just throw that cup on the floor,' says Guna. 'You just throw it on the floor and what will happen to it? It will break into pieces and pieces. And then what? You tell me this. Will it be possible to put it back together again just as it was?'

Guna leans forward and continues in a low tone, drops of sweat appearing on his forehead.

'It is very, very easy to break something,' he says to Rajan, enunciating each word with a hissing disdain. 'Very, very easy to break something. It happens in seconds. But putting it back together is completely impossible. It can never be the same. You need to think about this thing – you can break your relationship with me very easily, if you take offence for something, yes, you can stop calling me brother, respected elder brother, and you will feel very fancy for a while, of course, that is right. After all, you will say, he is not related to me by blood, from now on he is dead to me. But then, you have to understand, you can't just put it back together as you please. All the pieces will be too small, it will be broken in such a way, some pieces will go missing even. It is very, very easy to break something, and then it is too late.'

The performance is perfect, the dramatic pausing is worthy of a climactic showdown in a movie. The two of them move apart and enact their tasks in silence after this final speech. Shan watches them as he discards the shells, hiding a smile. Their relationships contain the same sticky recriminations and celebrations as a joint family back home, where the needs of daughters-in-law, sons, parents and grandchildren all collide under one roof. And why not? They are sharing a room after all, some kind of intimacy is bound to come about with this sort of situation. Part of him envies it.

'You know,' says Guna suddenly, unable to sustain the attempt at dignified silence any longer. 'You know, some of us can be taken from here at any minute. Look at fucking . . . fucking bloody Heman's sister!'

A chill descends over them all with this mention, and the smile leaves Shan's face. He suddenly wishes he was out of the room, away from this, not party to the whole thing. He knows the story, it has been discussed often enough, even though he has never met this sister, or even Heman – a cook in a restaurant somewhere in South London, known to Guna through his networks back home in Wattala.

The sister's story is not a good one. Rape at the hands of three government CID officers sent to investigate her home in Wattala while her husband was out with their three sons. The officers then dispatched her to a remote camp for questioning, and from there to a hospital where she managed to buy her way out, and on to London, by using the title deeds to her home. All so that she could be brought before a British judge whose speech contained a detailed explanation of why her 'fabricated story' was 'ludicrously lacking in credibility'. From what Shan can gather, and he always listens to this particular cautionary tale for any clues that might help him, her big mistake was not telling of the rape initially. Instead, she yielded to the usual vagaries of shame and fear, and this meant that later her story was deemed inconsistent.

She is being sent back this week. Guna talks about it all the time. How Heman has been telling him that he fears his sister is actually suicidal now, she keeps muttering about how she wants to leave the place of detention mainly so that she can walk out in front of traffic, trains, whatever nonsense in the lead-up to the flight, even the official psychiatrist has heard her say this and written it in some useless report. Her husband and sons are still missing back home.

Shan puts his thumb and forefinger together and begins the task of removing the spindly antennae of the prawns. He can't help but think of his own vulnerability, the fact that he is still illegal. Guna, too, is equally in danger of deportation of course, with no formal acceptance into this country yet, and that is why he is chewing his lip with tension as he speaks.

'What if they come and take me just like her?' Guna says to Rajan. 'Then what? You have your passport, you have no problem.' Gone is the bravura swagger that usually inflates his speech. His voice becomes very small, like a child who has only just realized his own weakness. 'But what if I go? You will be sorry then, or what?'

Before Rajan can respond, Tuli pops his head around the door of the kitchen.

'All OK?' he asks, beaming at the three of them, proffering a jaunty thumbs-up to accompany the question. He opens a bag and shows them three cartons of Marlboro reds.

'Just got these from the butcher, OK? I'm leaving them behind the bar. Tell everyone special rate, yes? I'll sell them myself if any customer wants them. But just say now if any one of you here wants your own pack and we can work something out.'

'Yes, boss.' It is Guna, still subdued but perking up, wanting to get in first. 'I will have one pack. For sure I will have one pack.'

'Of course,' says Tuli, ripping off the cellophane and opening up the long box as he speaks. He taps the end so that a pack of twenty pops out, glossy and sharp under the tube lights. 'Guna, are you sure you want one only?'

Guna nods, endowing the movement with a sense of benign confirmation. Shan swallows, and then pushes himself sternly to get the words out.

'Actually, sir . . .' he says.

Tuli grins at Shan and simultaneously throws a pack at Guna, who laughs in spite of himself, raising a pair of hands, gloved in yellow rubber, to catch the pack just in time. He falls back slightly with the momentum of the packet and exclaims, a fielding cricketer who is surprised by his own catch.

'Aha!' he says, smiling. 'Thanks, boss.'

'No problem,' Tuli says. 'Leave the money in the usual place. OK, Shan, hello, tell me, go on, how many?'

'Actually, boss,' says Shan, 'I was wondering if I could talk to you about something.'

'Be my guest!' says Tuli, putting his arm around him with sudden bonhomie. 'We haven't got that much time before the early dinner shift, but come, let's go upstairs! In fact, you just go up, Shan, and get yourself a drink. I will come in one minute.'

He knows that any meeting with Tuli involves a dance of some kind with regard to sitting in the correct place, and this meeting is likely to be no different. He makes sure he is standing, as if by chance, to avoid the embarrassment of being asked to move to a different chair by the boss when he enters. The Brit waitress Nia disappears down the stairs as Tuli enters.

'Hello!'

Tuli walks into the upstairs room and immediately commands the space, gesturing towards a small table in front of the bar and dispatching his floor-length leather coat onto a stool. It is the coat of a gangster.

'And how are you today, Shan?' Tuli is cheerful, as if he is on holiday. 'What will you drink?'

Shan is about to finish his shift but is unsure as to the etiquette. His preference is to drink water, but Tuli is already pouring himself a drink from a green bottle with the word 'Martini' printed on the label.

'Sir . . .' he falters. He moves his head in an uncertain figure of eight, to indicate acceptance.

'Come now,' says Tuli, arranging Shan at the table. 'Would you prefer some water?'

Shan nods with relief, and they begin.

He has been working with Tuli to try and locate his family, and he knows straight away from the neutral look on the boss's face that there is no news.

Tuli walks over to the wall of windows at the other end of the room and opens one. They are misty with condensation, the steam filters the red neon blur from the shop opposite. He stands near one of the tall plants, spiky-leafed thing, set in a large ceramic pot on the floor, and taps a pack of Marlboro against his palm. There is visible pleasure in him as he lights up, inhaling deeply, making a clicking sound as his tongue hits the roof of his mouth. He holds the smoke for a few seconds before blowing it out through the side, there is a kind of suspense to the whole process as Shan watches, waits for the cloud to emerge, fill the air and dissipate. Kind eyes, the man has, and they open up slightly as he turns to meet Shan's gaze. His movements are leisurely, they indicate that there is all the time in the world for this conversation. And indeed, Shan admits to himself, there is a certain ease between them now; it has taken them months to get to this point.

'OK. Just give me the basics again, lah?' says Tuli. 'I'm sorry to ask you, man, but it's just in case there is some other lead, something we've missed.'

There is always something new that comes up when they do this, some new stone of a fact, some quartz element that glints with promise, and so Shan has no problem with going through it again, it is all worth it, even though, inevitably, there is the needling pain in the nerves as he does it. A small operation without anaesthetic, you could say. Something necessary.

He saw them for the last time on the day that the agent came by with the papers. It was 13th May, he remembers that much and Devaki was still not speaking to him, refusing to discuss the possibility of his leaving, finding things to do in rooms other than the ones he would enter. They had argued it out but they were stuck in an impasse – he was so convinced that it was the right thing to do, and Devaki so angered by the fact that he seemed to be serious about going that she couldn't actually communicate with him. It was a Sunday so she wasn't in the lab. Instead, she was making pickle – bottling mangoes and chillies with various suspensions – less taciturn than at their worst point of communication but still unyielding in terms of disagreeing with his plan, and Karu was in the house too of course . . . somewhere, playing. This is the moment of suspended animation in Shan's memory, a single scene in which each member of the household is going about their business. Pause and repeat.

It was about noon when the agent turned up, he said an opening had come up for that day itself, that Shan wouldn't have to wait for months as he'd hinted previously. An extra three hundred thousand rupees and he could go now, he said, in the next couple of hours, right in this batch of ten people leaving Jaffna today.

And so to a decision that is now soaked in regret. An ugly, incendiary petrol bomb of a memory. He unlocked the security box. It was easy enough with Devaki keeping herself to herself like that, and then he walked out of the house with the jewellery in his pocket, without telling anyone.

'To protect them,' he says to Tuli, who nods with reassurance, understanding that now, as always, Shan has to reinforce this fact. There is a rare quality of acquiescence in the man's face, thinks Shan, as he stumbles over the shame of the telling, as he has done before. A feeling that he will always assume the best intention for you, not the worst, and that he will hand this confidence back to you, for your own usage, with grace.

'I knew they would come looking for me, those SLA guys I told you about before – they were coming every week or two by that point, harassing us, that's why I didn't tell them where I was going. I didn't want to put them in danger. Devaki, Karu. I never thought that I would . . . lose them. I knew there was some risk but the agent said I could bring them here within a week of arrival. That was the whole point.'

Yes, they both know that Shan took his wife's wedding jewellery, her only valuable possessions, left her with nothing. Yes, it was because he thought he'd buy them all safe passage, step by step. Got it. And there is the inhalation of smoke, the impassive face of the boss as he waits to hear something more.

He goes back through the old wounds. Shan's father went missing about six months before this date. He was coming up for retirement. They had him in there for four days of beatings and torture, in prison, the government officials who came one day to ransack the house, look for weapons that they claimed he was hiding for the Tigers. Shan doesn't know if his father had weapons in the house – it feels very unlikely that he did – but he knows that

Tuli understands that it doesn't much matter. They were after him because of his last big article, an exposé of the execution of five students by the army in Trincomalee.

Discarded from a jeep in the dust, like a big old bruised aubergine rolling off a vegetable cart, that's how Appa came home. Dark welts on his skin, burgundy in colour. Don't look directly at them or it will burn you, that kind of bad, if you can imagine it. Your own father, so vulnerable. There wasn't time to see the driver. And then, while they were still gathered round him in the uproar of shock and relief, three of his colleagues came to see him that evening with a letter for the United Nations High Commissioner for Human Rights in Geneva.

'We the undersigned humbly request you please take measures to Protect Journalism . . .' it said, before naming those lost in the spate of recent murders in Jaffna and nearby states. 'The Pen is manned at the Gun Point. We would like to express to the entire world why they are silent in this matter?'

Eight days later, after Appa's signature on that petition in curling sky-blue ink, it happened. Executed by unknown forces. He was walking to work, it was very easy, he was without protection, what to say? They came on motorbikes and disappeared in minutes, while the morning coagulated its heat around the dead body.

His father now appears in the Wikipedia entry, 'List of people killed by Sri Lankan government forces'. He is mentioned as one of two minority Tamil journalists who used to work at the pro-opposition Sinhala-language newspaper *Satana*. They are not fancy people, most of the journalists in the list, at any rate. Like Appa they were on small salaries. A sheaf of contacts as large as you like, but not moneyed.

Shan used to look at this list daily when he worked in the Internet café. Then he would search his father's name relentlessly on the rest of the Internet, still does, but there's not much else about Appa online, just three-line summaries of the events, the body wrapped in a white sheet on the road, patterned with a haphazard mixture of bloodstain and mud. He has gone through so many phases of looking, when it comes to this picture, from rank aversion to obsession, that it has become part of his daily environment. He can never be anywhere without thinking of it at some point.

He stops, looks Tuli in the eye.

'You know all this,' he says. 'You know it all. You've got the names of everyone I remember, the journalists who brought the petition. The government officials who named themselves, not the gunmen obviously, I don't know who they were.'

It is not just the story of Heman's sister that gives Shan the fear. He has heard from enough people how important it is to remember things – the ones who travelled with him and those who he has met in this country who couldn't make their stories patch up exactly the same way every time. And he knows that he is like the rest of them, that pain has cut small holes through his thoughts so that key facts are missing. Boring, obvious, concrete facts that have disappeared through these gaps, making him seem suspicious and cagey to the observing eye.

He fears going to court because of this, even though if he is to believe in this idea of 'leave to remain', then it is very likely that he will have to go to court soon. But even without the fictions that he has introduced in the hope that Tuli can get him through the system – presenting the terror of Appa's cell time as his own, for example – the body of the real, true story is dismembered by anxiety, it is always a little different when he tells it. And that is a problem, of course.

'Yes,' says Tuli, 'but you have to just keep going. Trust me. Say everything you can remember to me. What, how, when, where, something new will come. It always does.'

Shan nods. He's a funny guy, this Tuli character. A Tamil from Singapore, whose parents were schoolteachers, they themselves grew up in Malaysia, he has never even been to Sri Lanka or India. Studied here at the London School of Economics, and now, by all accounts, he has made a real success of life here in the UK. They are probably the same age but you could say they have nothing in common.

'But look, if you don't want to go over the last phone calls right now,' says Tuli suddenly, cushioning his tone with reassurance, 'I really don't mind, Shan, honestly. If you don't feel up to it, we can do it another time? It's up to you?'

'Well . . . boss, I have felt very alone here without my family,' says Shan, uneasy at the forced spill of emotion.

He looks at Tuli, still smoking in shadow at the window. There is the suggestion of sympathy around his mouth, he gives a short nod to continue.

Sometimes, knowing that he has omitted the *seeni sambol* from his life, the really tasty stuff, the sour-sweet spice, Shan senses that Tuli is disappointed: the story that he has presented is too generic, impersonal. He doesn't present the texture of their home after Appa was taken for good, the experience of losing Amma so soon afterwards, to that disease, it had seemed so inevitable that she would die too, part of the hopelessness that permeated the whole house. There is no snapshot possible of the horrific void, he is not going to attempt it. So instead, Shan talks about the present.

'I don't know how we will find them. My child, my wife. And I am in a kind of ditch. It is like being . . . sometimes like . . . waking up in the cold snow, being fully exposed, without a . . . without a raincoat?' he says. 'Or even a jumper?' He regrets the comparison instantly. It is vulgar. And yet it is an accurate image, one that has been pulsating inside him every morning for the last few weeks since things got worse. Six a.m., and in the half-light of consciousness before waking, it is the same nausea every day: he is lying in a dugout, a low grave of sorts, his body covered over with the thick, white, insidious weight. Inches and inches of overnight snow. In the final moments of sleep, he tries to move his limbs, and cannot, the cold renders them inert. He lies there, in vest and underthings, impotent, gradually realizing that it is too late, the climate is freezing, it will take too long for it to melt.

Part of the dream is based in the pure physical fright of cold, how it had felt as though it was maiming him when he first arrived in this country. That deep freeze of his insides: as if sub-zero liquid coolant was being piped through his veins directly into his heart for the long hours each night, until dawn.

It was a mistake, a mistake, a mistake to leave without Devaki and Karu. There, let it be said.

'I'm sorry it is so hard,' says Tuli, returning to the table and stubbing out the cigarette in a small, ugly ashtray, moulded in thick glass. Shan stares at the ridged circles, waits for words to populate his mouth. He is done trying. Tuli encourages him to continue by briefly skimming his hand over his shoulder. 'Shan, look, just talk without worrying, if you can. Don't censor yourself. Part of it is just that talking helps, sharing what you are thinking, whatever, it can lighten the weight of it. The other part is to do with actual details, but you can't make them come on demand, you just have to go easy on yourself in that sense and understand that you have been through a lot – it's naturally difficult.'

Shan is tense, the embarrassment is right in his backbone. This is not something to share with this man, this genuine, useless description of his snow grave. How has it happened? He looks out at the street. A lamp post throws shadows on the buildings, none of this gives him any understanding, there are no footholds into the unknown, it remains something to approach with great caution, fearfully black, a slick of gleaming tar. The window of the restaurant on the other side of the road is flickering, superimposed with the reflection of the Chinese food shop opposite, the sign of green and red lights, intermittent cars.

And then he remembers something, hands it over grudgingly as though it is a gift for Tuli rather than himself, irritated by the false hope that tends to come with these memories.

'That superintendent who was a block away from our house,' he says. 'The one who came over and beat Appa at home once with his cronies. His child was at the Catholic school. I still can't remember this guy's name but I have just remembered that the girl was about thirteen, fourteen, and the school was called Holy Family Convent.'

He watches the information log itself in Tuli's brain.

# NIA

There was a Tamil girl at school, in the year above Nia, her father worked in the petrol station near their flat in Bettws. Her name was sinuous and exotic, it made her ripe for bullying. Cynthia Suntharalingam. But she was unapologetic for it, and instead became famous for admonishing her naysayers by explaining that her surname had the same number of syllables as Arnie Schwarzenegger – just try harder and you'll be able to pronounce it, she'd say, with an acerbic grin, almost yawning. One day you'll get there. And it had become a feat, to pronounce her name as casually and effortlessly as possible, when it was passed around the playground. This particular memory of her, mildly perplexed at her detractors, obviously full of better things to do than engage in such childish nonsense, was the most enduring, and Nia thought of her often.

She wasn't quite friends with Cynthia but you could say that they had a mutual respect for each other. It was difficult for Nia to really be friends with anyone due to the home situation, but she and Cynthia could both smell the outsider scent on each other, and so they circled one another with a significant level of curiosity. Cynthia was the reason that Nia had first tracked down *Das Kapital* in the library – Cynthia let it be known once that her father had taught himself English by reading that particular book during five years of imprisonment in Sri Lanka before she was born. Now, he seemed to be bringing his two daughters up alone – there was no mother on the scene – and Nia knew not to ask about any of the details, it was clearly a no-go area. There was just the information that Cynthia volunteered now and then – it was important that Nia realized he wasn't just a petrol attendant, her father was doing an evening course, training to become a social worker, some scheme sponsored by the council. He had been in prison for being a 'rebel' of some kind and she was proud of this fact. On the other side, she knew that Nia was half-Indian, even though she looked otherwise; she knew not to ask much more.

Once she told Nia a crazy story that frustratingly disappeared into the ether before she could understand it properly: something about her father driving with both daughters to Germany to 'collect' a man, using a car that he had borrowed from the owner of the garage at his workplace. On the journey, her father told Cynthia (seated in the front seat in a 'disgusting' mohair cardigan and calf-length tweed skirt that he'd brought home from the charity shop) that if they were stopped by officials, she was to pretend to be his wife, and her younger sister to be their daughter. He handed her a pair of reading glasses to complete the outfit, and off they went. Once they had the guest in their car, and had left Germany, she should return to being herself, he said.

Like with all of Cynthia's stories, the minute Nia began asking questions all her words turned to powder and were dispersed on the wave of breezy laughter that would come her way.

'Aw, mate,' she'd say. 'It's bloody hysterical, honestly. Where to begin. So funny! Another time. Ha ha ha ha ha!'

Oddly enough, Nia could imagine getting into these kinds of shenanigans herself, and on one level the three of those Suntharalingams weren't so different from her, Mum, Mira and their little squashed triangle of dependency. But in reality, that triumvirate family was more the symmetrical opposite to theirs – like those pictures where if you squint you can see either two faces or two vases, depending on how your mind sees things. Their arms were linked so tightly and tenderly, everything they did seemed to be unquestioningly in service of this ring of blood and its survival against all odds. It astonished Nia, even shamed her slightly, in ways she didn't understand. They were beyond the law in some sacred, honourable way.

Working in the restaurant, seeing Tuli's comings and goings made Nia think about the concept all over again. You need a victim for it to be a real crime, her mother was fond of saying. No victim, no crime, surely that's obvious? But she didn't agree with her version of this particular philosophical argument. In truth, the idea of 'victimless crime' was more than just hypothesis for her – it was almost a religion.

One of her worst memories was the day it went wrong at Asda. Her mum was full of positive energy, parking up with half a tank of petrol and slamming the big empty shopping trolley with a pound coin to unleash it from its chain. She and Nia left Mira in the car, it wasn't so usual to take her with them for this kind of thing, where Mum had planned it all in advance, and Nia had been informed of her role. It wasn't that Sharon didn't know what she was doing, she had achieved it successfully at least ten times in Nia's own estimation, at least. But if you win at roulette then of course you keep playing, and the odds are the odds each time. They walked in and Nia was giving her best effort at being the cute mama's girl, laughing at her mum's jokes and pointing at random items in the Tupperware aisle. Hanging off her arm, wishing that they weren't pretending, that this comfortable, idle meandering portrait was actually their life together.

She saw her mother put her hand in her pocket to feel the quarters of aluminium foil that she had packed in at home and too soon they were heading for the booze section. A little bit of foil on each plastic tag is all you need, Nia knew that by now. So it was the full smorgasbord for them – whisky, vodka, champagne – it all made its way into that gaping huge maw of a trolley till it was three-quarters full of those bottles. Then, on top of it all, the usual staples – bread, fruit, veg, nothing out of the ordinary. Some middle-class touches like houmous and sun-dried tomatoes to aid the whole look. In the past Mum had just walked out of the shop with that huge trolley of goods, right past the self-checkout, big smile on her face, and through the doors without a single beep. An astounding experience, exhilarating, even for Nia, every time. She had driven the whole set of bottles straight to the guy at the 7-Eleven in Bettws, barely keeping a couple of the cheaper bottles back for herself, and exchanged them for cash within half an hour.

Can it really be that easy? Well, it was . . . until it wasn't any more. The last time they did it, Nia saw security coming for her mum when they were a good few yards away – a man and a woman in full uniform. It was a huge store, one of those gigantic buildings off the motorway, it was madness really, what they were doing. Nia saw them out of the corner of her eye and before she realized it, something in her knew to hang back, let herself disappear into the crowd by the checkouts and then out while they were with her mother, to the car park from the other exit, to get to Mira.

'Where's Mum?' Mira said, and first Nia lied of course, something about how she had run into someone they knew, but then she started shaking when she realized that they were stuck off a motorway in a car that might have been full of petrol, but that was devoid of a driver. They slept in the car that night, it seemed the easiest way. They could have rung one of her cronies but Nia was too lit with rage and it was evening time, anyway, they had come at the end of the day in case they were reducing all the food or throwing it away. Mum always brought the foil on these trips, but five times out of ten they didn't do it if conditions didn't feel right.

So, it just seemed simplest to recline the seats in that empty car park and pretend they were camping. That's how she sold it to Mira, to get her to stop crying. She said, imagine that we're lying back in two deckchairs, just do it, Mira, do it now, I'm telling you, or else.

Nia had her earnings from the restaurant now, and those days were behind her, but she still found it hard not to slip in an extra pack of crisps, or a pack of salad at self-checkout when she was buying food. Something light that was undetectable. Sometimes she did treats – a flapjack or brownie, a pack of cookies from the bakery – but more often than not it was just random, because it was left over, you could say, from a darker time. She never stole anything worth more than a pound or two, and they were usually frivolous extras.

She knew she was different from, say, Grace, the woman in her fifties who visited the restaurant sometimes because she was being represented by Tuli, one of Patrick's church flock. It was an oft-discussed case, mainly for its absurdity. Grace had been slapped with a court order for stealing a Mars bar because, as she put it, 'It was the cheapest thing going for the highest calories available, wasn't it!' It had been three days since she'd last eaten at the time, and even though the offending item was just seventy-eight pence, the fines had spiralled because she couldn't pay them.

Nia hated herself for stealing. It was the bruise of her private shame. But in another way, when the sky blushed pink that morning in the car park at Asda, it was a brutal reminder of her familial betrayal, how she'd disappeared like a slug through the side exit of the supermarket and left her bewildered mum to her fate with the police. Cynthia Suntharalingam would never have left her father to the pigs like that. Nia cried silent tears for her mother that morning in the car, her head levered back with the front chair in the reclining position, Mira curled in a foetal crescent next to her

On a lower shelf, behind the bar upstairs, there was a black folder she had seen Tuli go through many times, with thick elastic snapped round the front. It was not in a locked drawer or anything like that, but it was clear that it was private. He often took this folder out when he had visitors. Now, troubled by the business with the Hungarian, Nia often found herself eyeing up this folder, wondering whether she could catch a glimpse of what was in it, as she walked by, finding herself slowing down to listen in a little more on his conversations. But she wasn't remotely successful at seeing or hearing anything useful. She couldn't figure out if this was because Tuli was aware of her attempts to eavesdrop and look over his shoulder, or because ultimately, there was nothing there. Still, she found herself thinking about the Hungarian compulsively, the drug dealer too, and waiting for a night when the boss was out, so that she could explore a little more freely.

On the night in question, Shan was in the kitchen, rolling out the dough with that heartbreaking conscientiousness he had sometimes. His face was drawn, weary, lacking the more vivacious, optimistic expression he'd have when Ava came for her shift later. Nia envied Shan a little for his friendship with Ava, it seemed so genuine, and any attempts she'd made to bond with Ava had not been successful. She'd made a clumsy attempt at helping out when she'd seen her struggling with filling in some forms once.

'What, you think I can't read or something?' Ava said, giving off static a little, but in that way she had of being annoyed and pleased all together in one full choc'n'cream Swiss roll of a sentence.

'Ava, come on,' Nia said, looking into those blossomy eyes, crinkling her own to show that she was with her. 'How is it possible for me to think that!'

But she hadn't let Nia get involved, and she'd known not to push too hard. It was the same with the cooks – she wasn't one of them, and after the conversation with Guna it was clear that maintaining a respectful distance was the thing that kept everyone most comfortable.

She was reminded of this fact when she saw Shan in the kitchen, and rather than trying to strike up conversation, she just nodded at him and hovered near the dishes. She suddenly knew that he wasn't going to give her anything other than the formal quick whisk of a nod that was his standard response. There were other cooks talking and they stopped the minute Nia walked in, even though they spoke in their own language. There was no way of starting any kind of dialogue, let alone an interrogative one regarding the boss. After a while, she couldn't stand it any more, the awkwardness of being in there, and she gave up quickly. Instead, she found herself heading upstairs.

She knew Tuli wasn't in the building. But there was danger in the decision – his staff were all so dedicated to him. How strange it was that she counted herself amongst that flock even as she thought it. She had to be careful and move quickly. The black folder was lying on the low shelf next to the fridge, same as always. She moved the elastic over the corners and let it spring open, knowing she could stop soon enough if she heard footsteps on the stairs, thinking she was able to get away with it for a brief, intense period.

Bills, bank statements, nothing for the first long minute. A page-length receipt – a term's fees for someone called Muttiah Kulasekara to study veterinary science in Kent. And then, just as she was wondering what it was that she might be looking for, she found it.

*Mr Tuli,*

*I write, only to tell you, in words, of the event that we spoke, as per your request to put it on paper. I thank you of course for the sum of five thousand pounds you have given me at a rate of zero per cent interest to be paid back at the sum of 50 pounds capital per month. We will discuss this arrangement after twelve months on the date of 12.03.2004.*

*Thank you,*
*MR SHAN*

The calculation didn't take long. One hundred months was a very long time. It was difficult to understand what it meant. A loan for eight years or thereabouts, with pitiful amounts coming in every month. What was the point?

Beneath it, another piece of paper:

*Mr Tuli,*

*Here is the information that you have requested.*
*In the cell they did the following for three days.*

1. *Whipping with wire: In this I am held by two men while the third throws wire or plastic pipes fast against my back again and again for maybe twenty minutes. This happens three times in three days.*
2. *Under Water: This is the practice of holding my head under the water so I cannot breathe then letting me go out of it at last second. This they did only once.*
3. *Rope neck: Again they did this once only to give a big shock. The rope is tied around your neck and the two men hold you with a third man pulling and pulling the rope tighter to stop your breath.*

4. *The plastic bag: In this bag they put the petrol and tie it around your head for you to breathe the fumes. Sometimes, instead of petrol they burn chillies and use the bag to hold the smoke near to the face.*

5. *Wire on fingers: This is for leaving and going – they tie the copper wire around your fingers very tight and leave you for a while, so they do not have to be in the cell.*

*I am sorry to say that I cannot write more detail to you because I wish to forget these occurrences and make a fresh start for myself. I hope to find asylum for my wife and child once they are located.*

*Also, as we have discussed, this paper should not fall into the wrong hands in Sri Lanka, where the government is responsible for the horrific acts, and I am trusting you on that aspect to keep my name out of this and for that I will withdraw my surname here.*

*Thank you once more.*
*MR SHAN*

Then finally, scrawled on one of those orange Post-it notes and stuck on top:

*Is it the kind of thing you need or tell me if it is too much?*

She thought of Shan standing downstairs, the way she'd watched him just minutes earlier rolling out his dough so methodically. The words were jumping up at her in this horrible, stabbing way: fumes, neck, whipping, wire, rope, fingers, breathe. She put the folder back and began to rearrange the CDs in case anyone came upstairs, her hands trembling with a kind of shameful insistence, as though they were intent on giving her up. A wife and a child, for crying out loud, he had a kid back in Sri Lanka?

The way it was written out – so clearly and distinctly, those words – it made her both believe it and not believe it at all.

# SHAN

In Archway, he sees the scooter-kid on his way home. He is in the park, waiting with his mother at the bottom of the gigantic slide, the one which begins so high against the clouds, rooted in huge paving stones of natural rock, as though it is in some kind of national park, and ends on the ground in ignominy, its dull metal surrounded by potato-crisp packets and cigarette butts.

When the boy's friend reaches the bottom, he shouts 'HUR-RAY!' and taps his ice cream lolly against the lolly that the other boy is carrying as though they are clinking glasses together. The mother is there, an encouraging tone to her voice as she sits on the side, the boy's scooter between her legs.

He looks at the kid and thinks, this is your life, your actual life, these are your memories. My life was what at your age? The magic of badminton in the street park at sundown, burnt grass on the face, nosediving to win, tussles and fights, shuttlecocks and companions. My father's eyes when I got the top mark at school. What did I dream of, hope for from life, before this all began? How to find that person?

'CAN I GO NOW!' the boy shouts at his mother, his high baby voice still mesmerizing to Shan: a stream at altitude, slipping over the words 'CAN I GO, MAMA! IS IT MY TURN, MAMA?'

She nods and he begins his ascent, clambering amongst the rocks on the landscaped incline. Shorts and socks, little bare knees. Shan can see the concern in her face, the way she steadies herself to present a light-hearted smile and wave when he turns around.

He looks up at the sky to check for rain. It's difficult to stop the habit of imagining that the universe turns on a spine of logic. That physics idea of every action having a reaction. If he helps Tuli do whatever it is that he does – you could call them 'good deeds' for want of a better definition – then maybe somehow, someone, something will notice and he'll get his kid rebounding back to him. He is momentarily as superstitious and vulgar as a Hindu from Benares, imagines his own boy dropping out of these blackening clouds on an elaborate gold chariot like something out of the *Mahabharata*.

# NIA

The words in the letters kept on visiting her as she performed her chores that day. Shan . . . to think of him was to feel the prick of tears, and blink them away each time. She avoided the kitchen for as long as she could, and when she finally went in, forced by the need for oil and balsamic as the first customers began to arrive, she avoided looking at him. It was a bit dehumanizing, but poor fucking bastard is all she could think.

She was waiting for her moment all afternoon, to get to a point when everyone had gone, where she could ask Tuli some questions. But she couldn't reveal that she had been snooping around like that, of course. She still had the juddering heart, kept having conversations with him in her head, an argy-bargy in her brain where she was imagining what she might say, what he might say. It came back to the same question as always – what did he actually *do* when it came to all these people, where did his money come from, how did it work, was there anyone he wouldn't help?

Then, as if he could read her mind, he came to find her at the end of her shift. He put a CD on, smiling at the cover, as if at a private joke. It was music that made you think of the opening titles of an epic film – a marching, semi-triumphant sound that announced its own demise even as it celebrated it.

'Leonid Kogan playing Lalo's Spanish Symphony,' he said. 'One of Ava's friends brought it in.'

Nia nodded. He knew that this was all new for her, she didn't know much about classical music. A sweet, twisting violin began to pierce the space around the main thrust of the orchestra, gradually making itself known, supple and strong.

'Want to go for a drive?' he said, standing and looking out of the windows at the back. The glass was spotting with rain again and there was something sublime in how the red and yellow lights outside were permeating each individual bubble of water with colour.

'Sure,' she said, as the violin turned to yearning, and then frivolity. She undid her apron with a flourish, like a waitress in some arthouse film. 'Let's go!'

She couldn't work out why he wanted to keep her close. Did he really want her company? Or was he trying to figure her out – was he uncertain about her in some way? She hoped for the former, but couldn't quite believe it. Still, she wanted to go with him. It wasn't just that she fantasized about confronting him in some way, it was more that in the nights since they had been to the skip, she had lain awake, thinking about that trip, turning it over, in all of its uncertainty, wondering if it would happen again. Now here it actually was – unforeseen and slightly unimaginable – the chance to be with him without anyone else.

They were in his car, and he was strapping on the seat belt when his phone rang. The ringtone was an operatic anthem, the kind of track that Pavarotti might sing in a stadium full of fans. Cascading notes, revelling in the brashness of the melody.

'Shan?' he said. 'Calm down, man. Calm down. What's happening?'

# SHAN

He reaches home and his door is bolted, they have changed the locks. Oh, God. Oh, no.

For a moment he sits on the floor, treats his own body as part of the litter that is around him. The concrete of the corridor is closing in.

Then he stands up, takes a gulp of air, and phones Tuli.

'He's locked it,' he says. 'It's over, boss. New locks . . . I'm sorry but what . . . I am sorry . . . can I sleep in the restaurant tonight?'

He bites his tongue as he says it. Shame. For letting it go this far.

'Come back, man,' says Tuli. 'I've got a solution for tonight. It's OK. Get yourself here quickly.'

'Boss, thank you, I can't express . . .'

'Just come. Don't worry. Do me one favour. When you get there, talk to Ava. I'm not actually going to be in the restaurant itself, but I will explain to her. There is a small hotel here, I know the doorman, his name is Jaipaul, we call him Big Paul. OK, so he sometimes tells me if he has empty rooms there after eleven at night, and he usually does. You need to be careful, but he'll show you what to do, plus there's a whole thing, strip the beds in the morning, special place for the sheets, yes? He'll explain it.'

'Boss, I do not know how to thank you, I—'

'Shan, stop it and just come. Have a drink when you get in to Vesuvio, take it from the bar, try and relax. OK. Got to go.'

'OK, boss.'

He walks fast, feels the adrenaline, gives thanks for the fact that he has an Oyster card for the tube, it means he can go, and it has meant it before, that he is not trapped in one place when things get critical.

★

The moment is outlined as a thermal heat pattern in the map of his mind, with a hot orange-red border – the exact, violent minute when he took to that boat and left them, against everyone's wishes. They all know, everyone knows, that he did it partly for them, partly for himself, there is no way to disentangle the motivation and purify it. But he thought they would be together soon enough and he could sort it out then, once they could see that he had done the right thing. He didn't think he would lose them. And now, Devaki won't respond, to the texts or the phone calls, and he is reduced to this mental squalor. It was a mistake. As simple as putting money on the wrong card when you play the game 304. A mistake because he can't go back, but he doesn't know how to bring them here, forget that, how to find them, even. Tuli says keep going, keep believing, and Shan keeps pricking open his veins and giving him blood, just in case, just hoping that something is there. Betting on your own memory. It is enough to send a man to insanity. Sometimes, when his resolve falters, he thinks why not just slit your veins open and be done with it, let the whole of this sorry life experience spill out at once, just nobly acknowledge that it will kill you. Settle into that kind of sleep. Why not?

And what is life without them? Just, all he gets is the occasional shouting conversation with Gauri, their hard-of-hearing neighbour, full of useless facts, no information on their whereabouts, just the same terrible story of how they both disappeared months ago, Karu's cricket bat still visible in the yard, his bike against the fence. Sometimes he rings his wife's cousin, sometimes one of her former college professors, asking for the numbers of her college friends. Nothing from any of them. Are they lost, these people that constitute his family, or have they ostracized him, without letting him explain? When he thinks of it, the fury in him suggests he might survive, as if the anger might brutalize the sorrow, punch through it and allow him to breathe.

But the anguish is taking him down, and as he looks up to the clouds, he feels a dismantling of his entire self, the sheer force of the knowledge. He takes the certainty, and instead of running from it, pushing it down to the lower levels of his mind, he just holds it like a bomb in his hands and allows himself to touch it. They are not special: Devaki, even Karu. They are dead, both of them. As dead as Appa, Amma and all the others.

# NIA

On the street corner: a modern hotel block with a small glass door. Behind it, a man with a small child at the reception desk. Nigerian. The girl had braids and red ribbons, she looked like she was drawing or writing in a notepad, she was maybe about seven years old and her feet didn't reach the floor. Around them: the clean, shiny surfaces reflecting the overhead lights.

'Are you in a hurry?' Tuli said.

She shook her head, confused as to what he might be planning. They had been in the car for just five minutes before stopping, and she had been turning over questions in her head, hoping that one would present itself as an obvious starting point.

'Do you mind if I go in the lobby, here?' he said. 'It shouldn't take too long.'

She watched him walk through the doors, extending his smile, his whole body even, the way you would a ticket for a ticket collector, making the start of the conversation as easy and inevitable as possible. They talked for a good ten minutes, Tuli leaning over on the bar with his back to her, jiggling his ponytail whenever he nodded, the leather coat skimming the heels of his boots. Occasionally, she could see the man's face, his lips moving quickly, the child watching them both with her cheek balanced on her fist, elbow on the counter. She envied it – the way in which he just entered people's lives like this. The child was giggling, eyeing him with what looked to Nia like curiosity, but it could easily have been trepidation, there was no way to tell at such a distance.

'Ten o'clock at night is too late to have his kid at work with him,' Tuli said, shaking his head when he returned.

'Why is she there?' She couldn't figure out if Tuli was judging the man, or sympathizing with him.

'I think he's pretty much separated from his wife too. They've been here a good five years, maybe seven even, they have grown apart, he says. He's doing these long hours, shift work, she's been handling the child. That kind of thing. In other news, you know what he told me? The Chinese grocer, the one opposite the restaurant? Quiet guy, you know, doesn't talk too much. This fella just now, he said the grocer was being attacked the other day and Guna went and beat the guy up, lah? He is very loyal in his own way, it doesn't surprise me. So, good on Guna you might say. But then finally he just went too far, Guna, well . . . he then urinated all over the guy, the one who had broken in and all. Did it when he was lying on the floor apparently, after the beating.'

He raised his eyebrows in a strained manner, as though hoping it could mitigate the pain of having to speak this detail.

'What the fuck?' Nia said. 'Guna?'

'Yes. Guna. It's bad, very bad.'

'Bloody hell. Are you going to let him go?'

He turned, with a blank gaze, so that she wasn't sure if he had heard her.

'Let him go, I mean, Tuli, he can't work at the restaurant any more after this kind of thing, can he? Fucking awful!'

He looked away and she could see him taking his time with the answer, chewing it over. She looked back at the hotel. The concierge was still visible through the glass, looking at the same computer screen as though no time had passed, but his daughter had disappeared. Nia was gripped with an irrational need to know what the kid was doing. Sitting on the floor now, with drawing or homework? Gone to the toilet by herself, her father unable to leave his workstation unattended?

Finally, very carefully, but with an acid tone, as though he had no interest in her reaction, he spoke.

'You must realize, of course, that you are speaking from one hell of a special place. You don't know what he's been through.'

She flinched. There was a fullness in the car then, it was clear he didn't want a response, that he didn't want to think about Guna discharging himself idiotically over another human being, but also, that there was nothing for her to say that might be relevant to him. She was twinging with the harshness of his response, he hadn't spoken to her like that before.

The car was still stationary, he had not started up the engine, his body was just arranged over the wheel, on pause, while he stared through the screen with her at the different conglomerations of people in the pockets of darkness outside.

'Tuli,' Nia said, making a precipitous decision. 'I know about Shan.'

He mused over her words. For the first time she looked at Tuli and registered that of course, his face had a very strong similarity to the guys in the kitchen. It was easy to forget this, what with him wafting around with Patrick and running the joint, that lordly way he had of doing things, the fact that he was taller than them, and better dressed. He started the car up and began to reverse. A young couple walked out on the road behind them and he hit the brake abruptly.

'Yes? You "know" about Shan. OK? So give me some more, Nia?'

'I know you're helping him, and I want to help you.'

She felt so naive as she said it, but she got the words out and then repeated them with emphasis. 'How can I help you? I want to help. Tuli, man, just listen.'

'What do you "know" about Shan?' he said, taking up his habitual hunched position over the wheel and studying the windscreen.

'He's . . . here illegally,' she said, wary of his response. 'Shan. He wants you to help him . . . get asylum.'

'Oh. *Illegally*, is he?' Tuli mimicked in an almost bitter voice.

He went for another pause then. It lasted quite a while. She looked at her feet nervously, tucked one behind the other. She was suddenly very fearful that he'd ask how she knew this fact. She began to prepare a feasible answer – that she'd overheard Shan discussing it with Ava.

114

She turned to look out of the passenger window. They were parked by a beauty parlour. A woman was holding her hands out at the nail bar in the window, waiting for them to dry, the outstretched gesture of a pianist, a sorcerer even, about to release something from those fingertips. Nia caught her eye by accident and looked away.

'I want to help,' she said again quietly. He raised his eyebrows and nodded, urging her to continue, and something softened in the air. There was no need to worry. He would understand. The folder had been right there in the back bar, easy enough for anyone to flick through it.

'I saw the letter,' she gabbled. 'The black file . . . it was open . . . upstairs. I just took a look when I was cleaning the counters—'

Tuli turned to her.

'Listen, Nia,' he said, waving her words away. 'Be quiet and listen. One thing you have to realize is that *you* work for *me*. Consider this a formal warning. If I find you snooping through things again, you know what will have to happen. It will be a hell of a shame, but you'll leave me with no choice, Nia. Understand?'

She stared at him, the horror metabolizing slowly into understanding. It was clear that he already knew she had been into the folder. There was not a hint of surprise in his voice, only that thing which sounded almost like contempt, such was the finality of it. Had he brought her here, and led her to the confession?

'Tuli . . . I'm sorry,' she said.

He frowned.

'Just don't do it again,' he said.

Or it's over, she thought, wondering what exactly it was between them that could end, fearing it either way, watching the incongruous, pretty fringe of his eyelashes as he surveyed the world through the windscreen, face impassive against her apology. It could so easily all be over, just like that.

# SHAN

There's a kind of humiliation in the fact that Ava is the one taking him to the hotel room, but the night is full of djinns now that Shan has drunk a quarter of the whisky bottle. What to live, what to forget. Something, then? He saw her give the guy at the front desk a five-pound note, let her handle it all. So what? He is beyond thinking and doing.

To his surprise, as they walk down the corridor it becomes clear that she is going to come into the room with him. Has Tuli asked her to put him in the bed? he thinks. Surely not? How would he know that Shan is swaying on his feet, steadying himself against the dank wall of the corridor? The shame intensifies in his cheeks but he barely cares. Let it be so, then, let it be so!

But she doesn't seem to mind. Her mood, if anything, is playful. Instead of arranging the bed she jumps on it and kicks her shoes off.

But what are you doing? he says to her, making his eyes wide, willing them to captivate her, as though they are pieces of the moon. We are supposed to—

Oh, it's very bad, she says, raising her eyebrows, such a clean room.

In dream, he is able to assimilate it, her clothes are coming off, she is laughing at his bewilderment, her face framed in a soft halo of purplish white light, dear God, he thinks, it is her hair, not a halo, it is brushing her shoulders and then she is sitting there in her bra and knickers, on her knees, discarding finally even these flimsy items with the same cheerful insanity till her body is before him, certain and firm as a rock itself.

He runs his hands along her thighs, holds them so they are either side of his torso and puts his face on her stomach, above her mound. He is so hard it hurts. Everything is a hallucination, the softness of her breasts, the way his fingers touch the small tips of her nipples in slow motion.

There is no rubber. When he goes to withdraw she says no, holds him tight against her.

So she *can* still have children . . . or does it mean she can't? He turns his face to the side and pumps, guilty and obscene, Devaki's face, his mother's too, ghostly shapes flickering under his lids, and then the sweet release, the chance to lie with Ava in his arms in clean sheets, naked and sweat-rinsed and all of him touching all of her. He is alive for one moment. He is igneous rock, he is molten lava, he is fluid and fluent and can be part of the river of change that runs through London town.

In the morning they have to leave with care, the sheets need to be stripped, replaced with the ones in the cupboard so that it seems no one has been there.

They part outside the tube.

'It's not going to happen again, is it?' says Shan, looking for something in Ava's eyes.

She smiles, shrugs, puts a hand through her lilac-grey mane.

'Who knows, mister,' she says, but she looks sad.

'What, Ava?' His voice is full of want. He knows that it didn't work between them, the physicality of it, his desperation has made the whole thing void. He remembers, twinges at how he burrowed his head into her stomach, like a madman burying his head in the desert.

'Nothing,' she says.

'Tell me,' he says. 'You want a baby?'

'I can't have a baby, don't worry,' she says. 'You're not going to end up with a little frog. I paid a lot of money . . . to try for them to do it. With the donor. Sperm donor. I saved up over a long time. But it didn't work, is no good. And I accept it. What you gonna do, eh? You try, and you see. If it works, it works, fine, but if it doesn't you have to be ready for this. So for me, is OK.'

But has it really stopped you trying? he thinks, as he watches her leave. It must have been part of it, part of the reason you came to bed – you have not ever desired me in that way, surely? But also, he knows that for Ava it could easily have been a moment of why-not. A little fun, something new, why not, no big deal? He recoils as he remembers how quickly it happened, the act itself, it was a matter of minutes, the whole thing, it is so easy to imagine a world in which it had not happened. If only he had not done it. What did he think, that he would be able to crudely stitch himself onto her life, now that his own is gone?

Her figure moves confidently through the street and it seems as though she carries the night itself away with her, the whole grey sky could be a fairy-tale cloak on her back. She disappears around the corner, and without her eyes as witness, their union is gone, just like that, smoke in a breeze. Ava Amada. He did not think it was possible, but he is more alone than before it happened.

Around him, people connect up the dots of their lives as they hurry along the narrow pavements. Purpose. They have such purpose. On his head he feels the cold, patterned mantra of this country's rain. He misses his child. He has no idea where he will sleep next.

# NIA

They drove on, he was hunched once again over the wheel. She waited for Tuli to speak, scoured his body language for clues. Sometimes she really couldn't work out if he was a thirty-three-year-old play-acting at being sixty or the opposite, a sixty-year-old soul forcing himself into the confines of a young man's mind, body and spirit. But always, when she was in the car like this with him, the night outside seemed spotlit, there was the feeling that they could get sucked into any one of the million stories that were unfolding across London in that very moment, that every single story was epic in its stature, each one worth telling.

That kindness in him, she had witnessed it so many times. She willed it back. Kept her mouth shut.

She thought about that crazy dull-eyed teddy bear he had tucked behind the bar. The one that came out for big celebratory dances – a major chess win, a successful funding bid for Patrick, some employee's family member getting married or into college back home – that kind of thing. As tall as a one-year-old child, the bear would romp to a string symphony or eighties love ballad in the slow blur of candlelight. Tuli's joyful puppeteer grin dancing across his handsome face as he wielded it, cigarette in the fingers of his free hand.

Eventually, he parked up. It was a street that she didn't recognize, under a tall, solid iron lamp post with that very white light coming from the filament. He turned his face, grinning in a way that sent relief catapulting through her. It was his old teasing expression, ready to rib her for the strange quirks and tics she housed.

'What's wrong?' he said. 'You're scared of me now?'

A titter of a laugh escaped her, slightly hysterical.

'Calm down!' he said, the first word high, sliding down to meet the second. 'You don't need to go to pieces. Keep it together, Nia, come on! Keep it tight.'

She punched him then, lightly, on his arm. It was a risk but she had to check, somehow, that the elastic wasn't broken between them, that it was going to be all right. She was angry too, he had scared her.

'What!' he said, still smiling, and she knew as soon as he said it that they were playing a game, in which they weren't to mention what had just passed. Those private letters she'd read, her transgression, it was all too weighty to be brought back into this arena.

'I don't bite,' he said, holding her gaze, pulling at the brake of the car.

She held the stare, returning it with a hidden vigilance, suspicious of him now, but also feeling the spiked points of his eyes on her, there was something charged about the unfamiliarity of it. She imagined kissing him, she would feel his hard teeth against her tongue as she did it. He would be the recipient rather than the giver.

'Do you like graveyards?' he said, releasing his seat belt with a click, and she smiled inwardly. She had a floating sensation as she got out of the car, a gauzy sense of the desirability of her body – its firm, swollen, erotic curves – as though she was living in it for the first time.

'I don't know,' she said. 'Maybe.'

She realized soon enough that he meant for them to walk around the perimeter of the graveyard; it was too late of course to enter the massive grounds. The tombstones were huddled together like little stone families. She stopped herself from sliding her hand through the railings and pulling at the grass, feeling the damp texture against her palms, ripping at it even and brushing the lines against her cheek.

'Ask me something,' he said.

'What?'

'Anything. Ask me anything. Anything you like.'

'OK. Tell me about your childhood.'

He considered it for a second.

'Sure. What would you like to know? Go ahead.'

She asked him what kind of building he'd grown up in, what his parents did, what kind of school he'd been to, that kind of thing. She was careful to avoid anything that might reveal that she was trying to uncover subtext of any kind. If he thought she was attempting to find out his secrets it would end the conversation.

'You're really very British about this,' he said, musing over the questions as they walked.

'Is that a compliment or an insult?'

'Hm. Both maybe?'

'British how?'

'It's class,' he said, as though it revealed something he hadn't associated with her before. 'Quite a conventional line of questioning, isn't it? School, parents, house and the like.'

She didn't contradict him, and he gave her some answers that were a little unsatisfactory – they didn't account for the flow of money that he seemed to have going on at the restaurant – he seemed to have emerged from confusingly ordinary beginnings. His parents were schoolteachers, he had gone to a public school in Singapore, run by the state until he was thirteen, it was what he called 'mixed' – this, he seemed to mean in terms of affluence or poverty, but also, in terms of ethnicity – Chinese, Tamil, Malay and more. His parents had come over from Malaysia when he was young, and yes, they were Catholic. He had come to the UK for his first degree, in law, and stayed on.

Then, she hit on something. He had been in the army there, straight after school, enforced national military service for two years upon graduating from high school. Hated it, he said, the regimen, the machismo, the cruelty.

'Ah!' she said, revelling in a new understanding. 'The rules! All those rules, waiting to be broken once you got here, yes?'

He laughed. She listened, but there was nothing jagged in the sound.

'Sure, detective,' he said. 'You're like that, aren't you?'

Like this, they talked, walking the circumference of that place, a pilgrimage which felt holy to her in some way, an acknowledgement of how this piece of caged land was holding those completed, important lives in its confines.

Nia remained light, careful, the smarting memory of his warning in the car still with her.

# SHAN

He is making his way back to the restaurant on foot, for want of any other ideas. He feels the threat in his stomach, a glassy hunger after the whisky. He is without initiative. *Muyarci illātatu.* He is drifting back weakly, like an empty plastic bottle inching towards a beach at low tide.

'Have ten pence for me, do you?' says a woman lying in a door-way near to the station. She has an orange-brown sprawl of hair, peppered with white threads, is slumped as she speaks the words. She stares at one of her hands, twists it with a bemused look, as though she can see it moving in slow motion. She is wearing those odd gloves that have the fingers cut off. 'Got to get something to eat. Ten pence . . .' she says mildly, trailing off as though she has forgotten the script. Or realizes how pointless it is, thinks Shan, reaching into his pocket for a coin that isn't there. He can only feel a few thin coppers of different sizes, they are not just insulting but useless too, you would need ten times as many to be able to buy something with them. The woman surely has no one, and it is the kind of rain where you can feel the water dripping right into your blood.

His phone beeps, vibrating against the fingers in his pocket and he pulls it out to look at the message. It is Tuli.

*Call me. He's found them.*

He stares at the screen for a whole minute as if the message might evaporate. He writes with a numbing violence in his fin-gers, a disorder that means he can't go through the permutations of letters needed to spell the word. Finally, he presses send.

*Alive?*

The phone rings in the palm of his hand, it is a long digital *dri . . . ing,* like the comic alarm on a bomb timer in a kids' car-toon. He raises the device to his ear.

'Yes, alive,' says Tuli, sending the words back to him in a cushion of velvet, two discs of pearl that he will return to survey over and over again in the ensuing days. *Yes. Alive.* 'Come now? To the restaurant?'

'Are they there?' Shan says, knowing the answer, his thin voice scratching on the air between him and the receiver of the phone.

'Not yet. We have to do some work to get them here.'

'Yes,' says Shan. 'Yes.'

And he is at the tube, now, his legs thawing into movement as he pushes through the people milling at the ticket barriers. *Whatever it takes*, he thinks as his shocked consciousness roars to take space, his gaze moving up the long steel girders in the giant hall of platforms as he descends the stairs. *We will do whatever it takes. We can do whatever it takes.*

# PART TWO

# SHAN

Question. How many times can you go over a one-minute conversation?

> S: Devaki . . . you are there?
> D: Yes, I am here.
> S: Oh . . . Karu is . . . OK?
> D: Karu is OK. He is with me. Quickly now, speak, there isn't long he says to me, one minute.
> S: Oh, God. Devaki? Did anyone hurt you?
> D: I am OK. You are OK?
> S: Devaki . . . I am so sorry.
> D: Don't do this now, there isn't time.
> S: (breaks down)
> D: Shan, he is saying to me to go now. I will see you in London.
> S: Devaki, phone number. PHONE. DEVAKI. TELL ME—
> Agent: OK? Then next I will call when the money is here. Don't worry. Everything will be OK.

Answer. You can go over it infinitely. You can go over the word 'OK' as spoken by three different people, a thousand times in one day.

This fifty-five-second phone call with Devaki takes place where everything takes place – on the decadent leather spread of battered sofas upstairs at the restaurant, when Shan has finished his shift. It comes at the end of a conversation between Shan, Tuli and a man called Tavan – a peculiar, staring, short Gujarati in silver-rimmed spectacles who approaches Tuli with a faux deference, and a light familiarity, like a family accountant. Shan sits and watches him obsessively, a girdle of strain around his chest as he breathes. It all matters so much and he can't do anything about it but listen.

The man, on the other hand, is relaxed enough to drink and eat without concern, piling in happily to some of the most expensive items on the menu without charge – the garlic prawns and lamb shank – but insistent on tap water only to go with them. He speaks in a series of short sentences, to-the-point kind of thing, but he fills them in on the situation with a distant tolerance, as though he is reading a shopping list and just has to get through it.

Devaki has been discovered in Munich by an agent in London who is known to Tavan, but (and he is at pains to underline this fact) not endorsed by him. This person – 'Pran' he is called – swears that she is not in danger and that Karu is safe too. Mother and son are sharing a room with four other people, and although they are not in a threatening situation, Tavan says, apparently some of their freedoms have been restricted. Shan winces when he thinks of this word 'restricted' and its importance, but some part of him wonders if they are safer like this, fed and watered and with somewhere to sleep, rather than wandering the streets and vulnerable.

They are 'restricted', Tavan continues, because this leg of her journey has come with a request for extra money, and Devaki doesn't have it. So, when Tavan put the description out through the networks – thirty-one-year-old woman, short black hair to ears, brown eyes, mole above lip on left side, six-year-old boy, who knows what else Tuli had given them after all his chats with Shan – they were waiting for it, when it reached them in Munich. Family involvement equals monetary possibility, and money is what they want, he explains.

And then, awkwardly, clearing his throat and glancing at Tuli, he comes out with it. They have issued a time limit of three weeks for the funds to clear, otherwise they say they will have to move Devaki and the child to a different location.

Guilt threatens to engulf Shan when he gets to this point – if he had left some more of her jewellery, not taken so much of it like a fucking idiot, would it have been enough to prevent her own journey stalling like this? But he hadn't known that after he left, Devaki would attempt passage herself with Karu. She had been so against the whole thing, how could he have known? All he can think is that some pressure must have built on her and Karu very quickly to force her to leave. Maybe the SLA themselves, noticing that her husband had disappeared, it is not as though they are slow in coming forward to harass people. Or the agent Shan used himself, what was his name? Sandro, Sandmar, Sand-something. Maybe he went back and told her that Shan was OK, promised to reunite them during those initial black weeks of his journey, when all communication was severed between them. He has asked Tavan for all these details – how, why, where, when, who, the list is sickeningly long – but the man has very little of it to hand.

The past is of little importance now that they are holding this ultimatum of three weeks over them.

'Like I say, they are not my choice of people, the guys holding her and the kid in Munich,' Tavan says to Tuli and Shan. 'They can be difficult. You should have come to me at the start, if you wanted to get her over.'

Shan bristles at this and holds his tongue. It is important that he gleans everything he can from this man, and getting angry is not going to help.

'Even this guy in London, the agent, Pran – I don't work with him,' says Tavan, reiterating the fact with more fervour than before. 'I'm just passing the information on, yes? This is not my connection, he just came out and called me when he got the description. We didn't get into all the bits and pieces, I just thought – aha – we've found them, good, this is what Mr Tuli asked for, and so at that point I came here to give you the guy's number, yes?'

Shan stares at the man, aghast at his avoidance. Why does Tuli deal with these people? Why doesn't he just do it himself?

'OK, man, OK, thank you, good work, it's very good work indeed, to have found them,' says Tuli in a pacifying tone that aims to both flatter Tavan and direct Shan's reaction at the same time. 'We'll speak to this guy Pran. Thank you. Bit by bit, step by step. Thank you for coming here straight away, I'm grateful to you, Tavan.'

Shan speaks then, he can't hold back. He knows the score, the boss explained to him in advance – this guy Tavan is someone he has worked with for a long time, completely trustworthy, always delivers what he promises, when people arrive in the country, he often sends them to Tuli for their first meal and orientation, la la la, he knows it all. But he has so much to ask.

'How are we to be sure we will get them here?' Shan knows that his voice is sounding like a blade, too sharp and devoid of softness or gratitude, but he can't help it. He is panicked rather than reassured and he can't speak fast enough to get it all out. 'We can send the money but how do we know they will not ask for more? How am I to speak to them? Are you sure they are not harmed? What was the route? Why couldn't I speak to them before? Why didn't he call me, your agent?'

'Sir, I have the number of the agent in Germany, but these are not my guys, like I say.' Tavan stops and swallows a drink of water, slowly, as if it will help him to be more patient. He is clearly dampening down his frustration. 'Respectfully, sir, I have come here to bring you these two numbers only – one for the agent in Germany and one for the guy here, with his name: Pran. He has asked you to call Germany first, and then to call him once you are satisfied that she is there and healthy, your son is also in good health, and that is what you should focus on. This man Pran will take the next round of cash here, and it is for you to do with Tuli Sahib. Like I say, none of these are my people, and I cannot be responsible for the outcome, I am just the messenger, and that too because of my respect and long-standing relationship to Tuli Sahib.'

'And really,' says Tuli, 'I am grateful for this.'

On it goes, round and round, until the man leaves.

And that is when they ring, Tuli dialling the number and twisting the word Devaki through the conversation with the man on the other end like an ancient charm in a stiff, heavy lock. That is when Shan speaks to her and hears his son's name from her mouth, watches his own shaking hand return the phone to Tuli as the realization trembles through his skin.

OK. I am OK. He is OK, you are OK? Meaning: I am alive, he is alive, you are alive? We are all still alive.

# NIA

Green felt summer haze, trees emanating pollen, the fertility dazzling. Thick scent of it coming right through the park over the streets, flooding the world with early-season heat. In those weeks the world seemed full of the same unseemly private expectation that a person has on an early date.

She went with him everywhere, now. Or at least it felt that way. Tuli regularly took her on his errands, mostly they seemed short and relatively innocuous. They went to a Chinese furniture shop to get photographs of a child framed before delivering them to the correct post box in a local council estate, went to the graveyard to leave flowers on a tombstone, to Tesco for a conversation with the cashiers that was inaudible to her but which seemed successful if you were to judge by Tuli's demeanour upon leaving, to second-hand bookshops (where she was urged to choose anything she'd like, even though no money ever passed between Tuli and the booksellers for these purchases), and to the skips and dumps of course. Every shop-owner or reception clerk seemed to think she was Tuli's new girlfriend, and she couldn't deny that she liked it. She felt herself animating under the curious, searching gazes. Even the cooks and Ava were giving her this new interest.

If she stopped to give Sue a tea outside the tube, or some loose change, Sue would take the opportunity to probe her for information.

'Are you in love or what?' she said, more than once, peeping at her from behind her glasses like she was a real curiosity. 'You look different. Or is it haircut? What is it, but, Nia? Is it a mystery?'

'Yeah, Sue, it's a mystery,' Nia would say, and when she smiled it was with an inexplicable thrill.

★

It was easier to ask him things now, outright, although he didn't always answer in the way that she wanted.

'How does Patrick help you?' she said. 'Why does he sign things for you?'

'Well . . . he's a pillar of the local community,' came the reply.

'OK, what else?' She said it with impatience, interrupting him before he could respond. 'What else is Patrick, besides a pillar of the community? What is Patrick?'

'He's . . .'

She answered it quickly, before he could continue.

'White,' she said. 'He's white.'

'Well, if you must! I guess he is! What's your point?'

'Come on. I know I'm not like Patrick. I can't sign things for you, endorse things. Give you my word as a cornerstone of the community. Is that what he's doing? It is, isn't it? False statements, are they? The ones he's signing?'

'Have you never heard of an indicator?' Tuli called out, suddenly distracted, it seemed, by the car in front. As ever, he managed to shut down the conversation before it went too far.

'You are white too,' he said, noting with surprise that Nia flinched slightly. 'And more than him, you are also British.'

These conversations became increasingly common. She found herself pushing him, to let her be more involved. Finally, on a particularly good day – a trip back from someone's house, a foreign student leaving for good, with the car boot full of discarded possessions, humming a tune at the steering wheel, Tuli had seemed to relent.

'OK,' he said finally. 'OK. Nia. How about we start with something? If you really want to help, as you put it, then OK.'

'OK,' she said. 'Great. Thank you.'

'With the Hungarian.'

She exhaled harshly.

'Why him! Seriously? Again? For fuck's sake, Tuli. How can you do this? How do you know you're not backing the wrong horse?'

'Listen,' he said. 'Just listen, Nia. This guy, the Hungarian. His problem is that he refuses to make his story the best it can be. Even Patrick has told him, don't mention hitting her, even once is too much. If you really believe the kid is best off seeing you for a decent part of the week, every week, if you are willing to live by that principle, then don't do it. The guy is like, I cannot lie, I just cannot lie. So if he goes to court it's basically a suicidal response. I had to tell Patrick to go see him and say look, it's fine to lie. You know? Patrick is there saying to him, come on! Here I am, a Catholic priest, telling you it's OK sometimes.'

He laughed, but only for a second, before turning serious again.

'If he goes to court, and says what he considers to be the truth, he's going to lose it all. The house, his kid, all of it. She's really something, his wife. She doesn't seem to have a sense of what's at stake, if he can't see his kid any more. Really. Her main thing is to take him for as much as she can in terms of the money. With anyone else, I would be saying, no way, absolutely, she has the right of way, she is the mother, in fact, I had another case last year literally, and I would not even think twice about helping the father get custody. I mean, in that case, he was a complete deadbeat and she needed a lot of help to shake him off. Which we did.'

She didn't have an answer, nothing had changed on that front. And so, this time, she went with a different tack.

'But he hit her, Tuli.'

'Yes. And I have to believe he won't do it again. I have to see that it is possible. And if it is possible then he deserves help.'

'You seem to think it's the right thing to do. But I can't see why he'd care what I have to say.'

'The fact that you're a woman – meaning, easier to trust – that yes, you're British and white at that, you carry a certain legitimacy, of course it all helps,' he said. 'In terms of him being interested in what you have to say about what is acceptable and what isn't. Sure it does. Of course. Think of yourself as a cultural ambassador. One who has his best interests at heart.'

They went through another silence, before she spoke. However much time she spent with him, Nia could not get used to the awk-wardness of these silences.

'What do you want me to do?' she said, finally.

'Just . . . talk to him.'

'What, tell him to lie?'

'Yes, if you feel it. "Tell him to lie" is one way of putting it. Or explain that there is something bigger here, something that mat-ters, that means a small lie, is OK, like Patrick says, you know, that type of thing. You have to think of the kid. All that?'

He finally started the engine, as if he was releasing her from hav-ing to make the decision. Within seconds she could see the familiar route to her flat unfolding, the big roundabout and traffic lights at the next turning. She thought about the Hungarian, his heavy face, looked for clues in the memory of his eyes, how they fixed on Tuli without wavering. She could divine something from them, surely.

'OK,' she said. 'I'll do it.'

She was tense, every muscle in her shoulders was straining as she said it.

'Calm down,' he said, frowning, keeping his gaze fixed on the road. 'Just take it easy. There's no rush. You have to really feel this, in your bones. You should only do something like this if you believe in it. You might need some time to think it through. Like we discussed, this is about being there, not walking by. And you should not be feeling like you are "backing the wrong horse" as you put it. I'm serious.'

It wasn't what she wanted, this take-it-or-leave-it attitude, the onus for the decision on her shoulders, it didn't relieve her discom-fort. But with him, why would it be any other way? Tuli knew she wanted to be in there, working with him, not watching from the outside any more, and if this was to be the test of her commit-ment, then she was fine with that, sure, she could put her money where her mouth was if needed, he'd see.

# SHAN

The boss is most often with the white Brit girl in the evenings at the moment, and he seems to have done something mysterious that means she has transformed from her former sullen self into a smiling dervish. *Veṛi piṭitta* – a crazy person – some idle unused part of Shan is pleased for her even as he is tickled by her.

'Do you think Boss is with Nia, now?' Shan asks Ava in a hushed tone. He can hear the rumble of voices upstairs, the distance from Tuli emboldens him to say more. 'With her like that, I mean? This is her idea, is it?'

He points at two new prints on the walls – a bewildering collection of boxes and triangles, flamboyant in colour but truly meaningless to him in terms of their overall effect. His raised eyebrows ask the question: are they really necessary? Ava is getting ready for the start of the weekend rush, and he is taking the time before his shift to help her with the tablecloths, smoothing them down at the corners and putting the menus out over the red-and-white chequered linen, ready for business.

'She is like a bee, on purpose drowning in a big bucket of her own honey,' Ava says in return as she pops a pale pink carnation into a vase on each table. A smug mischief puckers out her lips lightly, and Shan giggles in response, flushed full of well-being at the fact that they are still friends after their misadventure.

That Ava has not ditched him, that they can still talk, these are miraculous facts, all down to her lack of interest in their tryst. It is as if the fateful night's itinerary is a discarded menu from a long-forgotten dinner date. It seems inconceivable to bring it up, nor does he desire to do such a thing. She is even excited for him, genuinely, without sentimentality, a fact that shames and heartens him in equal measure as he moves through the slow unrolled hours of each day, waiting for news of Devaki and Karu but feeling awake and excited.

He is prised open with hope, it sits in him like a pearl in an oyster. His wife and child are alive.

Ava, by all accounts, now has a love interest: a man who turns up on a smart motorbike at all hours and whisks her off into the unknown, never even removing his helmet for a hello, how do you do, let alone ever entering the restaurant. Shan is pleased for her, of course he is, but he misses their conversations, and particularly the chess.

'Look after this place!' Ava says whenever she unties her apron and bounces out of the restaurant to join her companion, wearing her glee prominently as though it is one of those Radiance Facial Masques advertised at the beautician's around the corner. It is as though a magnifying glass is being passed over her entire self, her little tics and traits more accentuated than ever. A wink and then a warning finger is jiggling at him as she speaks.

'Remember the tiramisu. Is two days old, must finish it today, OK? Remember it, mister!'

Today, thankfully, she is here till closing, bundling in and out of the packed kitchen, doused in the crazed energy of the weekend crowd. She puts on her reading glasses as she deciphers her notepad, shouts out the orders so that the sound of her voice tunnels right through the steam in the room. He can see her small form glint in the reflection of the taps where he is washing a big frying pan and he marvels at how it no longer tortures him, he is just grateful for her friendship, can't quite believe that she is there. Friendship, Ma, you know? Friends.

'TWO FLORENTINA!' shouts Ava, grandiose and beaming, enjoying the drama. 'TWO GRANDE TRICOLORE! ONE GARLIC BREAD! TABLE THREE! TABLE FOUR, TWO MORE BRUSCHETTA. GET IT RIGHT, GUYS! YEAH!'

And more, and so much more there is to make, to fulfil, but Shan can do it all now, he is endowed with new levels of strength because life is about to change, the vortex inside which he has been trapped and whirling is now littered with gold leaf, he can almost taste it on his tongue when he speaks. Tuli has got him back into the Archway flat but he stays some nights with the others above the restaurant now; if he works late for the boss, his own piece of sleep is slotted alongside two other mattresses in one room, but his heart . . . it is brimming full. When they are all waiting to shave in the morning, taking tea in vests and shorts, as they queue for the bathroom, he can barely contain himself, he is like a man walking around with a box of sweets wanting to say, 'Please do have one! I am celebrating the imminent reunion with my wife, my child. No, really! Please do!'

But sweets would be crazy, of course, *cerukku mikka* you could say, vainglorious. The whole plan is characterized by uncertainty, and he is working harder than he has ever worked in his life, to try to make up any part of his debt to Tuli, both in the restaurant and out. So when Ava winks at him, he finds that he is shushing her with his eyes, and gesturing over at Guna, Vasanthan, all of them bedfellows now, virtually, that he is silently telling her to mind these people crowding their shared kitchen space in their caps and aprons. Let's talk about it later, his eyes say to Ava.

How deeply they seem to work, his colleagues, all those arms presenting their united strength in white cloth, violently and speedily committing to excellence, to increasing the tips in the plastic bag behind the counter, to the hallowed path that will lead to the Pizza Express. They keep going, keep watching the ball, they never drop it.

And there he is, instead, constantly shuffling and reshuffling the hopes in his head, as though he can control the probability of Devaki's survival, of Karu's survival if he goes through the combinations, the possibilities of her route enough times.

Who knows, but now she is alive, Karu is alive, and it is the small vital flame that can be whipped into a tall fire of existence for them all. He just has to keep the flame burning. It is his job to get this sorted, not to descend into negativity. There are vials of anxiety that can poison his thoughts now if he allows himself – why can't he speak to her more, for example, surely there would be a way for them to give her a phone? But even as he thinks it, he remembers his own journey and how it was the first thing to go, along with his passport, the preposterous act of faith in handing it over, that mobile phone, seeing it disappear into a huge clear plastic sack of phones when he first got on that boat, without any hope of retrieval.

It worked for me, he says to himself, and it will work for her. They live, they are alive, both of them.

Sometimes when he walks the street at night, on the way to his next assignment for Tuli, his mouth threatens to snap open and release laughter, unhinged from decorum or sense, out into the volatile galaxy of stars, comets, asteroids above.

The men cleaning the shelves stare at him as he tails the aisles, but it does nothing to dent his good mood. Hawala, hawala, hawala! he sings to himself. They know why he is here, in this particular mobile phone shop, indeed he is back where he began, but really, how things have changed. There were so many options when it came to sending the money – he could have gone to the kebab shop, the snooker hall, the 7-Eleven, but he wanted to come back here, stand in and amongst the garish colours without the loneliness cloaking him like a shroud. Something, there is, about returning.

He has got the batch of notes in his bag. It is not heavy, in fact it feels as light as a bag of balloons, it is almost disconcerting how easily the money floats along on his back, how effortlessly he was able to accept this bag from the boss.

He is not going to think about the route that this money will take once the guy in Lanka receives note of the transaction, how it will fan out into tiny pieces like Christian confetti and be distributed to countless different groups, passed on through recruiters, transporters, hoteliers, corrupt officials, used to buy illegal visas, fake documents, to pay middlemen, sailing crews, ship-owners, the police and so much more. All of it is meaningless. What matters instead is that he has got the first batch of the money, part one, here it is – Tuli has given it to him.

Yes, he has it in his hands. Somehow, it is not an idea any more, he has it right there.

He saunters up to the till and nods at the man behind the counter, grinning at him in what he knows to be an over-familiar manner.

'Hawala,' says Shan. 'For Mr Shan. Thank you.'

The man stops watching the small screen that someone has attached to an arm of heavy metal, coming down from the ceiling. It is north-Indian fare, an endless reel of couples dancing through their courtships, one song after another. The metal arm is comical, semi-menacing, like the arm of a Bond villain who is particularly fond of desi love songs, thinks Shan, chuckling again, at the silly fizz of his mind's humour.

'You have the address, the number,' he says, ignoring Shan's premature display of gratitude.

Shan nods. It is very impersonal, this interaction, considering how intimate hawala is in its workings. Because in reality, no money is going to move across the ocean, of course, no three thousand pounds, no nothing. Instead, this man will tell his hawaldar associate in Sri Lanka to take the equivalent money in rupees, from his own account to the agent, and he will take on a verbal contract of debt, this shopkeeper will now owe the hawaldar three thousand pounds' worth, until something comes along to write it off. All of it, without a trace, just word of mouth – take this money to this person and write it down – it doesn't get more intimate than this, than the word itself. *Hawala* meaning trust.

Shan hands over his bag, and the man disappears to a back room to count it with barely a nod.

Trust, he thinks. Trust that they won't act like dogs and put them on a boat full of women being sold on, or one heaving with drugs carriers. But he knows, of course, as he stands there, drumming out his fingers nervously on the counter to the endless dancing on the screen, that it is unavoidable that some of those people will be with her, wherever she goes, there is no way of doing this without coming into contact with them, it is the price you have to pay.

The question is just . . . what? Exactly what? Meaning how many, what percentage? And his mind starts doing the sums again, metering out the cost versus the possible routes, punches it out like a rhythm of code that can bend happenings towards their best possible outcome, change the events themselves.

# NIA

She walked past one of Tuli's guys under the awning of the Aussie pub, recognizing him after a few seconds, a big muscleman Asian guy with a leather jacket that was too shiny, naff, big silver zip up the front. Soft-skinned chubby cheeks, thinning hair with side parting, staring at her with the classic form of seedy gaze: the unblinking steady stare approach. It was market day and Nia was humming, moving through the stalls on their road with a spring in her step. It didn't unnerve her. Men looked at them all the time on this street, all of the waitresses and sales girls, it was part of the gig, you were part of the aesthetics, free-to-view. She had got used to it by now, but very occasionally, like at this moment, she did stop and wonder why she, they, just accepted it.

Elene was in a state of euphoria as she ran into the restaurant, clutching the envelope, the brown A4 ripped open at the top to reveal a chunk of white, letting out little screams of revelry. Ava was out with her boyfriend, as was common these days, and Elene now rarely visited during her breaks from the café.

'Nia, you really did it!' she said, whooping and putting her arms around her. 'You did it! Thank you so much!' And then tears, as sudden and joyful as her little declarations of ecstasy. 'If you love me so much, I will cry, you be careful, eh! Oh, my God. What am I gonna do!'

Nia looked through the papers. There it was, all written out. A full chunk of benefit assigned to Elene for month after month in 2003. She was in the system. The same categories that had tested Nia's patience when she was filling out the forms seemed utterly glorious to her now, functioning as they did as part of a puzzle that had ended in victory.

'It is so so good. Then now I can do just one job instead of two? I should give you ten per cent!' she said, laughing and wiping her tears. 'What is the commission rate for the pimps these days, eh? I should ask Tuli, isn't it?'

They laughed and Nia looked around for him. Tuli was not in yet, but she wanted to show him her achievements, show off, you might say. It was her first success and she could feel it warming her central nervous system – ah, well, it did feel good!

'Come on!' said Elene, taking one of the CDs from behind the bar and putting it in the machine. 'Let us have a drink to this one!'

It was that song by Aerosmith, full blast of emotion, Nia had mocked Tuli for his love of the band many a time. Ava shared his taste for eighties power ballads and she had passed the passion on to Elene even though she was much younger. It was a match made in hell, Nia would say, when they put Bon Jovi or the Eagles on at the end of the night. But now, she was glad to sing with Elene, giving the lines some vibrato. They continued with this madness, lifting up glasses of Diet Coke and clinking them in time to the shouting verses until the first customers started trickling in.

It had taken just an hour for Nia to do the application forms with Elene. Tuli was the one who had entrusted them to her, after a good few rounds of interrogation.

'You're fine with this?' he'd said, before her shift had begun that morning. They were working on the decor, the *dee-cor* as he still insisted on calling it for her benefit, changing the layout of the wall hangings, experimenting with a new flower in the vases, a deep purple tulip with splotched yellow centre that she had brought in, three large bunches for the downstairs tables.

'You're absolutely sure?' he said. 'Don't get me wrong, I think it's good for you to manage this yourself, if that's what you want, you'll get a lot out of it. But in this instance, you have to be one hundred per cent sure you want to get into this with Elene, right? It's a big deal for her to come and ask for help. You can't back out once you begin, you know that?'

'Yup. Tuli, I already told you that.'

'You're putting her hours down as about twenty-five a week, yes?'

'Yes. It's fine.'

'Twenty-five hours.'

'Twenty-five hours, Tuli!'

'If you have a change of heart, come to me first. Don't just randomly change it on the form, lah?'

'I won't have a change of heart.'

He was right to check like this. When she had first found out that he was halving the hours for staff at Vesuvio on their benefits forms, of course she had been indignant. She asked him what he thought of the law: minimum wage, sick pay, maternity pay, paternity pay, holiday, striking rights, everything she wanted in her own contract.

'So I get that,' he said, when she went off on her high horse. 'But just go and ask any one of them. They are the ones who have asked me to change the figure, they are the ones who want it. As you know private rent is basically impossible in London and they have all the expenses you don't have – visa applications, sending money home – no waitress or bathroom-attendant wage can cover all of it. And in answer to your other fine points, yes, of course they are entitled to rights, and as you know, you have them all in your own package, but again, ask them – they get a lot of care in ways that far outweigh the things you are talking about. Take Guna, for example. His sister is getting married. He needs to buy gold for the wedding. It's a whole thing that falls on him, eldest brother, a whole heap of stress, lah? And he is expected back there for four weeks. So, it's understood. I'm going to help him with the gold and the time off, both things. He can rely on me. You think you could just up and leave for four weeks like that somewhere else? It happens organically, together you create a pattern that works.'

'But where do you get all this money from?' she said.

'What has that got to do with it? I thought we were discussing their conditions of work!'

'Yes, but while we are on it – did you just give him a heap of money for gold? How do you just manifest this stuff?'

'Hmm . . .' And then, after consideration, 'OK . . . so in Guna's case it is a loan but sure, I would be happy to just give it to him if he was to ask. But he hasn't. And while we are on this point – you must understand that when I lend people money, honestly, the majority of people do pay me back. Often they will try to pay back more than has been arranged, in some way. In fact, that's a very common occurrence. I am always getting big donations when people feel like they have made it big, further down the line!'

'Where does the money come from, Tuli?'

'There's no big mystery. Don't worry.'

'OK, so just tell me then.'

'I'm afraid you can't know everything, Nia.' He stubbed his cigarette out, suddenly spiky with impatience. He walked out of the room then, a shadow marking his face, and it was clear that the conversation was over, she wasn't to follow him.

# SHAN

He checks the address twice when he gets to the apartment block. Tall, wide white stone steps take him to a covered archway at the entrance. It's a much fancier affair than he'd imagined. He had thought that this visit would be to someone in the estate across the other side of the square. Instead, he punches the security code into the aluminium plate on the voice-box and can see his reflection in brass door fittings. He looks at the ground for much of it, is wary of being seen, but assures himself that Tuli wouldn't have sent him if there was any danger of hidden cameras. Sure enough, the giant red door clicks open immediately, leading him into an entrance with majestic ceilings and grand stairs.

Steady, thinks Shan, straightening himself to ascend the levels with a nonchalant look on his face. This preparation means that when he does indeed bump into an elderly gentleman with a small dog on the third floor, he can smile in the light, dismissive manner that is required for this job.

The key fits the lock but when he turns it right and left it is in vain, he cannot get the door to open. Again, he tries and the key just reaches the end of the rotation with a thud. Hard, he pushes it, straining his fingers with frustration and then he stops, suddenly fearful of breaking it. He breathes slowly for a few seconds, wipes sweat from his forehead and then puts it in again.

This time he can feel the satisfying shift of the heavy mechanism, which turns just as it should. Patience is all, he thinks, smiling with relief, he is in!

The woman has a lot of books. His eyes scan the shelves which go the whole length of the walls. Lot of plants, too, some of them on their way to the high, vaulted ceiling, which has a raised, thorny design built into its whiteness, repeating along the border.

Some of the plants are smaller and nestle on the floor amongst their tree-like companions; they are all growing from painted ceramic pots. It must be a 'look', he thinks, because the whole of the living area is arranged to face these rows of books and foliage. The sofa is situated with its back to the window, and has a checked wool blanket folded neatly over it. He looks out of the window and sees the distant tall blocks of flats, repeating themselves in perpetuity against the horizon, so familiar to him now and so different from the one in which he is standing.

He doesn't sit. Instead he checks his watch and goes to open the door of each room, as he has been instructed. Kitchen, bathroom, bedroom. There is no one there. These rooms are immaculately clean, but there are definitely a few signs of life. A recently used teabag in a dish on the kitchen counter. Some fleecy cream slippers on the carpet near the bed, the sole of one is upturned. A newspaper in the toilet, folded on the centre spread.

And then the bell rings.

Here we go, thinks Shan. Come on, man, you can do it.

He stands in the living room with the door open, and the bell goes a second time. A break, and then a third ring, before the key goes in the door.

The man who walks into the hallway is much bigger than he had imagined. He jumps slightly upon seeing Shan, who shudders too, irrationally. Shan is annoyed at himself. He is the one who is prepared, he has been waiting for the guy – why be so jumpy and that?

'Who are you?' The man speaks in a deep voice, cautious and measured. He looks huge to Shan, bulging out of a massive black leather jacket with a silver zip, more than six feet tall at least, and most surprising of all, he is desi, as brown as they come, but he is the Brit-born type, one of those accents, swollen full of condescension. In his right hand there is an orange folder, full of papers.

'I am here for Tuli,' says Shan.

'Oh,' says the man. He pauses. There is the lightest sense of a frown appearing in his forehead. He is quiet as this happens, has a listening face, as though the perplexity will lead him to an understanding of what to do next.

Shan decides to take the initiative.

'Madame Evie is not here,' he says, giving the man a stare that he hopes is quietly confident.

'OK,' says the man.

'You should not enter her apartment with your key.'

'Hmm,' says the man. 'I need to see through her window to the gutter on the back wall. It is for the good of the building, which is my responsibility.'

'No,' says Shan. 'No. You will not come here and threaten her any more.'

'Threaten her?' says the man. 'Threaten her?' He laughs, raises his eyebrows in a mocking fashion. 'You think I have been threatening Mrs Lehman? You are mistaken.'

'No,' says Shan, firmly. 'You have been pressuring her to sign the documents of building works. And it is her decision. She does not have the money to do it. You want to do it? Then you pay for it.'

'Ha! What are you, her guardian angel? Ha!' The man looks Shan up and down as though he cannot imagine why he is having to interact with such a puny specimen.

Shan is suddenly a vat of liquid fury.

'YOU SHUT UP!' he shouts. 'You cannot do it now any more. She cannot sleep, she is not that age to decorate this building, she is trying to live the peaceful life only. You leave her alone. You shut up!'

The man steps right up to Shan and pushes back his shoulders, as if to show that he is dwarfing Shan with the action.

'How dare you,' he says.

'How dare YOU!' says Shan.

'This is between me and her,' says the man. 'She is the freeholder of her flat. It is nothing to do with Tuli, you can tell him that.'

'You have bought all of these freeholds!' says Shan. 'You have been keeping on buying all of the freeholds of this building and you are punishing her because she is the last one, she will not sell it to you.'

'It is her duty to perform the upkeep of the building—'

'NO!' shouts Shan. 'NO. She is seventy-eight years old. You shut up. You should be ashamed of yourself. She is an old lady and you beat her with this again and again so she cannot sleep, she cannot eat, she cannot live happy in her own home alone. You should drown in your own shame. NO MORE. Enough, now.'

He peels away, and pushes past the man to the kitchen, registering the guy's surprise at the sudden movement. When he returns, he has a knife in his hand. It is the first one that his hand could feel, blindly in the drawer. As big as a bread knife but with a smooth edge, the kind you would use for chopping vegetables.

This is power. The man is looking scared. Oh, yes, he is terrified! His little eyes are sinking into his big cheeks.

'What?' Shan says. He just holds it in his hand. Puts his index finger along the line of the blade and says in a very quiet tone, the voice with which you might lull a baby to sleep, 'What it is you are looking at, eh?'

He hears himself speak and stifles a laugh. To some extent, he is modelling himself on Kamal Haasan: otherwise known as Universal Star, *Ulaga Nayagan*, the one and only. The thrilling, contrary, iconic hero – a Tamil legend who has made his name in more than two hundred movies – he is thinking of Kamal when he is about to assassinate Gandhi, or about to beat himself up, play all four identical Kamal quadruplets, or a serial killer, even the film where KH plays a heroin addict who buys his drugs from someone disguised as Ronald McDonald.

Look, Kamal-annan would play this scene by playing with the knife itself, in chilling fashion, and that is exactly what Shan does.

'My God,' says the man, backing away. 'Take it easy.'

His eyes show that he is genuinely fearful, mostly because he believes Shan to be a lunatic. There seems to be no doubt in his mind that Shan is capable of using the knife.

Shan begins a slow nod, stroking the knife all the while. This is pleasure.

'Calm down,' says the man, backing towards the door and opening it. He raises his hands in a placatory fashion, opens his mouth as if to say something, registers the knife once more and thinks better of it.

Once the door is shut, Shan puts the latch on inside and punches the air. His mouth is open, but no sound comes out. He laughs like the loon that the man imagines him to be, noiselessly and with delight. He has done it. For today at least, he has won.

# NIA

'You think I lie?' said the Hungarian, proffering the question with an amiable disinterest and looking over Nia's shoulder at Tuli with such intensity that she, too, turned instinctively to survey the dark familiar shine of his leather trench at the bar, the short ponytail quivering slightly in the dusty atmosphere. He was smoking and looking through the folders, pretending to ignore them. She stared in a kind of attempted companionship, as if she was seeing it all for the first time – the proprietor with his relaxed, magisterial stance.

'OK, I get it. You think I will lie.' The Hungarian nodded, urging her to agree with him. She heard herself continue in an odd, formal voice.

'I'm just saying that it's probably worth forgiving yourself that one lapse—'

'Lapse? What is lapse?'

'I mean that one mistake that any of us is capable of—'

'Yes, a mistake.' He snuffed out her sentence with the same cheery dismissiveness, looking around the room for distraction, wondering when he would be released from humouring her.

She was blushing, she hadn't wanted to say the crap 'any of us could do it' line, but she wanted to make him believe that she was sincere. Nine days since she had promised to speak to him, and inconceivably, the big moment seemed to be slipping through her fingers now that it was here.

'I'm just saying that—'

'You want I lie in the court, yes?'

'Well, I would say more that you think of how to make the best case for custody, and what to leave out, given that you know what is best for your child. I'm saying that . . . that I understand that you are a good father.'

She wasn't beyond hearing and seeing herself the way he might, a nineteen-year-old waitress soothing him in this absurd, condescending fashion. But he didn't react. Just gave her a nod and a couple of high, pinched notes in his throat to signify that she was entitled to her opinion.

'Mmm. Hmm!'

This is how the strange, circuitous dance between them continued, until the Hungarian took his leave, pushing back his chair and whistling upon exit, smiling his goodbyes to Tuli and blowing Ava a kiss as he went through the door. He did not turn to make eye contact with Nia. She watched his departing form, unsure whether his confidence signified guilt or anything at all.

That evening, they had a whole table of lads in from some match up the road and the place was seething with half-cut testosterone. You could pretty much smell their needs, they were so desperately on show – fun, food, flirtation, all before midnight, please – and though it was tiring, it occupied Nia, the whole dance, playing the foil to Ava's fencing stance, smiling through the raucous applause when they were commending her put-downs.

'You need to watch it if you want dessert, mister!' Ava said, when someone tried to snag her attention with the epithet 'Darling!' She rang her words out with a righteous certainty, as if someone had slapped her arse. 'You'll be gone out of this place without tasting "Heavenly Vanilla" on your tongue, can you see it on the menu? And it is very HEAVENLY, by the way.'

'She's right!' Nia said, keeping it simple and upbeat, trying to reduce the time spent at the table. They had never discussed this aspect of work, the way in which they fell into a kind of peppy burlesque double act on these occasions, for the big groups and parties. There were a lot of trigger words to choose from if you were looking: Darling. Angel. Sweetheart. Babe. Baby Doll. Sugar. Pet. And many more. Ava winked at her when she was coming out of the kitchen.

'Playing the big men,' she said, raising her eyebrows. 'They pay their money, they need to play, so what, let them play!'

Tuli was in a non-interventional role, sitting with Patrick on the leather sofas by the bank of windows upstairs for much of the evening, while Ava sweated with her through the steam of the encounter below.

Nia was watching them pretty regularly over the evening, whenever she came up for bubbly or mixers, and the two of them would go quiet whenever she entered the room, as though she was interceding, pushing her way in.

'Well, Nia,' said Patrick with forced cheer when her shift was over, 'what'll you drink, dear?' and she realized from his tone that they were doing business of some sort, and the ideal scenario would be one where she left them to it, rather than stuck around as she usually did.

'You OK?' said Tuli, looking up from a pile of papers to give her a quick nod.

'I'm going to head out,' she said, covering a mild disappointment when he nodded again. It wasn't the end of the world by any stretch, it was just that he was so unreachable when he was like this, and there was nothing you could do about it.

She was going over things in her mind when she left that night, ruminating on her life and how it was going to turn out. That's the only excuse she had for being so distracted.

She was wearing a short skirt, yes, and it was summer, so she was without tights. The mind always goes to the clothes you were wearing. Surely it is the same for everyone. It shouldn't be the case, but it is.

So, the long and short of it was that she realized someone was following her within seconds of turning down one of the alleys from the restaurant.

'Hey!' came the voice, and she ignored it. By this time she thought of herself as well-versed in shaking off this kind of straggling attention. A quick look around, crossing to the side with the street lamp and holding her phone to her ear as though talking to a cohabiting partner. The usual drill.

'I'll be home in about fifteen, love,' she said to an imaginary boyfriend, waiting for her at home. 'Uh-huh. Did you get yourself something to eat?'

Sometimes when she left the restaurant at this time she tied her hair up with a band she kept on her wrist – it was a way of reducing flamboyance, that's how she saw it, but it was not possible to make that move at this point in the scene between them. Still, she kept her cool. She stared up at the filament inside the street light as she passed it, concentrated on the hot amber spiral inside the bulb.

'Hey!' It bounced over the air as she hung up and turned the corner onto a bigger street. In front of her was a phone box, windows taped up with escort cards. Without thinking it through too much, she went in and pretended to make a call, thinking this was an ingenious way to hang back, but of course, he came and stood in the doorway. She knew it was a mistake the second she did it, but it was too late. The way he was looking at her, she could see he recognized her and was waiting for return acknowledgement, meaning he was probably a customer.

'Hello, pretty girl,' he said. He was wearing a shirt that was half-open, chest visible, sweat patches under the armpits.

'Actually I'm done here.' She made a move to leave the booth.

'You're not going anywhere,' he said.

'Let me OUT.' He let her rebound off his chest as she pushed herself against him, threw herself twice against his body. He was tall, strong, lots of muscle. She made no impact on the torso and even as she did it, she thought, how did it come to this? When did it escalate to this? She hadn't even blinked and now they were in battle. Outside, there were cars, somewhere, you could hear them, but hardly anyone audible on the pavement. No one in their vicinity, close enough to see them in that dark cuboid space.

'Look at you, with your legs out and all,' he said.

And then she remembered him. From the corner of the lads' table that night. Low key, but sticky with the eyes. Gruff with the demands for refills, as though he was quietly livid at being ignored by the group, by her and Ava. Or that's how it seemed now.

'You're fucking having a laugh,' he said. 'Look at you.'

She turned her back to him and used her mobile, resting her hand against the big phone installed in the booth. She rang Tuli's number and waited for the answering machine to kick in. Through the glass pane, chopped up by the grid of business cards for topless masseuses, she could see two men walking towards her – young lads, out on the piss.

She whacked on the wall of the booth then, rammed her fist on it so hard and magically, yes, it was open sesame: the huge stubborn form of the guy peeled away from the entrance in seconds. Then: a whoosh of air into her lungs, and a scattergun mania dispersed inside her as she took the breath in.

'He's after me,' she said as she slipped out onto the road, positioning herself as an obstruction on their path. 'He's trapped me in the phone box. Help me. Help me! Help me.' She was half-laughing, the relief was so great, but it had the unfortunate effect of making her seem a little doolally.

He was shouting then as he left the scene, her companion, in that same gruff voice.

'LIAR. BITCH LIAR.'

And just like that, he was gone, *disparu*, off to attend to his business somewhere else.

'You all right?' said one of the boys. Lumberjack shirt, a lot younger than the guy in the phone booth and he was smiling and looking her up and down himself.

'What's your name then, love?' he said, and she saw him looking at her legs too, those fucking bare legs, and she ran. There was nothing threatening about this one, but she couldn't take the sickness that was rising in her. She ran onto the main street, with its weak blare of traffic and light, towards the hope of noise, ran away from them, cursing herself as if in one of those dreams where you suddenly discover that you are naked – those legs, not clothed, were now her whole body, like she had it all for show on her face, two tits for eyes like that famous painting, the one called 'The Rape', her mind hammering it out stubbornly, like she was the only one to ever think these words: *What did you expect, going around dressed like that? Asking for it. You dirty fucking slag.*

# SHAN

Crying, screaming even, silent lips against the front window, her mouth is open as though performing some kind of Halloween joke. It takes his mind a chunk of time to catch up with the visual, some seconds for Shan to realize in horror that Nia is calling for him to open up the restaurant. It is only luck that means he is still here – he has just locked everything in painstaking fashion, abiding by the copious instructions from Tuli, finally preparing to make his way out through the back. He has checked the ovens, the freezers, the essential supplies in the cupboards – all of it with the diligence that is necessary for the last, lone inhabitant of the restaurant each night.

'Thank you,' she says as she falls in through the door, glutinous slivers of tears down her cheeks like the tracks from a snail. 'Thank you. Sorry. Thank you.' She takes an upturned chair from one of the tables and puts it gingerly on the floor. She sits in it, puts her head down between her knees and heaves and heaves.

It takes him a while to offer her a hug. It's not just that he is awkward about being physical, it is the fact that he is of the opposite sex, there is a paralysis that takes place as he hears her story, the shame of being a man. Particularly nauseating is the knowledge that it was a customer, that her job has reduced her to this, and he can't help but feel culpable even though he is not, of course, the boss of this establishment. But how many times from the kitchen even, have they tolerated, encouraged, the over-familiar overtures that come towards the female staff? Awkward smiles, nods, winks of camaraderie when customers get rowdy with Ava and Nia. When Tuli is around he usually steps in if things start looking improper, but which of them in the kitchen would dare to take that role in his absence?

'Don't tell anyone,' she says, over and over again. 'Don't tell anyone.'

Her cheeks look sore, she has blotches of red creeping over her tanned skin, the movement makes her look like she is blushing, expressing an embarrassment which will not fade. The big dark eyes that are usually lost in their own trance of thoughts are turned on him now, darting from side to side as she speaks. It is as though she must tell him everything she is thinking straight away, or she will implode with it.

'I knew it was a mistake, I knew I should have put my leggings on. I shouldn't have taken the shortcut, it was lazy, it's too late for the shortcut. I shouldn't have gone in the phone box. Stupid. Stupid.' Shaking her head and staring at her knees.

It is this persistence, the way that she seems so set on making it her fault, that finally melts his reserve.

'Come on,' he says. 'Stop now, Nia. You are not to blame in this.'

He puts his arm around her shoulder, wipes away her tears with a red napkin and says the only thing that comes to him.

'Want to eat something?'

She nods like a child, a quick shuffle of her forehead, and holds the napkin to her nose.

'Want something different?' he says, using a voice that he has not used for a long time, the voice he would use to soothe a baby, a consolatory, indulgent voice designed for one particular baby, in fact. A Karu-friendly voice. He pats her arm as he speaks. 'Not pizza pasta, hah? Something with some masala in it?'

'Something . . . Indian? Something Sri Lankan?' she says.

'Something Indian . . . Masala omelette?'

Her face breaks into a smile and he quickly thinks through the ingredients. There is some coriander left in the cupboard, he is sure of it. Red chillies for certain. No spring onions but red onions will do the job.

'My father is Indian,' she says, as she eats, tucking her hair behind her ear. 'This is delicious. Thank you.'

'Really?' He does not hide his surprise. It is genuinely the last thing he'd have thought possible. He looks at her face and bends her features to fit this new information. Long, fine nose, the elongated lash ridge above the eyes. Yes, if you were to imagine her darker, he can concede that the same face . . . it had the potential to move in that direction, towards the east coast, maybe.

'Yup,' she says, nodding. 'Bengali. But I don't know him. Never did.' She makes a sharp 'shhh!' sound as her tongue feels the chilli and grins, taking a swig of water.

'Wow.' He shrugs, it is a moment of true amazement for him. 'I did not know this. And your mother?'

'Oh, she's a drunk. An alcoholic!' she says lightly, ribboning the words with a light laugh, watching for the response to come to his face. 'An alcoholic, it's a drug like any other.' He does not know if she is anticipating shock or pity but he gives neither. She lets out a sigh, but her face is too young to be world-weary, the expression slips off it in seconds. It's a lot of information that she is coming out with, but it does manage to do the job of breaking through something between them. Before he knows it, they are exchanging histories and he is telling her about his own family.

'How did you meet your wife?' she says.

'She was part of a group of friends when we were at university. I went to a classical music concert one night back home with some friends and she was there.'

A haunted look comes over Nia's face, as if she has just remembered the incidents of the evening, and it suddenly occurs to him that he has been remiss.

'I should call the boss?' he says, shaking his head at his own ineptitude. 'Sorry, Nia, I should have called straight away.'

'No – don't call him.'

'Why?'

'Just. He has his own life. Don't hassle him with this.'

'But surely . . .' He is not sure how to phrase it. 'Surely . . . you are part of his life?'

She gives him a frown.

'What you mean by that?' she says.

'You are . . .' He struggles, uneasy with the direction that the conversation is taking. 'You are like, how to say . . . with him?'

She bursts out laughing then, in a semi-hysterical fashion, as though he has delivered a wonderful punchline to an absurd joke.

'Oh, no,' she says, beaming. 'I'm not with him like that!'

'OK . . . OK . . .' He beams back at her, not sure why it is funny. 'Ha!' he exclaims, hoping it will relax her.

'What about you?' she says, with a mischievous flare to her eyes.

'Me?'

'You and Tuli?' she says. 'With Tuli? Ha ha, only joking!'

It takes him a moment to understand. He laughs then, right from his belly, and she joins in. Somehow the whole thing is wonderful. It is juvenile and nonsensical and glorious. Every time he catches her eye, they set off again, laughing and laughing, until she is bent over on her chair and the tears start coming out of her eyes once more.

'No, no, Nia!' he says, putting his hand on her arm to steady her. 'Don't cry now.'

'It's just funny,' she says, wiping her right eye, starting off the giggles again as she registers his concern. 'Don't worry!'

'OK.'

He is suddenly aware of the chill in the air. It is very late, must be coming up to one in the morning.

'What about you and Ava, though?' Nia says, raising her eyebrows.

'Ava?' He is blindsided by how direct the question is, was not expecting it.

'Yes, Ava.' She is unapologetic, waits for an answer, bold as anything. Shan looks at her. Initially he is wary, and then, unable to think of anything appropriate, tired of caution and its attendant loneliness, he just comes out with it.

'Well, I actually tried it – we tried it – Ava and I tried it.'

'Did you!'

'For one night only, we tried it.'

'Did you really! Wow, Shan.'

'No, but, what, it was a . . . not good. Very awkward.'

She seems surprised he has confided in her like this, but urges him to continue.

'Actually, I thought my wife was dead, you know? I thought, well, my father got killed, I didn't hear from her for so long . . . Devaki. My wife . . . But she is actually alive, it is so . . . just . . . so thankful I am, but I feel guilty, when she comes here next week – she is coming I can't believe it – how to look at her, I want nothing more than this moment where I see her again but I am ashamed. See, the thing is that Ava didn't really mind at all, you know? She thought it was fine, just friends – not anything like that between us, so I don't know why but I am nervous to face her still, Devaki I mean . . . nervous but desperate to face her . . . to just see her . . . and my son . . .'

And so it goes, into the night, with Shan wet-eyed, untangling his thoughts like this in front of the Brit waitress Nia, who strangely doesn't seem so fully Brit any more, while she sits hunched in her chair, dabbing her nose with the napkin, nodding and encouraging him to say it.

# NIA

She rang Mira the next day when she was between shifts. She didn't want to talk to her about it, but she did want to hear her voice. She was eating her lunch at Vesuvio upstairs, and Tuli was nowhere to be seen. It was a relief to her that she hadn't left a palpitating message on his answering machine, she knew that much. And that Shan had taken his place, been the person to absorb the story, who'd have thought? The revelation of him and Ava. That night of shared confessions, candy-light with comfort, but so much like a dream this morning, until Shan welcomed her with a golden smile when she walked through the portal of the restaurant. This was new, and a confirmation that their paradigm had shifted – him communicating wordlessly with a nod that he was glad to see that she was perkier, less emotionally bedraggled today.

Mira's phone rang for a good thirty seconds before she answered.

'Hello?' she said, with that upward questioning lift that people use when they don't know who is at the other end of the line.

'You can see it's me ringing,' Nia said. 'What's with the formal voice?'

'Are you ringing for a fight?' she said.

'No, plum face, I'm not ringing for a fight.'

She must have heard that there was something doleful in Nia's tone because she asked the next thing carefully, as though she was treading on eggshells, not resentful for once, more like she had to go ahead and do it because it was important, even though it might hurt.

'Are you . . . OK, Nia? I mean . . . on your own there?'

'I'm fine!' Nia said, almost too loudly.

'Seriously, though, Nia, why don't you come and see us?'

'Aw, don't start that again!'

Mira laughed. It was something beautiful to hear. It was a

private reference for them, from the film of *The Jungle Book*, the bit where the vultures sit in the tree and wait for Mowgli. As kids they had watched the film almost every week on a DVD that had come their way. They knew its map of scratches by heart, the moments when it would seize up, sat ready with the remote each time to forward it through the frozen frames on to the next glorious chunk of moving scenes.

'Are you OK?' Nia said, suddenly fearful of the answer, pressing down the rising nausea. Don't say you've been doing the skips, she thought. Don't tell me anything that I can visualize too clearly.

'Yeah, we're good,' she said.

'Really?'

'Really. Mum's got a job.'

'What is it?'

'Driving.'

'For whom?'

There was a pause.

'For Affie,' she said. It was the taxi driver who carried drugs to people on the side. She didn't need to know any more.

'OK then. OK. Are you going to school, by the way?' Nia said, as though it was an afterthought, in the voice of someone who is winding up the conversation.

Another pause, and to be fair, Mira didn't lie just to break the silence. She appreciated that.

'I love you, baby,' Nia said, feeling herself disappear into a sodden quicksand of sentimentality.

'Nia, don't go.'

'Bye, baby,' she said, putting the phone next to her plate and looking long and slow at the remnants of spinach-and-feta parcels, the two olives stuffed with pointed tips of garlic, emerging like Halloween nails from the faded green flesh.

That night she heard herself say these words as she cried.

'Mummy. I'm so tired, Mummy.' Just shaking and saying the word 'Mummy' like a baby.

She knew it was a fantasy that she was calling on – this shape of an imagined mother. She knew how futile it was, and that she was nineteen years of age, too old for this sort of imagining, but no one could see her and so she whispered the word, in all of its baby-ish simplicity, let it go round her mouth like honey. Mummy.

# SHAN

There are six of them, and they move like an army. For a flicker of a moment he realizes that all of them are black, which strikes him as strange when he registers their charcoal uniforms, the plastic visors closing in their faces, sees the blue rectangular patch sewn onto their uniforms and the words 'IMMIGRA-TION ENFORCEMENT'.

He freezes. The tablecloth is tight in his hands, Ava has the other end, and all he can think is, no, no, no, there is nowhere to go, they can see me and I can see them.

'POLICE,' they shout.

He is dressing the table closest to the payment counter, and if he were to drop the cloth and run, it would be nothing less than an overt admission of guilt. He can't look at Ava, for fear of disclos-ing himself through facial expression. Guna is in the kitchen, he thinks. He will have bloody escaped, but I am stuck here like a fucking sitting duck.

No, no, no. Not now, not after everything that has happened. They can't take me away. What was it all for? Not for this.

'EVERYONE STAY WHERE YOU ARE!' shouts one. The lights are reflected in their helmets, they are robots, human machines zipped up in black, walking towards him; he is back in the hell of his nightmares – who is there to protect him now?

'STAY IN YOUR PLACES. NO ONE BEYOND THIS LINE.' Two of them turn and lean over, quickly pasting a zigzag of yellow tape to the door. Another releases the blinds. Shan is scanning them for weapons, he can see two canisters in the hands of the man who is guarding the door. Do they have guns? Knives?

Tuli steps forward. Behind him, Nia is rooted in place, standing right where she was polishing the counter. Like him, she is trying not to move. Only her nostrils, slightly flared, reveal the intensity of her effort.

'Hello there. How can I help you?' Tuli first chooses to address them as though they are customers looking for a nice table. 'Please, do let me know what you are here for?'

'Lu-ci-ana Martinez,' the first man says, reading the name from a booklet in his hands.

'OK,' says Tuli. 'There is no one by that name here.' He is brusque, it is a voice that suggests that they are released from their duties. Everyone can get back to doing more important things, now that this has been revealed to be a mistake.

'We want Lu-ci-ana Martinez,' he says again. He is a bulky man, with broad shoulders and a close-cut hairstyle.

'Pardon? You want who? Is this necessary? This mass of you? Why the helmets? Are you under the mistaken impression that we are armed for some reason? We are a small restaurant, not a drug cartel or Nazi hideout.' Tuli is spitting out the words now, compressed pellets of disgust. Shan finds himself trembling as he hears the sarcasm, he knows that it is covering an anxiety, the man never speaks in this way.

'What is this regarding?' Tuli says. 'Who are you?'

'Lu-ci-ana Martinez,' says the man again, stepping to the side of Tuli and walking over to Nia. 'Show us your passport, madam.'

Nia is provoked out of her silence. She widens her eyes in outrage.

'I'm Welsh. What you gonna do, arrest me for crossing the Severn bridge? I don't carry a passport because I didn't think I was living in a fucking police state.'

Shan stares at them – there are so many of them, all dressed like they are going to war. Oh, but what is this bloody fucking preamble, is it some kind of cruel trick, before they start on the cooks? He tries to make eye contact with Ava now, but she is looking away, furiously attending to the flowers in the vase on the table, folding the cloth napkin and placing the triangle precisely underneath the cutlery. Don't move, Ava, he tries to say with his eyes. These people are dangerous, you don't want to annoy them, you need to stop . . . for all of our sakes . . . but then, how could you know that? He tugs the tablecloth but she won't look up.

'You are from the *immigration* office?' says Tuli, conceivably just loud enough for it to be audible in the kitchen. Shan knows what he is doing. If Guna is still there, well, he'll be gone by now. 'Do you have documents you can show me?'

'We are here to investigate your employees,' says one of them, flashing a paper at him, a half-smile revealing his contempt for the question. The other men discuss Nia amongst themselves. They form a line, blocking her exit.

'She's a bit young,' one of them says. 'But she does look Colombian, doesn't she?'

'For ff . . .' says Nia, holding back the word in her teeth. She chokes as she speaks. 'My name's Ni-a Wa-lker. I'm Welsh.'

'Calm down,' Tuli says, catching her eye.

One of the men who has not yet spoken raises his eyes when he hears her voice. He takes his helmet off and leans against the counter with a thoughtful expression on his face. The man next to him does the same.

'Say something else, darling,' the first man says. 'Keep talking for a bit longer, if you wouldn't mind? Tell me your address if you can.' To his colleagues he says, 'She does sound Welsh, to be fair?'

'Please, do let me know if I can assist you as her employer,' Tuli says. 'I have her passport photocopied upstairs, if you want it. She's British. Shall I get it for you?'

'Ha,' says the other officer. 'Not falling for that one, mate.'

He casts his eye around the room as if wondering whom Tuli is trying to hide.

'I'll go and get the passport then,' says Tuli, disregarding the comment. He walks off towards the stairs and speaks again, almost mimicking his usual courtesy. 'There is no one by the name of Martinez who works here. You have the wrong place. Really, I would love to be able to help you out.'

The first officer moves over with the first bulky guy, and together they block the stairway, standing side by side. They are like chess pieces, thinks Shan, the bitter gourd of revulsion curdling in his stomach and trouncing some of his fear. They move so casually across the board and destroy our lives, just so.

They begin their automated sentences again.

'You must stay down here while we complete our investigation.'

Tuli lets out a sound of frustration, in spite of himself.

'Please!' he says, and then, turning, he does something that Shan has never seen before. The boss shouts, and it is truly terrifying, he feels something give way inside him when he sees Tuli buckle.

'WHY ARE THERE SO MANY OF YOU? IT IS NOT NECESSARY! WHY ARE YOU DRESSED LIKE THIS?'

'Sometimes things get difficult,' the man at the stairwell says, holding his hands up in front of his chest to prevent any further forward movement. 'So we come in a group as a precaution.'

'You can put your hands down. I am hardly going to throw myself against you!' Tuli says, his voice quieter now, but unsteady.

'Look,' comes the reply. 'Think you are special or something? Do you not realize that there are things that we know about you? Sit down and shut up.'

Before Tuli can reply there is a noise at the front door that makes all of them turn. It is the sound of a door slamming.

'TO THE DOOR!' comes a shout from one of them. 'STOP! SUSPECT LEAVING THE PREMISES. STOP NOW.'

Shan turns swiftly and sees that the person disappearing through the front door is Ava, she is no longer with him at his side, fiddling with the cutlery, he is there alone. The yellow tape is curled on the floor, in sticky, ineffective plastic spirals. Everything is confusing him now, his thoughts are blurring as he watches them all bash their way out through the front – those big officers, Tuli caught in the fray of them, pushing his way out too. It is so contrary to his expectation – he can't work out if this is all trickery, some slippery elaborate smokescreen before things finally turn to him.

Now, he thinks – run for it now – through the kitchen and out the back, there is still a chance. Maybe they haven't even noticed him. Maybe he can do it?

But they are all pouring back into the room, they have separated into the conquered and the conquerors. The boss and Ava are being held by the men in their army gear, they are being pulled back into the building. Several of the men are still wearing their visors down, as though they are in the middle of a riot rather than a restaurant. Shan can see the whole of Vesuvio reflected in those plastic jaws, lit up, distorted, bent out of shape.

'Ava,' Tuli says. 'Ava. Officer. Let me speak to her. Ava, just one second. Tell me. Tell me!'

'Mister, you need to let us do our job,' comes the response from one of the men. 'Miss. You need to stay with us.'

'YOU SHOULD BE ASHAMED!' Tuli hurls the words hard at them, rains them down like shells from a tank, the rage is throttling him now, he is breathing in a sordid, ragged way.

'ASHAMED OF YOURSELVES. WHAT DO YOUR MOTHERS THINK OF THE WORK YOU DO? LOCKING PEOPLE UP AS IF THEY ARE VIOLENT CRIMINALS?'

Tuli lifts his hands up, but his arms are still locked in the grasp of the two men who are with him. For a brief, hideous moment, Shan wonders what the boss is going to do with those hands. Don't let this go that way, he thinks. Please, no. No. No. No. These men, you don't realize, they will overpower us. They have come from the government, the logo is all over them, they think they are invincible, that is how these people see themselves. Someone has told them that they are the good guys, like those superhero films, where the audience is instructed to cheer for each and every violent act committed in the name of freedom.

Ava is looking at the ground, her hazy pastel-tinted hair falling in obstruction over her face. Five feet high, she is, if that, but five men stand around her in a circle, two of them locking her wrists together with steel now and pushing her down onto a chair. She looks up at Shan and her eyes tell him all he needs to know.

# NIA

Nia could see from Tuli's face, as they put the cuffs on Ava, that it was as much of a shock for him as it was for her and for Shan. The three of them were united by the slow descent of understanding. Tuli's face had collapsed, he couldn't do anything about it, Ava kept nodding miserably whenever the officers asked her a question, even though they all wanted her to stop. Every time she moved her head in assent, Nia could see Tuli flinch.

'You are Luciana Martinez?'

'Yes.'

'You are here illegally without a visa?'

'Yes.'

'You came into the country how exactly?'

A gulp, and then silence. Those green eyes, staring up at Tuli and then back down to the floor. His face was grim, one-dimensional, now that he had regained a measure of control.

'We'll need you to come with us, Miss Martinez.'

An almost immediate intervention, then, from Tuli.

'Where is she going?' he said. 'You have to tell us. Where you are taking her!'

'We don't HAVE to tell you anything, sir. PLEASE SIT DOWN.'

'She has the right to representation,' Tuli said.

Ava waved her hand.

'No. I don't want to go through it all, Tuli. Is finished. I'm tired. Is over.'

'How did you come into the country?' came the question again.

'In back of a lorry.'

'When did you come?'

'One year five months since now.'

'How do we appeal?' Tuli said again. 'Where is she going? What is the protocol to speak to her there? Will she have her phone?'

The questioning officer ignored him. A small movement passed through the line of men behind him – as though preparing to pull together and restrain him if things were to turn difficult.

'Can you confirm that you have been using a stolen passport, issued in Madrid and belonging to Ava H. Amada,' the first officer said.

She buried her head then, in her hands, and started trembling, her nutty arms so lean and small in that sleeveless shirt she always wore. Nia knew she could not reach her, the circle of guards around her was impenetrable. It seemed crazy to watch her life atomize in front of them like this – Shan was just standing there with his mouth open, frozen in one spot. Tuli wasn't going to her either.

'To repeat. You have been using the stolen passport of Ava H. Amada, issued in Madrid?'

She nodded again, and with that one swoop of her small elegant head, bathed in grey softness, Nia could see Tuli's heart break just a little.

'Ava H. Amada reported the theft of her passport six months ago – is it true that you were living with her at this time? She was your flatmate in Enfield, is that correct?'

'Please, if you could bear with me for one minute,' Tuli said, finally. He stood up and three men went to him immediately, he had hands on his arms and shoulders within seconds.

'Please,' he said. 'We can do this in a civilized manner. I just want to get a piece of paper, a pen. PLEASE.'

There was a muttering between a couple of them, and then one of them eventually produced a pen for him. Tuli took a leaflet from his pocket and began writing on the back. 'This is my number, Ava, if you don't have your phone,' he said. 'Ring me as soon as you can.'

She took it, but she was just shaking her head now, biting her lip, sitting in that chair, her eyes brimming but no tears falling.

Nia was staring at Tuli as they walked Ava out onto the road.

There was an officer pressing in on either side of her tiny frame, someone had untied her apron and left it on the chair. Tuli was standing at the door. He pressed his fingers to his forehead and dragged them down his cheek, he was going over it bit by bit. Where and when had he been duped, how had it got past him? He would have registered that passport of hers with HMRC, like he had done for Nia – national insurance, PAYE – the whole deal. It wasn't just that he could have helped her if he'd known, it was much simpler than that. Surely he was also angry at her, at being hoodwinked. He simply couldn't accept the betrayal. Why wouldn't she have confided in him like the rest of them? He sat down in a chair by the counter, his tall body diminished, head bowed, and closed his eyes.

There was silence for a good few moments after they left. Nia and Shan stood in the emptiness looking at each other.

'Boss . . .' said Shan, finally. His voice was a whisper.

Tuli opened his eyes, moved his lips.

'Don't worry, Shan,' he said, sighing. 'Don't worry.'

'Boss, you want a drink . . .' Shan said. 'Water?'

Tuli shook his head. He took his phone out and began searching through the numbers.

'Boss . . .' said Shan, swallowing tensely. 'Will they come back, you think?'

Tuli looked up, a little jolted, as though he had just remembered something.

'Shan – of course – you just leave now – obviously. Sorry. I was just trying to remember the name of this lawyer . . . Sorry. Look, it's very unlikely they will come back but obviously just leave now, lah? Guna has gone, I heard the back door go when they came in. So I think it's just you, so go now?'

Shan moved his head in acquiescence and began walking to the kitchen.

'Listen, we'll talk about it later, Shan,' Tuli said, getting up and putting his arms on the guy's shoulders. 'But just quickly. If that happens again – you're here to pick up the trade, yes, remember?

You're not being paid, obviously – your applications are in for asylum, all that as we discussed, and you're here just learning how things work in a restaurant while you wait. It's the *plausible defence*, remember? Everybody needs a *plausible defence*. That's ours – just picking up the skills, I'm just giving you something to do, you're passing the time, that's all.'

'Yes, boss,' said Shan. He disappeared through the back and it was just the two of them left. Tuli sat at the table by the bar, and began rapidly going through his phone again. Nia didn't know what to do. She still had the can of polish in her hand. The place was so silent. Something had happened which could not be revoked. A razing of Ava's existence here, in these few seconds.

'I can't believe it,' Nia said, finally, awkward with the words, but unable to just leave him there without saying something.

'Can't believe what?' Tuli said, still looking at his phone.

'That she's illegal. Ava. I just mean . . . it's a shock. She has another name, another identity—'

'I need to talk to her,' said Tuli, still focused on the phone, as though it might ring in his hands at any second.

'Yes, I know. But I mean – she's admitted it, she was nodding when they asked her, Tuli—'

'I need to talk to her,' he said, flicking his eyes up briefly at Nia. 'Otherwise we are just sitting here bitching and that never helps.'

'Are you OK?' Nia said. 'It must be a shock for you, Tuli—'

He made a sound of exasperation and lifted the phone, suddenly, as though he had made a decision to call someone.

'What a fucking stupid thing to do,' he said. 'Above all, this whole thing is just stupid. What was she thinking? I need to talk to her.' It was as though he had forgotten that Nia was in the room. He was fighting to regain control of the situation.

'She took someone's passport,' Nia said.

'Yes. And that person can get a passport again very easily. In fact, I guarantee you that she already has one by now. It's a disruption, yes, a small disruption of a couple of weeks and about seventy-five pounds. She shouldn't have just taken it, is the thing.

I mean, it's a stupid move, she should have just asked her flatmate directly instead. That would have been much better. Of course. Then they could have done it together.'

He dialled the number and held it to his ear, used the other hand to get a pack of cigarettes out from his jacket and propel a single orange-tipped stick of white out onto the table.

'Hello?' he said, lighting up and pulling hard on the fag, blowing the smoke out sidelong, as though playing a mouth organ. 'Sriharan? It's very urgent. Thank you, man.'

# SHAN

He is never going to see her again. The journey home has a funereal, sombre quality about it, but he has to undertake it – what else is there to do? There is no point making a drama about it. He is too proud to suggest that he sleep in the flat above the restaurant today, when there is no formal reason – he is not even doing an extra job for Tuli. Some of them are a little jumpy in there, after today's events, but he could do with being around the seamy familial warmth of the other cooks tonight, instead of being alone. Those smells mixed up into body odour – cinnamon, black pepper and cigarettes. He covets their cosy familiarity, the cycles of prodding and debate. He could be sitting on one of their mattresses, talking about Devaki and Karu rather than getting confused by all this wasteful emotion he is feeling. He could even be celebrating his own narrow escape – not one officer looked back at him upon leaving the restaurant – imagine? If they return, I'm ready for them, he would say, if he was in the flat above Vesuvio. I know their drill now.

Instead, he is thinking of her. There is no point in texting Ava, everyone knows that once you are in custody you don't have access to your phone. They will have taken her to get essentials from her home, on the way to the detention facility, and then, tomorrow or within a couple of days, she'll be gone. It's probably the place that is close to Heathrow and she is one of those inside who are listening to the planes overhead, wondering which shrieking machine will be for her. Like she said, it's over.

What are the pieces that go to make a person? How many of her anecdotes were true? A family of grey-haired Colombians running a hair salon in Cartagena rather than Valencia? A sister trying to leave her beating husband in Bogotá, maybe? A childhood drowning accident in the Atlantic Ocean rather than the Mediterranean Sea? Or it could all be made up, every last mesmeric twisting part of her history. Scheherazade, plaiting words to prolong her life?

There is no way to fit her together, and now she is gone, taking that beautiful, metal-studded smile with her.

Who is he to her, after all? What are they to each other, what *were* they to each other? Not the fabled mingling of red earth and pouring rain, that is for sure. *Luciana Martinez.* He says the name once, lets it resonate through his mouth, in all of its exotic strangeness, and attempts to discard it from his mind.

He hasn't seen the boy for a while. Somehow, he almost doesn't recognize him. Where have you been? Shan wants to ask of the mother, as the two of them come towards him at the crossing the next morning. The traffic is as it has always been, the soft-cheeked man in his wheelchair goes by still, the huge trees of deep green, fanned out like gigantic feather dusters, the high stacks of shoebox flats and their railings – it is all identical, but when he gets closer he sees that something is off-key. The boy is in an argument with his mother, he is not sailing past on his scooter, instead the mother is pulling him along with a kind of silken braid that she has tied to the handlebars. The boy's face is pale, creased up, unhappy. He drags his little foot with anger so that it scuffs along the ground under threat of damage.

'Why won't you just put your foot on the scooter?' says his mother, the frustration submerging her words so that she trembles as she speaks. 'We're going to be late.'

The boy shakes his head, keeps his foot on the ground, harder now, so that they can't move forward.

'Baby, stop it!' says the mother. 'This is not OK. What am I supposed to do?'

'Carry me,' says the boy.

'No. Your legs work fine, you can do this. Come on! Don't make me angry!'

'No,' says the boy. 'No cars, no road, no people, no lights, no pavement, no . . .' 'Pee-pole' for people in his rounded accent. He looks around and adds on some more things in his vision.

'No trees! No sky! No bicycles! No lamp posts. No nothing. No nothing!'

He starts crying. She crouches down.

'What's wrong?' she says.

He coughs – a long, staggered chesty cough that makes him retch slightly, so that Shan worries he might vomit. Then he astounds Shan by going again, in his flute-like glissando of a baby voice so that it sounds out like the simplest poem in the world:

'No cars!

No birds!

No road!

No diggers!

No nothing.

No nothing!'

Tears are slipping out of his eyes as he says the words, his face is so small that they slip right off his jaw into the unknown.

'You won't listen. You carry me!' he says. 'Carry me or I'm going to do no people again, I'm going to say no people, no nothing.' He gives her a tragic look – threat mixed with pain and tears – and she picks him up, crosses at the traffic lights the second they change, dangling his scooter off her right arm.

What a verse, thinks Shan. A stance of clean protest. No nothing! Bravo, he thinks, well done, little boy, although there is undeniably a melancholy dissolving into his spirit and clouding him up like aspirin in a glass as he gets his free newspaper and doubles back to the bus.

# NIA

In the days that followed, she imagined that only something as dramatic as a flock of birds, let loose into the quiet of the restaurant, could dispel the thick cogitating darkness that hung over them all. An intervention from the world beyond – a vast murmuration of songbirds, fluttering and warbling away their fears – that was what they needed, to look up from their tables and forget themselves. Even when customers were there, the atmosphere was subdued. Tuli was withdrawn and coiled up in himself. Shan spoke even less than him, and the cooks had dampened down their banter in the kitchen. It felt like bad taste to smile or joke or even comment on the food, when the world outside had revealed itself to be so hostile; only a fool would relax after being reminded of this.

# SHAN

The waiting has quickly become like a cling film over his daily life. He can see through it, he can conduct himself as necessary, he can even breathe through the small hole of hope in it, he has to, but all feeling is preserved, visible but inaccessible. Sometimes he begins an hour and he thinks, already I have just done only thirty seconds, there are still more than fifty-nine minutes to go. I could get through the next three minutes and there would be fifty-six minutes. And so on, with a kind of semi-suffocated automation as he looks each day at the large clock on the kitchen wall. The chopping continues, the kneading of dough, the freezing of ingredients. The vanity of sweat left on a forehead, not wiped away, just there in defiance, as evidence. Evidence of what? That he is going through pain? He does not have an end date for Devaki's arrival with Karu, or the chance to talk to her. Does he want everyone to know his hurt? Would that make it better?

The cooks are tiring of his distance, he almost misses the old interrogations. And chess with Ava is a distant memory. The conversations with her are the ones that he does miss, he must accept it: no more Ava. But the biggest surprise of all, there is Nia. And how different it is, in some ways a relief, to exchange a few friendly words with her now and then without implication or need.

'Why you checking your phone so often?' she says, balancing plates as she goes through the doors of the kitchen, giving him a big smile, full of a welcome cheekiness, like a niece teasing her uncle, treading the boundary wall of his irritation. 'You'll drive yourself crazy, Shan, man! Come on, give yourself a break.'

And in return he smiles, gives her a nod of agreement in the shape of a figure of eight and tells her not to worry, welcomes the interruption, the way it eats up a few seconds, takes him out of himself so that when he returns to counting the minutes that are left, there are fewer of them, and in that shortening of time, he can countenance a kind of hope, a trust that it will be OK, all OK.

Hawala, hawala, hawala, he says to himself under his breath, repeating the word as though he is counting rosary beads or chanting Allah, drenched in the same insanity as religious believers, making his own raft from it, one that is strong enough to keep him afloat.

They are in the local church, bagging up packets of pasta for sixteen different food boxes, when the words come out of him without preparation.

'I can't take it any more, boss,' Shan says finally to Tuli, who is ticking off a list of goods. 'Can you ring him, please. He'll answer the phone if you call.'

Around them, green-shirted volunteers throng the aisles and pews of the church. Everyone is busy, engaged in the production line that is the weekly food distribution: happy-seeming and fulfilled in the moment. Shan is in favour of it all, truly – he can feel the majesty of the place with its high slanting ceiling and peaceful glass murals, stained with the colours of boiled sweets. The people around him are radiating the same kind of light that reflects off their idols, but instead of sculptures frozen in mother–child moments of familial tenderness or guru–disciple benevolence, these guys are doers, bathed in the joint glow of group action, the satisfying, practical build of all these food boxes.

Today, though, he can't shake the pothole memories of his journey to this country, the ones he doesn't allow very often. They mostly centre on smell. Crammed into the back of a van, no windows, overpowering human sweat for hours. Sleeping on a towel on a toilet floor in Hungary, the unholy stench of it. His mind transposes Devaki to these situations, puts her in without concern for her dignity. Karu is not in these images. He can't help but think the worst today.

'Boss, sorry to ask . . .' he says, uncertainly. 'I just . . . can't keep waiting . . . you know? It is too much for me. And he doesn't answer when he sees my number. The agent, this guy "Pran" . . . he ignores it — but I think he will answer if it is your number because . . .'

He trails off. In the distance he can see a familiar face. It's the man he followed on his salmon-stealing trip for the butcher. Standing in line with at least fifty other people, there is a white woman who has covered her head with a scarf in front of him. Presumably she has done this out of embarrassment at coming here for food boxes, as she is also wearing sunglasses indoors. The man seems shorter some-how, squat, less confident in his movements. As he inches along, Shan can see his right hand shaking a newspaper as though it is a musical instrument or a fan. It looks like the same free newspaper that Shan himself reads on the way to work.

He turns back to Tuli.

'Boss, when he sees your number he will answer . . .' He doesn't want to say what they both know — that the agent will surely take the call immediately because Tuli is a source of business. This Pran character will have marked up Tuli's number as important, like everyone else in the man's orbit.

Tuli puts down his clipboard and places both hands on Shan's shoulders. There is no indication of what the boss is about to say, which way the dice will fall. The man is calm as anything, in spite of not being allowed to smoke in the church, although he does disappear every now and then to smoke outside, returning with a very mild tobacco scent on his person that is pretty much his per-manent smell. Behind one ear, a pencil points backwards at his ponytail. He seems very tall to Shan in this moment. Imposing, with his rolled-up black shirtsleeves and gentle, assured smile. Trying to keep things light, even though he holds Shan's life in his hands, that is how it feels.

'Shan, of course,' he says. 'Give me five minutes and we can do it.'

Five minutes! Why in hell didn't he ask him sooner? He is almost tempted to touch the man's feet as though they were back home, throw himself down in that old-fashioned gesture of gratitude, respect, servitude, whatever you want to call it, but he knows it is not appropriate, it would freak the guy out. Shan shakes, trembles with frustration at his own pride as he continues to stack each of the sixteen boxes. His eyes well up suddenly. Why didn't he ask him sooner? So many nights are now routinely devoid of sleep because he can't talk to Devaki. He still hasn't spoken to his son. Enough, he thinks, for fuck's sake, get it together. Just focus on the next steps. Concentrate, man. Don't screw this up.

There is a show he has seen on the television they have in the flat above the restaurant. *Who Wants to be a Millionaire*, it's the same programme that Bachchan hosts in India they say, maybe there will be a version of it in Sri Lanka one day too, who knows. There is a moment in each round where the contestant can phone a friend and ask for advice on the answer. When he watches the show in the flat, Shan is often overcome with a strange feeling of envy at the ease with which the contestant can just pick up a phone and ring a friend, get some advice, make a joke even. Know that he or she is not alone. It all looks so easy.

The similarity makes him smile right now, as Tuli nods before dialling the number, asking for a green light to proceed from Shan. They are sitting in the office of the church, the one that belongs to Patrick, located up a flight of carpeted steps, orange-pink, like farmed trout, at the back of the building, past a friendly receptionist who gives them the keys. The windows are large, the ceiling high, and so there is a lot of light in the room. Tuli sits on a small sofa, Shan is on a swing chair at the desk, which is dark wood, the surface nailed with a rectangle of green leather.

'Ready?' says Tuli. He is not playing it in the way of the TV show, not escalating the drama for the camera. Far from it, he seems very aware of the possibility of disappointment and is balancing this knowledge carefully, like an earthenware pot of water that must not fall.

'Boss, I know he might not pick up,' says Shan, wanting to re-assure him. 'I just want to try, you know? Just see in case.'

'Yes. OK, Shan, what are we going to say to him if he does pick up? You want to speak to him straight away?'

'No . . . no . . . It is better if you speak to him.' Shan stands up and goes over to the desk. It is very clean and ordered. He can see a stack of writing paper in the plastic jaw of a printer in one corner. Next to it, a small ethnic pencil pot in marble, red petals of a flower pressed into the side. A piece of paper on top of the printer proclaims, 'REFUGEES MARCH FOR JUSTICE!' Beneath the headline there is a list of dates and locations.

He picks up a pen. 'Shall we do it like this? I can write a question for you to ask?'

'Good idea!' says Tuli. 'OK, so what do we want to ask? In an ideal world. What do we want to know? Your top three questions?'

Shan takes a sheet of plain paper from the printer and writes a list in capitals:

1. WHEN SHE WILL GET HERE AND WHERE
2. WHERE SHE IS RIGHT NOW WITH SON
3. WHY I CAN'T SPEAK TO HER
4. HOW TO MAKE HIM ANSWER MY CALLS
5. I WANT TO SPEAK TO MY SON

'Four questions,' he says, handing the paper to Tuli. 'One demand.'

'OK,' says Tuli. 'Very good.'

They begin the call on speakerphone as planned but very quickly the man Pran asks for this aspect to be rectified. He speaks with a galling lack of urgency, in a drawl that is full of pauses.

'Yeah . . . I can hear myself,' he says. 'The phone. Put it on your ear.'

Shan groans inwardly. It's a mistake to make an agent suspicious. They are self-protecting leeches, transferring allegiance at the first hint of threat, disappearing to suck blood from another body without a second thought. But Tuli is adept at bringing things round, and soon his charm seems to have oiled the wheels of communication so that he is actually smiling on the phone and murmuring assent, after presenting Devaki's full name to the guy, Shan's name too, giving him a timescale and jogging his memory with the mention of Tavan.

'Devaki Devar, thirty-one with the mole on the—' says Tuli. 'Yes, right. Uh-huh. I see. Yes. OK.'

And then the call is over, and Shan can barely believe that the boss has let it end so quickly. But he can see Tuli writing down an address.

*Cardiff West service station M4 junction 33. 4 August. 9.30 p.m.*

'Calm down,' says Tuli when he hangs up. 'He wants us to meet him.'

'No!' says Shan. 'It just will waste more of the time.' A fist is scrunching up his heart like a piece of useless paper. He can barely contain himself. There is too much to lose. 'Boss, ring him back and tell him – boss—' He reaches out to pick up Tuli's phone which is lying on the sofa next to him.

'Shan, listen, just listen. He says he has them coming to him tomorrow,' says Tuli, putting his hand up to halt the intensity of the outstretched hand with phone. 'And he says he will try to bring them to us by the time we meet.'

'What? What is he meaning that he has them coming to him?'

Tuli looks pensive. A frown has formed between his eyebrows, and Shan cannot, for the life of him, work it out. The stasis in the man's delivery is suffocating. Should they be celebrating or what? How do people wait through these things? How do people live their lives when they are waiting? he thinks. What is the rule-book, the model? They have no choice, that is how the living happens. He feels a sudden dizziness, as his own lack of power comes to the forefront of his mind.

'And we find out like this, like we find out by chance? What does he mean, he has them coming?'

'Just that, presumably,' Tuli says, carefully repeating his words so that they are exactly the same. 'That he has them coming to him . . . and he will try to bring them to us . . .' He pauses, and says the remaining words almost to himself, with a question in his voice, revealing that he is also attempting to decipher it. '. . . by the time we meet?'

'What does it mean — they got the money then? They are releasing her? Where he wants to meet?' Shan's words roll on top of themselves, a motorway pile-up that renders them meaningless. 'What does it mean . . . why . . . where . . . he wants to meet? Does he?'

Tuli shakes his head, still with the frown. He knows something isn't right.

'Shan, just give me a second, let me think about this, lah? He wants to meet here.' He presents the paper with the address on it.

'When?'

'Tomorrow.'

'What! Where is it?'

'It's . . . about two and a half hours from London, maybe three . . . by car . . . in south Wales . . . '

'But . . . but . . . so soon?'

Tuli nods again, letting his discomfort show more easily.

'But, boss, why isn't it good?' says Shan, jumping up and shaking his hands in the air. 'He has Devaki and Karu and he says to meet him tomorrow, and you speak like this, so . . . so . . . why is this not a good thing? What else has he said that makes you be so . . . so . . . '

'Wary?' says Tuli, putting his hand up again and showing Shan his palm.

Even before he replies, Shan knows the answer. He sinks back onto the sofa.

'Because you don't believe him,' he says to Tuli, looking him directly in the eye.

'It's not that. It's more . . . we don't know him. Tavan doesn't know him. I'm just thinking . . . why so quick? Why tomorrow?'

It makes sense. Shan concedes. He hears himself spelling out his own fears and lets them mingle with those he can feel coming off the boss.

'Yes . . . why didn't he call us, this is it, yes . . . '

Tuli frowns again, lets another maddening pause enter the conversation. They sit in the stillness and wait together.

'It is more that I wonder why the request has been met like this,' says Tuli finally. 'Why it is so . . .'

'Easy?' says Shan, nodding, feeling relief now that they are talking openly. 'Why is it so straightforward? We ring and he has them, as if it is magic, and he is ready to give them to us in just twenty-four hours. Why has he been ignoring my calls? This Pran fellow. Why didn't he phone you at least?' He looks at the piece of paper with his final demand scrawled in what now seems to be a childishly naive set of capitals.

I WANT TO SPEAK TO MY SON.

Thinking back, Tuli's tone on the phone had been almost deferential. There was not the sense that he could have made this demand for Shan. Indeed, could he have made it for anyone? A slithering unease takes hold of Shan. The boss is not in control, or what? He is finding his way through the dark just like Shan?

'Yes,' says Tuli, 'why didn't he call me . . . but it's entirely possible that he could be completely for real. That's the thing, you see. There is always the chance that things are exactly as they seem.'

He looks up at the high ceiling and stares at it, eyes creased in concentration. Shan remembers where they are, in a place that many would consider to be God's house. For the first time he wonders, as he watches Tuli, whether the man is actually a believer – it has not occurred to him before, even though Tuli of course goes around with Patrick and frequents this church. Somehow, to connect Tuli's whole enormous approach to the world, his compassion and generosity in giving that sum of money to Shan, even – to connect it to those models of Jesus Christ and his disciples downstairs, frozen in such placid virtue – would be to diminish it. There is so much more to the man. He is not some property developer, booking his place in heaven.

'But what is the routine? Does Tavan normally call you when he does it?' says Shan. 'Tavan, when he brings people over for you, does he call you to let you know or you always have to call him? When you do this kind of thing for others?'

This time, the expression on Tuli's face as he looks for the words is genuinely alarming. Oh, God, Shan thinks. No.

No.

Shan screws up his eyes and lets his head hang against the bar on the back of the chair so that his face is the one that is now turned to the ceiling. He should have known. Think about it. The man is too nice. All those different forms and loans, the free legal help, the pizzas for pimps and addicts, that bag behind the bar with the brown notes floating in it like feathers from a mother duck. The cigarettes, the money, Ava, Rajan, Guna – what all he has seen Tuli doing – all of it is minuscule, small fish fry of risk compared to this bloody fearful task of getting Devaki and Karu here alive and free. Why did he ever think otherwise?

He doesn't open his eyes. More pothole images of his journey come at him now: his face against the engine of a motor in France, the heat of the metal burning him whenever his cheek brushes against it. Sitting in rows on the boat, all those men without their phones, unable to stand and shake off the nausea of the sea. And then, the stories that he doesn't read, the worst are in the paper – the one where a hundred men, women, children were stabbed and thrown over the side into the water by the men in charge because of an accident with petrol fumes. All to prevent them coming up on deck where they might be seen. He knows well this kind of story, even though he avoids it. By the time you avert your eyes from the headlines it is too late, the information has already gone in.

Devaki and Karu have only one more leg to their journey, they won't be on a boat, surely. So why is he thinking of these things?

Still, he knows one fact for sure – it is up to him now.

# NIA

Mira and Nia knew enough about their fathers to not pursue them. Of course, they turned up in fantasy – Nia's with his doctor's bag, placing his hand on her forehead during the sudden swamp of a temperature, tucking her up in a high single-bed unit, with a desk beneath it, a goose-down quilt too, naturally. For Mira, who knows, they hadn't discussed her own private version of this imagining for a long time, but when she was little, she'd talk about going to the Disneyland in Paris, sat on her father's broad shoulders like the kids in the adverts, so that she was towering up there, cheek to cheek with a big old Minnie Mouse or Goofy on stilts. Nia remembered being secretly pleased she hadn't gone for Butlin's, thinking that it placed them a cut above, this sign of discernment in her six-year-old sister's daydreams.

But in reality, they were in agreement that their mother didn't welcome the questions they had, and that there was no point in turning up the volume – they were looking for a quiet life, after all, and if they were the products of one-night stands conducted in a spirit of merriment and free-living then who were they to start reading too much into it all? Besides, if you were to contemplate the fact that they had different fathers, really get deep into it, there would be no way to join them up as tightly as they needed to be, once you started poking around. Nia often thought that they both didn't want to know too much for that reason as well.

It was pretty quiet in the restaurant when the woman came in. She was petite, with a dark-haired bob, very put-together would be the phrase – navy blazer and jeans with a crisp wide-collared white shirt. Maybe somewhere around thirty. Nia was surprised to see her come up the stairs – it was a reminder that they had basically left the place unmanned downstairs, no one receiving guests, even though the cooks were in and out of the kitchen. Probably one of them had sent her up.

'Hello there,' Nia said. 'Can I help you?'

And then she saw it on her skin. Right up in the sac below the left eye. A small cut, but a painful one, the kind that has spread redness to the penumbra below it like the physical, inky leak of a secret, an unwanted revelation. A black streak in a red scab about a centimetre long – tiny slit – hardened and shouting blue murder at her once she realized who she was, this woman.

'I am looking for Mr Tuli,' she said in one of those generic English voices: class-less, accent-less and as well-constructed as her outfit. It takes one to know one, thought Nia, and she could tell straight away that the woman had done a good ironing job on whatever her original creasing would have been.

'He's not here,' Nia said, loath to look at the woman directly. She took the notepad from her apron. 'Shall I . . . do you want to leave a number and I can ask him to ring you?'

Nia looked up, she was staring in spite of herself. There was no black eye, just this tiny slit and the red soreness beneath – she could have taken a razor to her face, Nia was thinking, and done this herself? But what was the benefit to her in taking such a drastic measure? To show Tuli that he had made a mistake? Really? She kept looking from the top of her cheek up to the eyes, which gave nothing away, surveying her face as though it was a piece of fruit. The woman smiled, watching Nia's nervousness with what seemed to be a kind of pleasure. Nia examined her even more closely. Was it a vindictive smile? But why was she thinking this way? Why was she so reluctant to believe that he could have hit her again? Men hit women the world over; what was this in her, that she couldn't accept what was in front of her eyes?

'No, he knows how to get my number,' the woman said. 'He can get it from Latvo. Tell him to call me as soon as possible.'

So it was definitely her, then. That was his name. The Hungarian. And this was his famous wife. Nia watched her walk away, dignified and straight-backed, that glossy bob curling under at her neck, you could almost see the cylindrical hairbrush in its blow-dried shape. Had she come to ask Tuli and Patrick to stop helping him? She turned to look at Nia once from the bottom of the stairs, as if to check that she was still watching.

After she left, Nia thought about her mother, how she had walked into so many doors, the many black eyes and bruises she had accrued over time. She should have been an expert on whether this was self-inflicted and yet, now that she was here, the Hungarian's wife, right in front of her, not just an idea but real, she was more uncertain than ever.

# SHAN

The boy is on the bus, seated in some kind of pushchair for which he is too big, and Shan is startled to see him as he presses his card against the payment pad near the driver.

Even though it has only been a matter of a week, ten days since Shan last saw him, the boy's face has faded immeasurably, there are dark circles bludgeoned over his eyes and the lids sag with fatigue. To see him is to see something fearful; there are still remnants of the balletic child sailing past on his scooter – the curly mass of hair, the long lashes – but it is as if the rest of him has been soaked in bleach; he is not the child of Shan's memory and the dissonance is upsetting, it makes Shan stop in his tracks, so that people queue up behind him, disgruntled.

At the base of the kid's neck there is a plastic tube taped against his skin that disappears into a small fabric pouch on his chest, gypsum yellow, printed with bumble bees, half-hidden under his tracksuit jacket.

The mother looks up and recognizes Shan.

'Oh, for fuck's sake,' she says, spitting out the words as though they are an inevitable outcome of seeing him. She too has degenerated in some way. Much like her boy she is a parched, discoloured version of herself. Oh, God, thinks Shan. The poor woman. Something terrible has befallen her, she seems so alone, so pulverized by circumstance.

'What the fuck you looking at?' she says, hurling the words at Shan so that there is no way he can pretend to himself that they are meant for someone else. Still, she looks so choked, there is so much of desperation in her eyes that it stops him from absorbing her words at first. 'I've seen you, always looking at him. You're always fucking looking at my kid!'

The boy coughs, a feeble repetition of muffled sounds, holds his hand up to his mouth in a half-hearted plea to his mother.

Her voice wobbles, raises itself up the steps of her anger and cracks with anguish.

'Fuck you,' she says to Shan. 'Fuck you. Hospital is a fucking nightmare, I fucking waited for two hours. Because of you people. That's right – you people. Just fuck off home, stop looking at us. Always looking at us, always bloody staring.'

The humiliation is instantaneous. He feels it pour in through an incision in his chest. He averts his eyes, presses the red stop button on the bus again and again, as the crowd growls and complains behind him, presses it till the driver makes the back doors open so he can get off, his eyes holding the tears in the way that you hold your breath when you are underwater, containing the swell until there is no one near him and then he is running down the street back to his room, the salt water already on his cheeks in rivulets of shame.

You're right, he thinks, I have taken something from you by living here, and simultaneous, in dream, like hands closing round a neck in threat, pressing as if they might close off the cord of breath, shut things down so fast, he thinks . . . but I can live too. If I live, does it really mean you will die, lady? If my boy comes here, my small tiger cub, my baby son, does it mean that your sweet boy will die? What if my boy had died there, lady, in my country? What then?

And still, as he runs, nonsensically, there is the image of himself and his loved people, ants swarming over a carcass, tiny filthy maggots coming out of this poor woman's mouth.

He takes his breath like a dog, he hyperventilates and waits for it to pass. His heart is a traitor, an informant battering at the door in psychosis, threatening to destroy him.

Well, I will live, he thinks, crushing his teeth together so hard that there is a ringing in his ears. I decide to live, lady. Whatever it takes.

# NIA

She was bursting with the words, she had rehearsed a selection of one-line openers in her head several times:

'Tuli, listen, the Hungarian's wife came into the restaurant and . . . I don't know if we were right to do it.'

Or:

'Tuli – I think he's hit her again, the Hungarian. There's a cut on her face.'

With both of these entries, she cast herself as a kind of detective in the situation, imagining that she would watch to see if there was any flicker of surprise in Tuli's face. Anything that might hint at his knowing more. But when he walked in that night, he seemed so brittle, so fragile that truly all thoughts of the Hungarian and his wife momentarily left her head.

'What happened?' she said, shocked by the bleak vacancy in his eyes, his blank fortitude, as though any other expression would just slip off his face in seconds. 'What's wrong?'

It was a while before everyone left – you could hear Elene joking with the cooks downstairs, who seemed to be having some kind of impromptu party for her success with the benefits coming through. They were grabbing on to good news, it seemed, their voices were puffed out and hyperactive.

'Leave it with me!' She heard Guna shouting excitedly under the floorboards. She began to fear that the night would turn into a late one, with a lock-in for Elene. His voice was bouncy with indulgence. 'You just leave it to me, Elene! I know what you like best. The ravioli, the sweet peppers, yes, ha?'

But there was unlikely to be a lock-in with the boss in this mood. Nia was distressed to see Tuli like this, his face drawn and brooding, so quiet and lacking in words, she wasn't used to it. But he wouldn't respond to her questions, just shook his head whenever she asked him if everything was OK. Instead, he sat poring over his phone and a couple of sheets of paper. At one point he rang Patrick, but he hung up when she got too close.

'Nia, just give me some time,' he said. 'I'll talk to you later, OK? Just steer clear of me for now, can you do that?'

'I was just going to offer you a drink,' she said, formally, as though they barely knew each other. And yes, you could say that she didn't really know this person in front of her that well, it was rare to see him away from the steering wheel.

When Shan turned up, sallow and distracted, his thick mass of black hair now damp with sweat against his skull, giving her similar blank eyes in response to her greeting, she said, 'OK, well, I guess I should leave you guys to it,' and began to take off her apron and hat.

'Stay, Nia,' said Shan.

Tuli looked up and across the room at him.

'You are sure?' he said to Shan.

'Look, I really don't mean to get in the way,' she said. 'I can just as easily—'

'Nia, just give us a second,' said Tuli, with the same mix of impatience and fatigue that he'd had since entering the room. 'Shan, what are you thinking?'

'Let her stay,' Shan said. 'She knows about Devaki and Karu. It's fine.'

They sat on the sofas at the end of the room. There were leaves yellowing on a couple of the plants, the long, lank pointed foliage of spider plants, with a musty smell coming off the papery thinness. Outside the window she could hear people yelling at the Australian pub, a skirmish at closing time that travelled all the way up the road from the corner, over the humid air to reach them.

They summarized events pretty quickly and Nia held her breath as she heard it, fearful of interrupting too soon. She had a mix of emotions going on in her head. The story they told her was crazy, straight out of a tabloid newspaper. And they told it like they were telling her the fixtures for a match – methodically, without any acknowledgement of the insanity of it.

At one point Shan left for the toilet and she grabbed Tuli by the arm.

'Are you serious?' she said. 'You've paid for his wife to come over with smugglers? With his kid? What the fuck? Are you serious, Tuli? How many times have you done this? Is this what you *do*? People who do this . . . you're one of them? That is what you are?'

'Look,' he said. 'Don't you understand – someone like Shan or Guna or anyone else – they are going to do this anyway. You know that. You know that the situation is dire in Sri Lanka, that people are risking their lives on a daily basis, come on, Nia. What do you think? That my being involved has any effect other than this: making sure that I can point them towards the most reliable, careful way of doing it?'

'Tuli, this is illegal. What are you thinking? Is this how you make your money? Is this it, after all, is this what we are talking about? How are you different from . . . from . . . ?' She was struggling, it was so unknown, unfamiliar. 'From . . . Somali kidnappers? How can you set yourself apart?'

He sighed, and rubbed the fatigue from his eyes. He was nowhere near offering any reassurance.

'Nia, I don't make money from this. I have two objectives – get them a discount, and get them someone reliable to agent the journey. Sometimes I lend them money too. But if you think this is about money then we have a long conversation ahead of us. What I've learned is some people are better than others, some have more integrity, some routes are better than others. If you're going to do it anyway then I would suggest that you go with this guy, not this one. It's a business like any other, people need to be careful. I do believe that the accountability factor is higher the more I am involved, people are more likely to stick to their word. I try to reduce the element of danger and get them something more reliable. I don't go there and manage the whole thing myself if that's what you are asking. But like I say, they are going to do this anyway, of course they are, you know that.'

'But how do you know they won't be trafficked? How can you be sure? Tuli, it's so dangerous – a woman and a kid, and she's been diverted, kept prisoner in a house in Germany. God, it's gone wrong – this is what I mean, fuck, it's crazy!'

'Nia, I need you to calm down. Seriously. I need that right now. I need you to leave if you can't be calm for me. I don't need you to be bringing this into the mix right now.'

Shan was returning from the toilet and he couldn't yet see that Nia was agitated. It would be awful to leave at this point. She could see the burden in his face as he crossed the room to them.

'No,' she said quietly. 'I don't want to leave. It's fine. I'm fine.'

And so she stayed and listened to the full story, witnessed all of their deliberations, as they measured out the possibilities.

# SHAN

You're going to allow yourself this thought, thinks Shan. The thought that you could kill someone. A pleasurable thought, one that contains vindication, a sloughing-off of all of the dead cells of his recent life. A thought that gives him the feeling of ownership over his own movements. The fantasy is one he has had before. It does not normally end in the purchase of a knife and yet here he is, going through the aisles of Robert Dyas, the shop near the restaurant that sells everything from toilet brushes to baking pans, until he is standing at the kitchenwares section looking through carving blades of all sizes.

To actually kill someone would mean he would become something else entirely. A supernatural creature, a killer – you imagine the word itself to be written in neon on the sky, to almost be science fiction. And yet this is not true, of course. His own father was killed with one of these things, with human hands, and the Internet image that Appa has left behind is not remarkable but humdrum – that dirty indelible pattern of blood on white sheets.

The knife he chooses is similar to the one that he held in Madame Evie's kitchen. It costs eighteen pounds and is vacuum-sealed in a tight plastic sheath with the words 'Forged Steel All-Purpose Knife' engraved in the dull metal. On the plastic is written 'Good Grip Pro'. He pays for it with a single twenty-pound note and discards the packaging in the bin outside the shop. The knife is already in his bag, he made sure to unwrap it in the shop as soon as it was paid for, whilst walking towards the exit, thereby preventing himself from being able to take it back to the counter and return it.

# NIA

'Do you know this place?' said Tuli, handing her a piece of paper.

Cardiff West service station. She was startled to see it written down.

'Yes, sure,' she said. 'It's not far from where I grew up. About half an hour. What are you going there for?'

'It's the meeting point,' said Tuli.

'Wow. Cardiff West. Bloody hell.' She was stoked, something so familiar from back home, and rearing its head in this situation? She had got to thinking of all the places from her past as though they were fictional names, or at least, signposts that would only figure in her own personal history. It was very rare to hear a Welsh accent that wasn't her own around the restaurant, let alone meet someone from her part of the country.

'You know it?' said Shan.

'Yes, yes, I know it well,' she said. Her mind was racing over the information – they must have chosen it because it was off the M4, maybe because it was likely to be quieter than the places nearer London, was that it? It was some coincidence though, it almost felt like a sign.

'Let me come with you,' she said.

'It's not going to happen,' said Tuli immediately, raising a small smile. And then softly, under his breath, 'That's a bit of a turn-around, isn't it?'

'Why not?' she said. 'It's my patch. I can do this with you. I want to help.'

'Don't get into it,' Tuli said. 'You know very well why, Nia.'

'Come on, Nia,' said Shan, frowning. 'It could be dangerous. Best thing is if you tell us anything you know about the place.'

She thought for a minute. Back home they would say you know

it like the back of your hand, that place, don't you, Nia love? Mum had gone through a period of going there for showers in one of the bleaker segments of time, when they didn't have electricity or hot water and she wasn't on speaking terms with her own parents. She had friends who had given her the idea, they were running a charity shop in Newport town centre, and had actually taken to sleeping in the shop because they had lost their flat for some reason. Anyway, the three of them used to head to Cardiff West for their toilette. Mira and Nia were very irritable in their teenaged way, resentful at their mother's hyped-up, buzzing navigation of their latest problem. There was always the chance you might bump into someone you knew there, someone from school would be the worst. There was the obvious fear that she'd drink something before setting out, and kill them all on the motorway. But then there was the chance to be clean for a bit, which always won of course.

'Let me come too,' Nia said. 'I can wait in the arcade or something. It's a big place, full of people, it's not going to happen indoors, under all those lights and cameras. I can just be in the service station itself, nearby, in case you need help. I can drive, remember?'

Tuli considered it for a moment, pressing his lower lip between his thumb and forefinger. It was long enough that she knew there was a chance he was changing his mind.

'What's the layout?' he said, finally. 'Who are the people who go there? Do you remember the petrol station? I'm wondering where exactly he is going to want to do this. In a sense, it could bode well that it is such a public place. On which point, I need to understand the dimensions a little more, so please, do just talk, say whatever comes into your head.' He nodded his head and lit up a fag before issuing some of his trademark single-syllable commands. 'Speak! Do. Please. Go.'

He's back, Nia thought, with a wash of relief.

They talked about Cardiff West for a while. She wasn't sure if there was CCTV there, but she knew there was a Costa, Burger

King, big bank of fruit machines. There was a Subway, and one of those mini Greggs at the petrol station. A shop with those neck cushions lined up outside. She and Mira used to shove them into each other's faces when they'd come out of the shower cubicle and were feeling lighter and more mischievous, having discarded something with the dirt off their bodies. She didn't go into this last part of course, sticking instead to the spatial layout and goods on display. Could it really be that Shan's wife and child would arrive there, of all places? She tried to imagine them amongst the sandwich and pasty shops, people pushing past them under the tube lighting. A Sri Lankan wife and child, having traversed so many continents, under such duress.

*Devaki.* Just the word itself was so unavoidably exotic, like a musical instrument hewn from bark.

At one point Tuli got up to attend to business downstairs. One of his homeless regulars was knocking on the door for pizza and she realized with a jolt that they hadn't put the margheritas out like they usually did at this time.

She looked at Shan and saw his face in the shadows. The expression was impenetrable, disappearing in front of her eyes, a train pulling into a tunnel.

'Shan, man,' she said. 'He's got this. Tuli. He's used to this, he'll get it sorted. Don't worry. This could be the end of everything you've been going through. I'm not saying to get ahead of ourselves, it's easy to say . . . still, this is Tuli we're talking about. It could be the endgame, don't you think?'

But his eyes just flickered over her, skittering across her shoulders and beyond, as though they were looking for something behind her, some truth to emerge from the gloaming void of that room.

# SHAN

The sky takes time to darken these days, and Shan presumes this to be the reason the agent has chosen such a late slot for the meeting. Still, they have to allocate a good four hours for the journey, including the process of extricating from the stranglehold of rush-hour traffic that goes to the outskirts of London. Tuli drives with a focus that is soothing, window half down so that he can tip his cigarette out of it, puffing smoke from the right side of his mouth. In the back, Nia is quiet, half-lying down, with her coat over her, seemingly asleep.

'What is the thing you are most worried about?' Tuli says to Shan. 'Let's get it out in the open and tackle it now, lah? What is the worst that can happen, in your mind?'

Shan lets a laugh bubble out of him, settles back into his seat, runs his fingers over the rigid buckle of the seat belt.

'Ha. Boss, what all you want to talk about that for, now? Really, the worst that can happen, you know what it is. There is no benefit to discussing it.'

'OK,' says Tuli, checking the rear-view mirror and then leaning forward over the wheel as if he is inspecting the bunched-up vehicles they can see through the windscreen, monitoring their small movements forward. Above them, the sky is without a single cloud, the colour distilled as one continuous pool of the same pale blue throughout. 'OK,' he says again, 'what about Devaki? What is she like? Tell me about her.'

Shan thinks for a minute and then relents. What else is there to do? The temperature is close, a little humid, and it is clear that they are going to be stuck in the traffic jam for some time.

'Devaki is tough,' he says, 'she's always been tough. When she was at university she had a reputation for it, didn't accept any shit from anyone. You know, the type to slap men who hassled her on buses. Right on the face, no hesitation, that kind of thing, a big fat slap on the cheek. I told you she studied biology, so, very male-dominated. Even in the research lab, before she had Karu, when she was working, she was I think the only woman. So, she had to build herself that way, she doesn't care what people think, what people expect that women should or shouldn't do, in fact, she is very . . . what is the word . . .'

'Independent?' says Tuli, smiling with approval. 'Fierce? She sounds great.'

'More like, that word where you know that a lot of what people think is stupid, so why get into it, you know?'

'Confident?'

'No, more than that.'

'Self-assured?'

'I am not sure of that word. Self-reliant, I would say yes, but try another,' says Shan.

'She sounds like a bit of an iconoclast, lah?' says Tuli. 'Someone who tips up what everyone accepts as the norm, yes?'

'Yes, maybe,' says Shan, liking the sound of it. 'In a class of her own, you can say.'

In this way, they pass the time, as the car goes through its perambulations, finally opening out onto the motorway, and the relief of straight steady movement, the white lines on the road disappearing under the body of the car over and over.

# NIA

A ripped-up sky, with thick seams of grey thread. Rainclouds all ready to release that heavy Newport rain. It felt like she was returning after forty years, not four months, when Tuli drove the car off the motorway, down past the petrol station into the car park at Cardiff West service station.

Half asleep, she is in and out of dream, remembering being eight, or nine maybe, and her first time running away. She hadn't reached Newport train station but it had been the planned end-point in her mind. They lived in a close in those days, all paving between the houses, no roads. Mira was very little. It was during an argument of some kind with Mum, Nia had slipped out the back and run through the pathways to the climbing frame near their house. A girl from school was already halfway up the bars, hanging backwards, ready for a modest back-flip. Sheri Wilson.

'Hiya, Nia,' she said, shaking her head so that she could see more clearly. She had two bunches, tied with pink-bobbled hairbands. 'Where's Mira?'

'I've run away,' Nia said, proud to flag up the distinction immediately and stamp the day with the gold imprint it deserved.

'Wow.' She was visibly impressed. 'Where are you going?'

'Not sure.' She fingered the two pound coins in her pocket. If she bought three bars of chocolate for her three meals, they could last her at least three days, she figured.

'But it's going to be good,' Nia said.

Sheri raised her eyebrows and widened her eyes with respect. There was no doubt between them that Nia was headed for greatness. As if to show Sheri her seriousness of purpose, Nia refrained from having a climb, although with the sun out, and the bars free from wetness, it was tempting to stay and play.

'Gotta go,' she said, giving her a wink and a smile, as though she was in Narnia or *Swallows and Amazons*, one of those old books in which the children run their own lives. 'Have a good one!'

In reality, she didn't make it to the station of course. After twenty minutes of aimless walking, she retraced her steps and went to the library.

They dropped her at the entrance and she made her way to Costa, as planned. There were no big goodbyes; if anything, all three of them were working hard to minimize any dialogue that might suggest this was anything other than a routine interval during a long road trip.

She nursed a coffee and attempted the crossword in a magazine that had been left on one of the tables. Over and again she pressed on the biro, carving empty lines into the paper; the pen was reluctant to release ink. She nursed a second drink soon after the first, so that the caffeine was swirling about in her brain. Around her, the wooden floor was full of the usual detritus: cracked white lids and squashed ribbed paper cups, a large spillage in the corner with wet napkins absorbing the dark colour, the occasional thin lozenges of sugar packets dotted here and there.

She knew her role, but it didn't make it any easier to pass the time. She was to check in regularly regarding their progress. It had been her idea, and Tuli had agreed.

'Don't be ringing us when we are with the guy, though, obviously,' said Tuli. 'We'll text you when we are going to leave the car to meet him and at that point you need to, you know . . . just wait, OK?'

'It's useful to tell her where exactly we are going to be,' Shan said to him. 'We don't know where he is going to say for the specific meeting point, yet.'

The first text exchange was straightforward enough:

- How are you guys doing?

- We are OK.

- What's your location?

- We are in the car park by Travelodge waiting for his text.

- OK. Is Tuli driving you mad yet? Haha

- No he is fine.

- He must have smoked about two packs of Marlboro by now, can you breathe OK?!?

- I am fine don't worry.

- OK will check in within the hour.

- OK Nia thanks

She had the urge to push it for some reason, by making the jokes, just nerves, she didn't know what she expected from the dialogue. She knew she was in touch for functional reasons, but she was trying to help take the edge off the wait was all – for Shan, for her, for all of them. She was scared of what might happen, and worried by the sparse way in which all three of them were talking, as though extra words might jeopardize the chance to be safe.

# SHAN

They sit in the cave that is the parked car, biding their time, waiting for instructions. Outside, rows and rows of cars. Shan can see the sign for a Travelodge, no neon on the words, the hoped-for darkness is right on them now. He thinks about the knife, imagines his finger running over the blade lightly. It is just a way to feel safe, that's all it is.

Eventually, the phone rings.

'Yes,' says Tuli, writing down coordinates. 'OK.' He punches into the sat-nav system and turns to Shan.

'He says it is five minutes from here,' he says. 'Text this to Nia.'

They drive then, making their way out of the car park with the moon above them, and down one dark offshoot of a road after another. Shan is a personification of focus now – his attention is entirely on every turn and twist that the car makes, nothing else. Each visible change in direction comes right through the windscreen to him and enters his chest as a pulse, a tiny electrocution to remind him to stay alert. Eventually, they reach a small petrol station, just the two pumps, one car, no attendants or lights.

Shan holds himself as carefully and still as he can. He strains to look in the tinted windows of the stranger's car. Tuli touches his arm before getting out of his side of their car. Shan dips his hand into his bag and takes the knife. He slips it into the waistband of his trousers, under his shirt, just as he has practised.

Be alert, he thinks. Stay alert. Don't relent.

They walk over to the car and the man gets out. He is tall, muscled, wearing a khaki bomber jacket, shaved head. Shan tries to look inside the car, heart flailing as he realizes there is no one with him.

'Pran?' Tuli says. The man nods.

'Where are they?' Tuli continues. 'You said you would bring them to us?'

'I told you I would try,' the man replies, 'not that it was definite. We have had some problems.'

A roar escapes Shan's throat then.

'NO!' he shouts. 'NO – MY WIFE, MY SON!' He pushes forward but Tuli's hand is holding him back.

Pran gives Shan a threatening look. 'We need more money,' he says.

'NO NO NO!' Shan is writhing, Tuli is in front of him. 'YOU DOG!' shouts Shan. 'DIRTY FUCKING DOG FROM HELL!'

'Where is she?' Tuli says. 'How do we know you have her? And the kid?'

'Get me more money,' Pran says, 'and I will bring them to you.'

'How – do – we – know – that – you – have – her?' Tuli repeats. His tone is clear and staccato, the words enunciated as a request for something very particular. A light comes to the man's eyes as he understands. He presses a button on the phone in his hand. Within one ring, it is on speakerphone and they can hear a female voice.

'Hello? Hello?' Then again, into the black air around them: 'Hello? Hello?'

It is definitely Devaki's voice. Shan lunges at him to get hold of the device but the man has switched the phone off, holds it behind his back.

And then, it is all blurred into one horrific smear of a shape: Shan pulling the knife from his belt, holding it out like a blind man with a cane, not knowing how to wield it, hoping it will direct him, the anguished shouts from Tuli who is pulling him back saying NO NO NO again and again, the knife falling from Shan's hand to the ground and that giant of a man picking it up in front of him and holding it in reverse threat.

'AGH!' shouts Shan as he runs at the man, pulling himself out from Tuli's hold.

'NO, SHAN!' shouts Tuli who is too late to stop him as he

runs straight into the man who calls himself Pran, with his arms up, trying to get the phone but knocking it to the ground instead, and then in the contortion of their two bodies, Shan feels the blade going into him, hears his own scream and sees his own blood released, seeping into the white of his shirt as he sinks.

# NIA

She knew from the moment he said her name, that it was the kind of call that no one wants to receive.

'Quickly, Nia,' he said. 'Shan's hurt. Your mother's address. Quickly. How long will it take from here?'

And oh, the freeze in her when she heard the fear in his voice.

'Tuli, what happened?'

'Nia, he needs help. Send me the address by text too.'

It was because he thought her mother was a nurse, of course. Back to the beginning, and that one little lie. Even as she gave him the address, began spelling it out, she could see her mother, opening the door in that wizened distracted way she had.

'I know the hospital is not an option but Tuli, my mother . . . she doesn't have the skills—'

'Nia, he's lost consciousness. Text it. I think he could be dying. If it comes to it, I will go to the hospital. Send me the hospital address too.'

'Tuli – no. My God. Tuli!'

And then, the gritty dragging sound before he hung up as though he was lugging something. Tuli's heavy, gasping breath – a primal sound – his own desperate, spasmodic glugging of air. Was he carrying Shan in his arms?

She can remember herself running, the banks of cars like long rows of teeth in the mouth of a gigantic beast, the black cavernous spaces that allow her to cut through, find her way out, so that she can begin following the instructions she has forced him to send. She is running down the motorway hard shoulder for some of it, a minute of it, clawing out her breath in a netherworld of huge lorries and diesel particulate, screwing up her eyes against the vindictive lights that continually emerge from the black. Nothing will stop. She is going down the lane on the right, running, running, unsure of whether the turning will ever come until she goes around a corner and screams when she sees them there, alone, desolate, in a lawless country of their own, Tuli heaving a body into the back seat, the legs falling out.

'No!' she cries, sobbing to see the blood on him. 'Tuli, no.'

# SHAN

There is pain but its violence is embedded in the cushion of darkness. He has failed them. He is conscious, he is not conscious. He sees the back of Tuli's head in front of him, the shadow patterns emerging on the windscreen, droplets of light scattered over the glass, and falls back to the deep, inchoate oil of his mind. There are no more thoughts.

PART THREE

# SHAN

He is lying in a single bed when he comes round. The girl with Tuli looks familiar.

'One sugar or two?' she says, in an accent that helps him click her into place. A bit like Nia, who is standing in the corner of the room, behind her. Same eyes. But the resemblance ends there, she is a skinny little thing, and tiny.

And then he remembers it all. Devaki. No Karu . . . He lets a wail escape him.

'Shan,' says Tuli, coming over to the bed and bringing his face close. He speaks in a whisper. 'Take it easy. This is very good.' His right hand is covering the mouthpiece of a phone.

'OK, man,' Tuli says, returning the mobile to his ear. 'Thank you, doctor.'

Shan looks down at his right arm and sees it is bandaged at the top. A horrible sting accompanies his slow understanding of the situation, the feeling of lemon being squeezed on an open wound. There is still a lot of blood seeping through his white shirtsleeve onto the cloth.

'OK,' Tuli says, nodding at the girl as he speaks into the phone. 'Direct pressure on the bandage. We can get to London in about two and a half hours, lah? But we need a bit of time to adjust. Is OK? Got it. Yes. Looks like that. Not into the artery. But a lot of blood.'

The girl holds the teacup out uncertainly in Shan's direction and Nia intervenes, decisively placing it on the table next to him.

*Shhhh,* Nia mouths, putting her finger to her lips to quell his attempt to speak. She puts a tablet in his mouth and gets him to drink from a glass. His top lip stays submerged in the water for a moment after he swallows. He wonders what will happen if he forgets to breathe.

'Mira did your bandage,' says Tuli, coming off the phone. 'Might I say, it's an impressive piece of work. I doubt your sister could have done such a thing, eh, Mira!' He puts his hand on Shan's shoulder and lowers his voice again. 'So . . . here it is. We were lucky, man. It looks pretty bad, I know, but they are superficial wounds. It didn't go very deep. We missed the brachial artery, that's the dangerous one. I've got a doctor, he's close to Vesuvio, he'll do this for us . . . we're good, Shan . . .'

Shan looks his boss in the eye and tries his best to understand. It is too much for his brain.

Tuli picks up a roll of medical cloth and winds it around the existing bandage at the top of Shan's arm, slicing off a piece with scissors, pulling the ends together tightly. Shan flinches, but he welcomes the firm hold. The giddy redness of the wound is blocked for a few seconds before it begins to slowly soak through, taking a much smaller circumference now for its territorial dark stain. He watches the little girl take the scissors and tape, the pink knuckles in her small hands as she chops and sticks everything into place.

'She used to do it all the time,' says Mira, looking over at Nia, whose face dissolves into blur against the wall when Shan tries to latch on to it. 'My sister. She's the one I learned it off. The first aid.'

'Why?' says Tuli. He has stepped back from the bed and is not looking at the girl as he speaks. Instead his attention is on a second phone, one that he is taking out of his trouser pocket.

'Because of Mum,' Mira shrugs. 'Mum was always hurting herself. Walking into things, falling over. You know. She had a bike for a while and fell off it a lot.'

Their voices fade to a hum as Shan's mind pounces from question to question. The man didn't have Devaki, he said Karu was with her. He heard her voice on that phone.

'Devaki . . .' he says, turning in his bed. 'Karu . . .'

'Shan, wait,' Tuli says. 'I have been waiting for you to wake up. Give me a minute.'

The girls leave the room and Shan frowns, clenches his forehead, wanting to lose awareness of the pain and his thoughts.

Tuli holds something out in his hand. It is the fucking agent Pran's phone itself. Nokia. 2002. Shan recognizes the model from his time in the mobile phone shop. Tuli must have picked it up when the guy ran off. He knows too, what he will find when he looks at the screen.

'Boss, but . . . it's the empty screen,' he says. 'He's cancelled it.'

Tuli produces his own phone.

'So, I checked the last dialled number,' Tuli said, meting out the words for Shan slowly, with care for his understanding. 'It actually took him about ten minutes to cancel the phone.'

Shan stares at the boss's phone as it comes to him, imperceptible droplets that are building to a small pool of realization.

DEVAKI PHONE it says in Tuli's contacts. And then, next to it, a mobile number with an area code that he doesn't recognize.

# NIA

She was about three dress sizes smaller than when Nia had last seen her, no joke. That would actually make her the mythical size zero, something where you can put your hands around someone's waist, stretch your fingers and they almost touch.

The flat was immaculate, unrecognizable. Not a thing on the worktops, wiped down till even the scratches were gleaming. Mira picked up a dustpan and began brushing the clean floor in a twitchy neurotic way that gave Nia the shakes. This was new, although Nia had heard of this trait in the kids of addicts. The desire for order. She didn't have it herself, the room in London was strewn with second-hand books and clothes, and she didn't associate it with her. Looking around at the broken-down place, with even less furniture in it now – the telly gone, no sofa – it made her attempts seem all the more pathetic.

'Where's Mum?' Nia said.

'She's out.'

'What do you mean?'

'She's been gone for days,' said Mira. 'Affie . . .'

'What! How many days?'

She shrugged. Nia stared at her, she was so small she could crush her with that stare if she wasn't careful.

'Mira, how have you been eating?'

She shrugged again and it was all Nia could do to stop herself from taking her by the arms and shaking her like a maniac. And then she was overwhelmed by a memory of their own mother doing exactly that, shaking Mira wildly in front of her, only a year ago, in this same living room.

'Mira, no . . .'

Nia began to cry and so did Mira, small bony little thing.

'Mira, you didn't start on it yourself, did you?'

Miserably, she shook her head. But she was holding something back.

'What?' Nia said, trying to soften her voice into encouragement.

Mira pointed at the booze table. About fifteen empty bottles of different types on there as usual, but also, there was a bottle of half-drunk vodka. It was this that she was trying to flag up.

'Mira . . .' Nia said. And she took her to her chest and hugged her so hard that she worried she might snap in two. Snap, bang, stretch, exploding candy, imagine if this was all a game.

'Get your things,' Nia said.

She nodded without resistance. It was shocking how quickly she ran up those stairs once Nia had given her the green light, as though that was what she had wanted all along.

# SHAN

'Hello?'

'Hello!'

'Hello?'

'Shan? Shan!'

He is ready to vomit. Where is she? Tuli steadies him, is holding the phone to his ear so that Shan can reorganize his good hand. And then he hears it. Like a pipe in the background, cracking and singing in the heat.

'Dada! Da-ada!'

'Karu?' he says.

Devaki speaks again and she sounds as though she is half-laughing, half-crying.

'Shan,' she says. 'I knew you would find us.' Then, off the mouthpiece, 'It's Dada!' She laughs again. 'I knew you would find us. Oh, Shan. My God!'

'Where are you?'

'We are in Munich in Germany,' she says. 'We are good, we are very good.'

'You are good?' He had not thought he would ever hear this word again in relation to them. This simple, solid, reductive, impossible word. 'Devaki? You are saying . . . good?'

'Yes, good! We have a room . . . we are safe. We have food, beds . . .'

'What?'

'Yes, I know! *Konjamum nambamudiyaathu* Utterly unbelievable!'

'What? How? Who?' He speaks the single syllables fast, knowing that he is tripping over her, rushing for answers. It is impossible to fully absorb that this might be a conversation that does not have a time limit. In contrast, she is replying almost gaily, winding sentences out like wool, oblivious to his urgency.

'Yes, they released me after you sent the money, and then Shan, you know what happened – I was with another woman who had a child – we both went to the Red Cross, and then they sent us to this organization called Respect and there they said—'

'They released you? The people holding you in that place released you?'

'Yes! Once they got the money! The money you sent, Shan – Oh, God, I can't tell you what it was like when we were waiting! Where to begin . . . Shan!'

'But . . . but . . . why didn't you call?'

'They did not give me your number. They said that the British agent would give it to you, something to do with the timing, was it . . . ?'

'You mean Pran?'

'My God, Shan I don't know his name! But it has all worked, yah! Here you are, I can finally hear you. . *Nampamudiyatu* . . . but it is true! God, Shan . . . I have so much to tell you . . .'

'I will come and get you.'

'But just wait . . .' she says. 'Just wait, wait. You need to get your own passport organized. We need to talk about it. Because I have claimed the asylum here.'

'What?'

'Yes, we went all together and did the forms, me and this other woman, I will tell you all about it – the process takes months but we are in the system now, it has begun, since yesterday—'

'You did it there? In Germany? But Karu . . . ?'

'He's got friends here, don't worry. There are three families in the building. Karu, speak to Dada?'

And then, impossibly, in full stereo harmony, that voice from the past, reaching right through to the present as rich and sweet as the solid sugar-cane *karumbu* after which he was named.

'Dada! Dada! Where are you, Dada?'

# NIA

There they both were, jarring the scene – sitting on and in her old bed, these two faces from her new life, set against that distant memory of a place: her bare box of a bedroom with peeling white walls.

Devaki and his son were both fine, was the gist of it. Free and safe and out of danger in Munich. But Shan was possessed – you could see him trying to figure it all – what, when, how it would pan out next. She went to the side of his bed and put her arm around his shoulders.

'She cannot leave Germany,' he said. He twisted his mouth in pain and she looked at the small cuts on his face, too small for bandaging, not yet plastered over.

'Not until she is securely confirmed to be a citizen,' said Shan, half to himself, half to her. 'Agh. You see? And I cannot leave here now, because I am also being processed . . .'

She nodded, holding the understanding in a way that she hoped was visible to him. There were great moments like this that could not rise up, full of truth and deception all at once. That was the pain of it.

'I will go to live in Munich, is that it?' He was still talking to himself, knocking his head back on the pillow and looking at the ceiling. 'I will live there with them in Germany and find some of the work there? Or will we wait to hope that it works for them to come here? I mean, who knows, right?'

He looked up at Nia then, as though she might be able to contribute to the discussion, release him from his fears. You could see what he was thinking – that he'd probably be leaving the restaurant, leaving Tuli, did he have it in him to start again? It was so immense, but you could also see that of course there was no question about doing it, he would do whatever was needed for them to be together, and all of his questioning was about trying to ride it somehow, this thrashing thing over which he had no control.

She could see that he was shivering. Tuli pulled a blanket up, over Shan's arms. It was an old embroidered thing, something she had owned for years. It's still here, she thought, looking around the room. This whole place still exists. She remembered reading with that blanket draped over her crossed legs. A solitary sentence, a paragraph, a single book – there must have been something that entered her here, and twisted the direction of her life.

'Relax, man,' Tuli said. 'Shan. Step by step. One step now, another step later.'

'Listen, Nia,' Shan said. 'I spoke to my son, you won't believe it. I spoke to Karu, he actually said to me on the phone one word again and again like this . . . "Dada? Dada? Dada?" . . .'

He paused, waiting for her natural amazement at this fact, as though the astonishment itself might form some kind of bridge, one that could carry him over the tumultuous rise and fall of his uncertainty.

But she was beyond speaking. She just nodded and held his hand tightly in her own. It was all she could do, to grip it like that.

She looked down at her fingernails and saw blood in them, dark maroon clots mixed with dirt. She shuddered, looking at Tuli's fingers too, they held the same. Of course. They had pulled Shan into that car together once she'd arrived, not knowing if he would soon be a corpse.

It was what she had wanted, for them to be united like this.

Tuli gave Nia a look of enquiry, she could see him trying to divine the meaning behind her silence. He stood up from the bed so that she could sit down but she just kept staring at him, his tall figure reaching up against the depressed low ceiling of her room, standing there in the lowlight with his sleeves rolled up, an unfamiliar austerity to his face. He had tiny lines of fatigue under his eyes, the smile he gave her was small enough to acknowledge the incongruity of the situation, the intimacy of him being right there in her home. He might as well have been Gulliver in the land of

Lilliput. She didn't know what he had gleaned regarding Mum from Mira, but she didn't really care, it was more something else that was bubbling up in her.

'We need to talk,' she said, after a long moment.

'Sure,' he said, putting one arm out and gesturing at the door. 'Where shall we go?'

She took him out to the corridor. Mira was in the other room, she could hear her packing.

'I'm . . . glad you are safe,' she said.

He smiled. It was a weakened version of his old cocky self, he wasn't pretending otherwise.

'I'm glad too,' he said. 'How about you? Are you OK?'

That did it. Her head was thrumming and she was shouting to overcome it.

'Tuli, what are you on? What are you fucking on? You play God and Shan gets stabbed – you could have both been killed – what the fuck, Tuli? And you're back asking if I'm OK?'

'Calm down.'

'No.' A long silence. Her fingers twisting together.

Finally she said, 'What is this? You think you're beyond it, beyond danger? It's a God complex or what? Playing with people's lives?'

He pressed his thumb and forefinger against his eyes. After a few moments, he lifted them and looked directly at her.

'Maybe I do,' he said. 'Maybe I have a God complex, sure. Maybe that's a whole thing to think about. Maybe it's a flaw. But you have to look at the whole picture.'

She began again. She was throwing the words out at him.

'The Hungarian's *wife* came to the restaurant, Tuli. She had a cut right here, under her fucking eye! And I was staring at it and staring at it, trying to work out if she'd done it herself or if he'd hit her again. And then I thought, what have I become? Why would a woman do that? Don't you worry about all this? About making a mistake? About getting all of it wrong?'

Her body was trembling. He put his hands out to steady her, but she stepped backwards, out of his reach.

'Yes, of course I do,' he said. 'Nia, of course I worry about it, you must know that already. You know that. But what is the alternative to trying? Do you have an alternative? What happened with Shan was bloody terrifying – do you think I would have taken a knife with me to meet someone like that? But equally, from his point of view, you go right in and ask him, does he feel that sending the money was the right thing to do? Was it worth it? Shan's kid is close now, very close. Away from the people who killed his father. You tell me: what are the limits? Is there some kind of a tipping point? Is reuniting a family worth it? You are right that it is a risk. I hope very much that the Hungarian has not hit her again and it disturbs me to think it is a possibility, correct, yes, all I've got is my genuine feeling that I don't think he would do that. I don't have anything more. But who does? Who really knows who is telling the truth? Is it worth the risk? Ask Shan, go in there right now and ask him? Fella produces a fucking carving knife from his trousers, and we're just standing there in this abandoned petrol station . . . bloody crazy . . . you're not the only one who thought it could be all over, Nia.'

She hugged him then and cried and cried, her face against his chest, wetting his collar with her salt water, soaking him with that love – call it what you want – brother, lover, parent, friend. She didn't care to name what was between them. She was just glad that he was alive. And that he would go right back to Vesuvio and undoubtedly start again.

'Why didn't you tell me about your mother?' he said. 'Is it drugs or alcohol? Or both?'

She shook her head, disentangled herself from his shoulder.

'Look . . . there's plenty of time to get into it. What about Shan? Does he need to go to hospital? Can he go if he isn't legal?'

'He seems OK for now. There's a Bengali doctor who comes to the restaurant, he helps me out sometimes – we'll go and see him when we return. I think it's under control. Mira did a great job, actually, you should be proud of her.'

Mira came out into the hall then, upon hearing her name, and she looked absurdly tiny standing there with two carrier bags in her hands, like a little doll going off to live in a doll's house somewhere.

'Mira's coming back with me,' Nia said, 'aren't you, Mira?'

She nodded.

'Maybe I can work in the restaurant,' she said, straightening herself up. 'I've done a lot of pizza work in my time.'

Tuli smiled.

'What about school?' he said.

'I'm not being funny,' said Mira, 'but I haven't been to school for a long time.'

Nia looked at her deeply then, clocked those small cheeks puffed out with determination, the defiant nubs of black pearl that she had for eyes, and just like that, without warning, she had a visitation, she could see her as an adult. It was something she had never been able to visualize before, as though she didn't dare to jinx the entire idea that she'd get there. More than that, she could see them both together in this image she had now of the future, just, sitting together at a table somewhere, and both of them fully grown.

# Epilogue

Does a thief steal expecting that he will be caught? *Akappaṭṭukkoḷvēṉ eṉṟē kaḷḷaṉ kaḷavu eṭukkiṟaan?* It is an old proverb, from his childhood, phrased as a question that Shan submits for consideration regularly these days, in the aftermath of speaking to Devaki. He has been trying to get her to spill some resentment, articulate the fear and hurt she must have stacked away inside. The chances to speak with each other are so rich and multiple now, after the long famine, that he just wants her to come out with it all in one big rush and be done with it.

True to form, Devaki will not oblige, of course, and why should she? There is no mention of their past, or even of the disappearance of her own hard-won career at the Durdans laboratory, 514 Hospital Road, Jaffna. She is more concerned with talking through the practicalities and concrete elements of her new life as it makes itself known.

'Bit by bit,' she says, when he asks her to describe what happened after he left Jaffna. 'There is a lot of time for all that. Did I tell you that Karu broke the kettle the other day? Really very naughty, you know, he was playing with Macha, that kid from down the hallway – together they need much more supervision than you realize!'

It is too big and painful to talk about just yet, is the truth, and Shan is happy just to hear her voice, the way it builds solid towers from details: lists of food, people, the artefacts in her orbit. He exists in the glass bowl of water and sand that is his life, a goldfish with no visible memory to impede each conversation with her, in a limbo that contains pleasure, so long as he keeps impatience away.

He imagines holding his little boy, against his chest, the flesh reality of it: lying down with those small limbs around him, clutching at his sides. Taking the boy's hand, and pressing the palm of it against his own cheek. He believes it will happen.

He knows that with Devaki there will be a full reckoning. When the strictures of time and space are removed, and they have the luxury of being together, she will no doubt unleash it, he thinks. Maybe he will tell her everything too. He craves it, hopes for a semblance of annihilation and rebirth in each other's arms. Who knows when they will meet. Till then, they have words.

He is standing outside Archway library and talking to Karu when he sees her. He manages a free phone call here, to Munich, most days now, before going to the bus stop; something to do with the Wi-Fi in this location, you can freely access it from the paved court in front of the door.

Without realizing, he nods and waves hello to her. It is an instinctive response, and his hand falters as he does it.

'Hello,' he says.

'Who is it?' says Karu. 'Is it one of your friends?'

'Ah . . . not quite,' says Shan.

The woman is walking behind the little boy, who zooms on his scooter with the old familiar glorious recklessness, takes a right, left and left again till he has quartered the orange bench in the centre of the square.

'Hi . . .' she says, tucking her hair behind her ear nervously, and Shan realizes she is addressing him.

'Karu, baby,' he says. '*Magan*, son, I'll call you later. I have to go.'

He hangs up, unsure as to the next step.

'I'm sorry for what I said.' Her lips are set in a horizontal line that is difficult to decipher. Initially it looks as though it could be an expression of anger or resentment, but he soon sees that she is biting her lower lip from the inside.

'No . . .' says Shan, shaking his head. 'I am sorry for your hardship.'

'No, I'm sorry. It was just a really difficult time, and I shouldn't have said it,' she says. 'It was before he had his operation and I was . . . out of order. So I'm sorry.'

'But he is so strong now!' says Shan. 'Very good!'

He waves at the little boy who is like one of those dancers around the maypole, circling them both and whooping, as though he is weaving a pattern of ribbons with his movement, binding them together.

She smiles and looks at the boy, and they both stand and stare at him like that, for a suspended moment, watching the kid glide through space with his right leg in the air.

# Acknowledgements

Much of this novel grew out of conversations with my friend Nirad Pragasam, and I am hugely grateful to him for that, as well as for the deep, extended dialogue around his publication, *Tigers on the Mind: an interrogation of conflict diasporas and long distance nationalism. A study of the Sri Lankan Tamil diaspora in London* (PhD thesis, LSE, 2012). I couldn't have done this book without him.

My thanks to Libby Attwood for alerting me to pertinent ECHR asylum cases. Also to Joanna Perry for her research into hate speech and hate crime at Facing All the Facts, Anna Skehan at the Migrant and Refugee Children's Legal Unit at Islington Law Centre, Annie Kelly for sharing her work on slavery and trafficking in the UK, Parminder Morgan at Freedom from Torture and to Nirmala Rajasingam.

I am indebted to the Society of Authors, Arts Council England and Royal Holloway English Department for the support of this book from inception through to completion.

My kind agent, Tracy Bohan, has put so much into imagining this book into the world, along with Andrew Wylie, and I'll never forget it. Mary Mount is a formidable, wonderful editor, and the novel was copy-edited by Mary Chamberlain.

It is impossible to overstate the help I received from my readers – Ian Breckon, Devorah Baum and crucially Tess – thank you for that brilliance and clarity.

For other conversations that have affected the texture of this book: Ana Amores, Rodrigo Davies, Gabriella Sharma, Narmi Thiranagama, Julia Miranda, Stephen Merchant, Yasmin Hai, Paul Berczeller, Krish Majumdar, Nick Laird, Dan Tetsell, Jonas Hassan Khemiri, Zades, Cynthia Shanmugalingam, Sonia Faleiro, Josh Appignanesi, Camille Thoman, Alex O'Connell, Jeremy Lovering,

Anna Whitwham, Matt Bryden, Harry Man, Ros Wynne Jones, Matthew Plampin, Susanna Howard, Adam Shatz and Johanna Ekstrom.

For solidarity: Mita Pujara, Kavi Pujara, Gerard Woodward, Adam Wishart, Bucy McDonald, Nina Miranda, Ben Markovits, Caroline Maclean, Roland Watson, Chris Hale, Pascale Burgess, Avni Trivedi, Ulrik McKnight, Mircea Monroe, Charles Tashima, Ritu Morton, Tim Armstrong, Juliet John, Lavinia Greenlaw, Jo Shapcott, Susanna Jones, Matt Thorne, Anna Davis, Jack Hadley, Redell Olsen, Eley Williams, Robert Hampson and Elizabeth Wilson.

For their nurturing hearts: my sweet parents, Mohini and Chander Lalwani, and dear Ama, Indu Sharma. Papa is always in my thoughts. My brother Nishant, you are that type of caring *badmaash,* it has always meant so much. Thank you also to kind Ishna Berry, Caroline Leslie, Brij Sharma, Rex Jackett and Izzy.

For lessons in how to love, whatever the weather: my gratitude to Anoushka, Shay and Ishika.

Vik – you took the many drafts of this book and helped me to transform them. For that particular deluxe VS blend of optimism, amour, empathy and insight, I have no words.